Inevitable

(Book Two)

MARINA RAYDUN

Cover art created by Rahul Philip. For more information visit: www.rahulphilip.com

First Paperback Edition: September 2016

For more information please visit:

www.facebook.com/AuthorMarinaRaydun

http://marinaraydun.blogspot.com/

Follow the author on Twitter and Instagram: @Author_MRaydun

ISBN-10: 1537017225

ISBN-13: 978-1537017228

DEDICATION

For my children, who I hope will love to read.

CONTENTS

NOTE:

Inevitable was conceived as the second installment in a two-part series. Part One—*Effortless*—is currently available in paperback and digital formats.

ACKNOWLEDGMENTS

Vadim—you are my husband, my best friend, and so much more. Thank you for your patience. I love you.

Donna Rello, my proofreader and my dear friend—I appreciate your work and your support.

Thank you, Rahul Philip, for designing yet another wonderful cover. Here is to many more to come in the future.

My sister—your faith in me is fuel.

Dr. Michael Yuryev—thank you for answering my myriad of questions about suicide attempts, liver functions, and psychiatric watches. It'll make sense when y'all read the book. It goes without saying that, should any information contained herein be stated in a way that is medically incorrect, it is my fault alone.

Tania, thanks for your help with the Spanish tidbits. I really, truly appreciate your time and value our friendship more than you know.

My friends Irena, Tania (yes, again!), Rosa, Igor, and Alina—thank you for always asking about how my writing is going. It really means the world.

And a huge thank you to my parents for believing that I can indeed do anything.

NEW JERSEY

Chapter One: *What Say You?*

I rolled the lint brush up and down my thighs, without a break, for what seemed like a solid minute. I'd found it in the bottom drawer of my desk, but it was not mine. Perhaps the teacher who used to claim my seat in that windowless closet of an office as her own left it behind when she retired to graze the greener pastures of a private school on Long Island (for twice as much money at half the classroom headcount, from what I remember hearing). I'd snatched it out mostly because I couldn't get my hands to stop shaking and needed something to weigh them down. My pants didn't even look like they had much lint on them, but I continued to mercilessly go at them, anyway, the act of it as fruitless as it was unnecessary. Each one of those ten days in Europe seemed like it was eons ago now.

Lingering in the wings never seemed this nerve-racking before (through it wasn't like I've had many reasons or opportunities to wait in theatre wings in the past). I never knew before that day that I even had stage-fright, if that was indeed what was happening. I hadn't stuck around in my musical theatre minor long enough to find this bit out.

I couldn't wait to get this thing over with; I still had quite a bit of packing to do, not to mention I had a plane to catch. Hand out diplomas in the morning, clean out my desk in the afternoon, board a cross-Atlantic flight in the evening—that was the plan. I usually missed my pink-walled office during summer breaks, but that was when my time off meant that I had to spend two consecutive months watching George salute the sun in exhausting repetition. I wondered if it'd be different now—my first summer as a teacher without the Kasuns in my life.

"You'll rub a hole in that thing," I heard a colleague joke behind me. I'm still not sure which colleague it was, never having turned around to check. I laughed in response, anyway, the applause in the auditorium too overwhelming for me to focus on much of anything other than absolutely having to remove every last trace of lint from my black, high-waist slacks. In a room jam-packed with future actors, singers, and dancers (as well as some waiters and bartenders, surely), any trace of nerves on my part would certainly be painfully obvious.

"You're up, Ms. Levit," another voice whispered

behind my back. Before I could turn around to see which helpful stagehand it was this time, I was nudged toward the stage. There was no time to give my chin that one final check for any stray hairs, though my fingers itched to do exactly that.

Regaining my composure, shaky in my overly ambitious heels, I strode on with enough feigned composure, I imagined, to make my college public speaking professor proud. When I finally reached the podium to receive my plaque, I realized that I was still holding on to my lint brush, my grip such that my fingers were pale and bloodless. In what I hoped would be considered amusing, if not necessarily discreet, I handed it off to Abbott as he passed me the award and kissed me warmly on the cheek. I, in turn, found myself holding on to him desperately then, his dress shirt smoother to the tips of my fingers than the handle of the lint brush; it was hard to let go even when it was clearly time to do so.

It was back in Heathrow that Abbott had first told me that I beat him for this honor after only four years of trying—that I was finally going to be awarded Teacher of the Year. It was still two months until graduation, but the votes had already been tallied. It was a close race, from what I gather now, though I could hardly pretend to care about the details at the time.

Finding out that I won such a sweet but useless title is all I remember from that entire flight back, actually. Seven and a half hours aboard a decked out Virgin flight and that's all I remember. It's a shame, of course, but my heart was too busy beating deafeningly in my ears for me to so much as notice the countless on-demand channels at my fingertips.

Shell-shocked stiff, I had to be helped from my position on the floor and up to my feet back in the terminal after I hung up with my mother. Her breathy voice repeating, "George tried to kill himself," rang in my ears over and over, louder and louder with each repetition. Jamie never left my side as we boarded, but if he wondered why my face was slowly sinking in on itself, why my pale coloring grew more translucent by the second, he did so mutely. Wisely, though having known me not ten days, he already knew I'd mutter it all out myself, eventually. A calm, if not calming presence, he stayed put, his blessed long fingers near mine but not daring to touch. Out of the corner of my eye, I could see that he'd picked up a thin section of his raven-black hair (just to the right side of his natural part) and braided it, just the way he now knew I couldn't resist. Mere hours ago, this would've made me uncomfortably warm, distractedly dizzy, but not then: most of my focus went into making sure I didn't retch, grateful for Veronika's ill-timed information dump for preventing me from making our last complimentary breakfast at the hotel.

"You did it, spring chicken! The torch has been passed!" Abbott had boasted at the gate door, slow to catch on to my dazed and confused expression, let alone ponder its meaning. He was perky, as usual—his gray mop of hair styled to furious perfection, his eyes bright behind his comically round glasses. And of course, he smelled like coffee and gum: a combination that, for the first time, was making me dry heave, my lip curling of its own volition.

"What's wrong, Miss?" I'd heard students (as well as several flight attendants) ask as I struggled to keep moving forward, following Jamie blindly to my seat inside the painfully lit Boeing. I'd moved on legs that did not feel connected to my torso, all the voices around me distant, as if I were drowning in a violent current.

"He killed himself," I'd mumbled, eventually, and when I did, I began repeating it over and over, my throat not my own. "He killed himself." Every time I'd said it (unsure who else could hear, if anyone at all, my voice too small), I grew dizzier. The plane soon began to moan as it sped up the runway, only preparing to ascend, but I'd felt my head roll as if we were already airborne.

It's still hard for me to parcel it all out: was I more scared or relieved?

Fear. It was mostly fear that I felt. I'm almost sure of it. One way or another, this was going to define me, I'd correctly suspected even then. I knew that I could say goodbye to any hopes of ever starting over now that George was truly gone, as ironic as it seemed. It would be difficult to shake my new description: the direct cause of her fiancé's death…a murderer of sorts. I'd always be yanked right back to that, to him, like a dog on too short a leash. I'd never again be able to hide myself in the roses on Jamie's arm without immediately seeing the skull peeking through. I'd allowed myself a chuckle at my poeticism as I blew my nose into a red Virgin napkin.

Still, as I'd downed a plastic cup of the tepid red wine that Abbott ordered for me in honor of my win (having waved the flight attendant over from his armchair directly behind my own), I'd also registered something akin to respect for George then: he'd finally followed through on something. Good for him!

I'd sat sandwiched between Jamie and Veronika, the seat beneath me vibrating with every light pivot of the plane as it struggled to level, and stared into the blank screen before me, my few scattered thoughts running on a never-ending loop, on constant replay. I could feel Veronika's habitually loyal stare on me, though I refused to give into it. I'd never be able to deliver on all that she was expecting of me that day, that week, or ever. I closed my eyes and imagined her skinny frame clad in clothes suitable for a girl at least twice her size, the perennially dry skin peeling painfully on the bridge of her nose; I prayed that she'd cut me some slack. Investigating Abbott's extracurricular activities would just have to wait. I'd have to talk to Paz, and I'd have to talk to Sophie, but I couldn't now (even though Sophie was already conveniently close to me—just a few rows over aboard the same plane).

Okay, maybe that's all I remember.

"You get an extraordinary gift today—you get to start over!" I said into the microphone when I finally brought my mouth to open at the sight of all the expectant-bordering-on-bored faces, a sea of white graduation gowns and gold tassels. They stared up at me, half smiling, half perplexed. Wearing my overpriced black slacks and a silk white blouse with an excessively voluminous mock turtleneck collar, my hair picked up just so, I hoped I looked both professional and old enough to receive this privilege from my very first graduating class. I met these kids when they were fourteen and brought them up into adulthood, which made me nervous. For better or worse, these were my kids; if they'd disappoint now, there was no way I could escape responsibility. This responsibility business was a theme of sorts as of late, it seemed. "I know it may not sound like much right now, but it is. Believe me, it is! At one point in time, you'll find yourself ready to kill for an opportunity to start over, so don't abandon this one, don't waste it. Use it! To the best of your ability—use it. As early as tomorrow morning, or tonight, even. Grab ahold of this rare gift, and squeeze all life out of it. Make it yours! This is your chance—"

I over-enunciated and tried to project to the farthest seats on the highest balcony of the Talents' tricked out auditorium, praying the words would travel back to me so that I, too, would actually hear what it was that I was trying so hard to sell.

Strain as I might, I couldn't see any familiar faces with the spotlight in my eyes. They were all a washed-out blur, so even attempting to differentiate one from another was not an exercise worthy of effort. I knew Veronika wasn't there, but Paz had to be somewhere in that field of white and gold. Ofir was there, too, as were Liam, Jordan, Riley, Wisdom, and Sage. Most of them, I had to grudgingly admit to myself, wouldn't miss this sappy and predictable (albeit also touchingly symbolic) waste of time for the world, so I had to deliver something remotely coherent. But my tongue seemed foreign.

Out of the corner of my eye I saw Abbott still hanging around in the wings. I could feel him watching me when he wasn't looking out for Paz in the audience, himself. This was his last official day as a teacher at Talents. I would need to find a new mentor come September.

"You can't start over, what a crock of bull," I'd scoffed reading my speech to him just the night before. "You're the same person no matter the day or location! Sure, they may no longer have to ask for permission to use the hall pass to go pee, but they will still be the same people. Okay, maybe now they have slightly more knowledge, and we all adapt, eventually, but—ugh! You know what I mean? I mean you don't actually change your skin with some kind of rite of passage. Just because you graduate high school—"

"Or try to kill your fiancé—"

"Yes, thanks, helpful as always. But the point stands—you're still you, and I'm still me. They'll try on a different routine, a different wardrobe for some time, but…we'll all continue to experience the same things because that's how we're wired…. If you feel like a loser, you always will. If you're unhappy, you'll continue to be unhappy, no matter where you are, no matter who is at your side, no matter what you do.... They'll keep searching to fill that hole, but nothing will. Hey, look—I left Javier in San Pablo airport all those years ago and now look where I'm going? Our life, it's all circular. We can't run because it's no different than staying in place, really, so why waste the energy.... Ugh, whatever, I'm so full of it," I'd groaned, plopping down atop of his still unfolded couch, my printed out speech in my lap, my red pen (the tip of it gnawed) behind my ear. I was rambling. Alcohol tends to do that to me.

If Abbott had to think about my existential crisis/nervous breakdown, he didn't let on. He'd just handed me another glass of red wine and sat down next to me, his arm quickly wrapping around my shoulders, just like old times. Like nothing ever happened.

"Look, you can't tell them that! Sweet Levit, they voted for you for a reason. Now, that reason may be that you are the hottest piece of ass there, other than Jamie and myself, of course, but chances are, they probably also like you! And even if the kids wanted to change their minds now, neither Jamie nor I are still technically employed there, so they are stuck with you on this one, spring chicken, for better or worse. And your job now is to inspire them with some bullshit one last time. It doesn't have to be true—they won't sue you for misrepresentation or anything."

I would miss my good ol' Abbott (and his accent) come tomorrow, I rightly suspected.

"I thank you, my dear graduating class of 2014, for bestowing such an honor on me. After all, you were my first—"

Knowing my kids well, I paused to allow for some laughter that came just as anticipated, as if it were timed and rehearsed.

"But you were, I swear!"

More laughter.

"When I met all of you, I was, as some may say, 'green.' Y'all were but fourteen, I was only eighteen—"

I was on fire! You could hardly hear how much effort I had to exert in order to produce every syllable, what it was costing me not to cry.

"I have watched you grow. I even think I made a couple of friends, though I guess we'll see if any of you will accept that Facebook friend request from me now that you don't need to suck up to me for a grade.... On the other hand, you know what—maybe you shouldn't accept that friend request.... Yeah, now that I think about it, just ignore it! You have to start over and there's no sense in bringing your past with you. I'm that past and I'll only hold you back," I announced, stifling a sigh that could only come out as fragmented and tortured as it felt. It was all lies. There was no storage cubby large enough for all of our baggage—it had no choice but to follow us around, no matter our intention.

Sweating under the stage lights, I felt as if my carefully applied makeup, including my mother-approved (via a Skyped conversation from London, anyway) scarlet lips, were about to melt and slide down my face. Breathless, unaccustomed to these many sets of eyes on me at once, I looked down briefly, letting my lids draw closed for a moment, but that only made me lightheaded.

"Forget me. Forget us! We were but your stepping-stones. It's time to start over. We'll always be here, unchanged, just the way you remember us…well, some of us will proceed to age at a rate that's more alarming than anything else, like Mr. Abbott, for example, but, for the most part, should you seek a respite, a place to come and rest from the real world—we're here. But try not to spend much time looking back. New chapter, new leaf, fresh start, and all that jazz! So, what say you?" I pretended to scream into the mic.

"Start over!" a unified chorus screamed back at me, right on cue.

Chapter Two: *The Walk Up*

Dr. Kasun (George's intimidatingly polite mother) greeted me downstairs, as if notified as to the exact moment of my arrival. I looked over my shoulder as I trotted up the steps, but Vlad was already gone. To be fair, he did only promise to get me here, not wait for me.

The Central Park-facing glass entrance to the hospital was lit almost egotistically too brightly. It hurt my eyes. After a long day (and a transatlantic flight), I had reluctantly taken pity on myself on my way over and discarded my contact lenses, so my vision was already blurry. I wished I could ask someone to take it down a notch with the display of electric capacity over there but suspected they had other things to do than to worry about my level of comfort.

"Dr. Kasun, I'm so sorry," I croaked when she was finally within my grasp. I reached out my hands to her, but she just grazed my fingertips with hers. They were cold.

"Helen, can you run up to the walk up and bring back a couple of things for us?" Her words were even, her tone—courteous, incongruous with the setting and the circumstances. "You know, socks, underwear, that sort of thing."

I nodded aggressively as she handed me my old set of keys, feeling a lump settle in my throat, constricting it painfully.

"I'm so sorry…about everything," I whispered, again, my voice breaking. I wasn't sure what exactly I was sorry about, but I bit my lower lip like a schoolgirl being chastised as I shuffled in place all the same.

"Right, sweetheart, I understand. This is not actually about you, I'm sure you know that. I know you feel you're supposed to apologize—it's your Soviet upbringing, I suppose, but don't. It won't help anything. If you want to be helpful, just bring back a few pairs of socks tonight. Your conscience will be clear then, surely," Dr. Kasun smiled thinly. Her eyes were rimmed red, but the rest of her was as immaculate as ever. Her colorless eyes were calm and bottomless, her hair was in a neat, low ponytail, and her light mint cardigan was buttoned just so. My mother never looked that pristine, I noted with some distinct tinge of jealousy. Were that I in George's place, my mom would probably look as if she were just electrocuted.

She began to walk away before I managed to speak again.

"I'm so— I'll be back soon."

"Very well. Call me when you're here and I'll come meet you," Dr. Kasun called back without turning.

"Can't I come up?" I asked in half-whisper.

There was no answer and, eventually, her mint shoulders rounded the corner and vanished from my field of vision.

~~~

After I finally summoned enough will power of myself to move from the spot where I stood rooted by Dr. Kasun's words, my eyes last to turn away from where my former future mother-in-law just was, I had to hail and then fold myself into a simultaneously stuffy and overly perfumed taxi, Vlad being long gone.

When I first saw him that afternoon, I couldn't shake the impression that he looked as if he were placed there—inside the industrial, less than generously lit "Arrivals" terminal at J.F.K.—against his will. His shoulders slumped, his eyes narrowed, you'd think he'd been waiting for us for ages. Our plane disappointingly on-time, being forced to stand there at gunpoint would be the only justification for the amount of exasperation written all over my brother's face.

"I'll drive you to Mount Sinai and then take your bags to mom and dad's," Vlad had informed me the second I approached him, my legs reluctantly obeying my brain's basic commands, awkwardly dragged behind the rest of my body. Jamie and Abbott were kind enough to frame me at my sides, as if I needed help remaining upright. Taking me in briefly, my brother deemed it appropriate to give me a limp hug. My arms were slow to reciprocate.

"Okay," I'd answered, unquestioning, into his coarse sweater. Catching Jamie's awkward stance out of the corner of my eye, I'd eventually, and warily, detached
~~~

myself from my brother. "Ummm, my friend needs a place to stay—" I had ventured in Russian, half abandoning the thought when Vlad, stunned, let out a semi-muted grunt.

"So this is why you were in such a hurry to go on this vacation? Because of this guy? Are you kidding me? There's a man half dead because of you and you're thinking of where to take your new boyfriend?" he had puffed, answering in his own laborious Russian.

Dizzy and dehydrated from having sat motionless the entire flight, drinking nothing but cheap wine the whole time, I struggled to find enough Russian words to string together in order not to have to use any English fillers for Abbott and Jamie to understand.

"Wait…what?" I'd interrupted my own derailing train of thought to stammer in English. "He's…alive?"

"Yes, what did you think? The idiot tried to kill himself with Tylenol. Shot his liver, from what I understand, but he'll live…I guess. I don't know. And I don't care, really. He's in the ICU, and apparently mom thinks it's imperative for you to be there, too, though I don't see why that'd be a good idea." My brother had sighed exasperatedly, then, visibly relieved to be back to the language that's been his primary for decades. "Look, I have a wife and kids waiting at home, and mom asked me to chauffeur you around tonight. Really, can't we just get going?"

My face red and my ears burning, I felt my heart

throw itself against my ribcage with poetic desperation. It was the heft of this relief that took me by surprise. Relief! For a split second, I allowed myself to consider that there could be some hope for me now. A fresh start could perhaps still be had, after all. Maybe Jamie's roses and I stood a chance at starting over together.

"He's alive?" I'd asked again, pointlessly, my voice barely an audible whisper.

Seeing my brother purse his lips and shake his head side to side, I was briefly convinced that if I squinted, I would be able to see his patience physically drain from him. When I tried to do just that, my eyes stung with dryness.

"Vlad, look, this guy is not my boyfriend. We work together, and he needs a place to stay. He just got divorced, but it's really messy—I'll tell you later. You say you are going to take my bags to Jersey anyway, so why can't you drive him to mom and dad's, too, and I'll come as soon as I can?" I had to stretch my Russian to its limit for this one. The two men stiff as columns at my sides would eventually need to be officially acknowledged. I still hadn't made any introductions.

"No." English.

I saw my brother examine Jamie to my right, his eyes moving up and down, pausing in the vicinity of my shoulder, where Jamie's long fingers were mindlessly wrapping themselves around my flesh. His ring was probably visible, too. I'd cringed.

"Abbott, can Jamie stay with you?" I'd asked without removing my gaze from Vlad's face, preemptively steading my jaw to prevent a tempting sob from escaping.

"No worries, sweet Levit. Of course Jamie can stay with me, can't you Jamie? I've got a couch."

I wondered what Stephanie would think about the proposed arrangement: the woman was toiling around with her luggage nearby, as if unsure if she were allowed to join our misshapen circle. If the dust would ever settle, I made a mental note to figure out how Abbott, such an overgrown hipster, ever wound up with this 80's suburban artifact.

Jamie's hair now just grazing the side of my face, I could only imagine him nodding in agreement. I'd physically ached to look up, to touch his cupid's bow of his lip, but feared that doing so would only cause the fog hanging over me to thicken and descend. And then I wouldn't be able to see anything at all.

"That's great, thanks, Abbbott. If that works, of course."

When was the last time we were on the same team? When was he unquestionably on my side last? Was it that one time in middle school, when this one intimidatingly overgrown girl named Erin threatened to have her cousins come beat me up for forgetting to pay her back the quarter I'd borrowed the day before (and all for some expired vending machine chips)? He'd picked me up after school that day, after I'd called him, panicked, and waited for me, ceremoniously, by the hood of his car, his fully reflective sunglasses on, his arms crossed menacingly across his chest, his crisp leather jacket. I, of course, had borrowed money from Jessica to pay Erin back with interest before I ever got in the car (and the cousins were nowhere to be seen), but to know that my brother rushed to my rescue had made not only my day, but my entire tenure at that school. It was easy to blame our distance on Alla, his wife, but that'd be too convenient. I was the culprit—I'd long ago given up trying to be the daughter my parents wanted, the sister my brother deserved. And now, I'd almost killed my fiancé. It was too late to beg for forgiveness.

Our staring match was over when I blinked and looked around the gray terminal. Veronika, I saw, was slumped in her mother's suffocating embrace to our left, her father patting her on the back, unnaturally, as if it were the first time in his life that he'd ever allowed himself the liberty. To our right, Sophie's parents were squishing her hair with their kisses, her cheeks pinched and stroked, alternatively. "Welcome Home" balloons were everywhere. Half embarrassed in front of my students for the stingy reception I myself was getting, and half delirious from the influx of information thrown my way in the last twenty-four hours (if not all two hundred and forty), I had lunged at my brother again.

~~~
~~~

Jet-leg catching up with me, adrenaline draining, I more rolled out of the cab than stepped out of it. My eyes as heavy as my head, I couldn't help but laugh when I saw that the landing at the top of the steps was empty—predictably, my bike was no longer there. If I had either the time or the energy left for a stroll around the neighborhood, I was sure that, within a five-block radius, I'd find a homeless man (or woman, to be fair) who'd been made a bike richer as recently as a week ago. George would not have waited more than a few hours after coming back to an empty apartment to make sure that anything of mine that hadn't been moved out by me would be moved out by him.

I stumbled up to the fourth floor, up the familiar staircase—its flights long, the corridors ominously lit—even though I'd so recently, and so vehemently, sworn to myself that I would never. My old key slid effortlessly into my old lock, remembering me instantly, and my old door yawned its welcome with unexpected ease.

The lights were on throughout the apartment, the whole place a mess. It wasn't the EMTs' job to clean, I shrugged to myself as I slowly closed to door behind me, making sure it wouldn't thud shut and wake anyone else. The people in the building had probably been through enough already. The girls downstairs were of that "shrieky" variety to begin with, from what I remembered, and discovering George's comatose body was probably not something that could serve to soothe their delicate psyches.

Fully dressed, my bag still hanging across my body like the thinnest, most impractical of shields, I kneeled on the floor to pick up our scattered photos (some torn, some burnt, as I discovered upon closer inspection). Dirty laundry surrounded me—a good half a dozen pairs of worn underwear and socks were littered throughout. All I could do was focus on the task at hand to keep myself from trying to do the math in the futile effort to figure out what exactly Jamie and I were busy doing at the precise moment when George was gorging on a questionable amount of over-the-counter pain medication.

A failed suicide attempt, I mused as I stacked our many photos in the center of the semi-circle comprised of George's stale socks. This was potentially worse than a successful one would've been, as far George would be concerned, I feared. If this were nothing but a cry for help, the fact that, as my brother informed me on our way out of J.F.K. and toward the city, those precious dancer girls downstairs called the cops when they heard him hit the floor with a thump would be, of course, fortuitous timing and a blessing of an outcome; but were George serious—on the off chance that he did in fact want to end his life for good—this failure would only bruise his ego further. He had to be able to do something right—his legacy deserved at least that small a victory. I allowed myself a snicker at my benevolence.

Somewhere in the piles of George's not laundered boxers I found a few of those lacy pairs of underwear I'd left behind. My kneecaps pressed painfully into the floor by my own weight, I tried to shuffle back, away from them.

Every birthday, every anniversary, like clockwork, I got lingerie. The man seemed to derive incomprehensible pleasure from watching me unwrap his delicate gift-wrappings as I feigned surprise at the receipt of yet another thong and balconette bra. Any romantic (as well as kinky) appeal of it all was lost after about the third such imposition. And the rules were soon clear—for any act of intimacy to commence, lace had to be involved; the romantic (as well as kinky) appeal of this too was lost after about third such imposition. These weren't gifts—these were little pieces of physical obligation wrapped in pretty bows, and there were times I was ready to kill for a teddy bear or another thoughtless throwaway gift picked up in the seasonal aisle at a Duane Reade over another frivolous pair of underwear. My friend Jessica tended to get those stuffed animals a lot.

"You know the rule," George would remind me when his hand would travel down my pants and find cotton in place of lace if I ever dared to pretend to forget. "You ain't getting any of this unless you comply with the rules," he'd tsk, pointing to his pelvis, playfully, as if this were all a joke.

Eventually, of course, I'd stopped complying, anyway. And, eventually, of course, I left. And then George tried to kill himself.

My sweatshirt now a makeshift laundry basket, I crept toward the bathroom with all these relics of the past.

I couldn't wait to deposit them into a proper receptacle. Bending down to unload the pile into the hamper, I got a whiff of the towel thrown haphazardly on the edge of the sink. It was the same towel that smelled of George's cologne that I used to wipe my face before leaving for Paris with Jamie. Jamie. Was I still allowed to think about him?

The scent of the towel made me dizzy. It should've been washed weeks ago, when George first left on the retreat that allowed for my clean escape to begin with. Making small, cautious movements, I threw it in with the rest of the clothes that weren't necessarily physically dirty, per se, but were designated as such, anyway, and waddled toward the bedroom.

The lights on there, too, I was greeted by more fossils—more photos, my old watch, his grandmother's quilt. I picked up the pieces of a broken mug that used to sport our photo on it (a grainy snapshot taken the very night we met, blurry on account of the fact that we were aboard a booze cruise), and allowed myself a minute's rest on the very edge of the musty pile of sheets, the unmade mattress that used to be our old bed.

I was tired, my limbs achy, muscles almost pulsing involuntarily from the many wakeful hours they'd had to endure. Suddenly, it was imperative that I close my eyes. I eased myself back to lie down, releasing the ceramic fragments in my weak grasp.

And then I tried picturing it.

What did he do, exactly? And how did he do it? Did he dump an entire bottle of Tylenol directly into his mouth or did he take a sip of water in between each recommended dose? Did he consider other ways? I didn't see belts or sheets or laces in the wreckage of the living room. No razors jumped out at me in the bathroom. But, then again, no empty Tylenol bottles were to be seen anywhere, either.

I felt sleep nearby, its tentacles working their way up my legs, wrapping themselves around my belly. Instinctively, I rubbed my face harshly to urge it to remain awake—alert. I didn't deserve sleep.

My hands smelled of the cash I'd forked over to the cab driver at the curb; I must not have washed them since the flight. At once, I was upright and back at the bathroom sink. Those twenty-eight years of being told to wash my hands in barky Russian weren't for nothing. I pumped the last of the Kasun's anti-bacterial soap into my cupped hands and waited for the water to warm just a degree above tolerable. Of its own volition my head leaned forward, my forehead now resting on the mirror. I closed my lids, my lashes brushing the glass, my breath fogging it up.

Frozen in a disorienting upright slumber, I stayed there for a time neither long nor short, nothing there to act as a reference, a measure, only fragmented images flashing before my eyes keeping me company: there I was on Jamie's chest, there I was on George's…and Javier worked his way in there, too. When I looked down at my hands, there was no soap left on them and my skin was red.

I shook myself awake. I had one last obligation to fulfill—to collect those socks and underwear on Dr. Kasun's behalf. But instead, I crawled back into the bedroom and reclaimed my spot on the bed. Without thinking, I felt myself curl into a tight ball on my left side, my knees folding into my chest as dictated by years of habit, my kneecaps pressing against the wall beneath the window ornamented with a fire escape on the other side of the façade brick, for old times' sake. I couldn't stay there, I knew. Still, I hugged the pillow that was still moist with George's sweat and let sleep pull me in, giving in much too easily. Dreamless and fitful sleep resulted.

My pocket vibrating was what woke me.

"Sweet Levit, is everything okay? Jamie was going to call, but I don't know if your mother-in-law is there—"

"She's not my mother-in-law," I mumbled, my brain slowly waking.

"Okay, didn't mean to offend. I meant George's mother. Anyway, we, or I, can come get you, if you want. Are you at the hospital?" Abbott sounded like the Abbott I always knew, and I almost said yes. But then I remembered Paz. And Sophie. Dumb and blind the entire flight over, I was finally coming to now.

"Abbott, why in the world would you talk to me like that? As if everything's the way it's always been?" I shrieked, my eyes stubbornly closed.

I heard Abbott breathe.

"Spring chicken, what are you talking about?" He feigned surprise rather unconvincingly, I thought. "I can come get you, drive you here, or to your parents', it's up to you, really—"

"Abbott, I don't want any rides from you!"

He'd given me rides home before (the walk up, I mean), but only whenever he had his car with him and the weather was such that I couldn't pass up the offer. I enjoyed riding with him. His car always smelled even mintier than his breath. His radio was always set to classic rock. I felt safe in that car. Safe and warm—its seats heated. The only downside was having to always leave my bike at the school on those days, which meant public transportation for me the following morning. Was that his M.O.? Who else was given these lifts, having to leave something that afforded them some semblance of autonomy behind? Was Sophie? Paz? Surely Paz was too sophisticated to fall for a two-door Acura.

"Sweet Levit, what's the matter?"

"Well, gee, I don't know," I puffed again, childishly. My arm was asleep under the weight of my head. I pumped my fist to get some blood back in there. "Where's Jamie?" I breathed when Abbott said nothing—an admission as loud as words could have never been, as far as I was concerned.

"Right here."

"Tell him I'll call him later," I instructed, flatly, my eyes now open and on the gate, the ripeness of George's sheets suddenly making me nauseous. "I have to go back to the hospital now."

"Where are you now?" I heard Jamie ask, that voice as plush and soft and dizzying as it was in my ear not so long ago. I was probably on speaker the entire time. Fuck, I thought as I took another whiff of George's sheets. Blinking, I imagined Jamie's face, his mouth so full and inviting.

I sat up, abruptly.

"The walk up."

Chapter Three: *Gypsy*

When I was little and would overhear my father giving someone directions to or from our house by referencing a "park and ride," I always imagined it to be a neighborhood amusement park that my parents simply hadn't gotten around to taking me to yet. Having to one day find out that it was nothing more than a drab parking lot near a bus or a train station was a bit of a letdown. Anyway, I hadn't needed to use one in years, and I wasn't about to start: I walked to the bus that Sunday morning.

There wasn't much time for sleep the night before, for which I was grateful. Having turned down Mr. Kasun's insincere offer to drive me "home," and refusing to call on Abbott, Jessica, or my father, it took me a long and petrifying lifetime to get to my parents' house by public transport that evening. Satisfied to find my bags (as well as all but the few boxes still at Abbott's) already there, I waved off my mother's late-night dinner, jogged up the stairs two at a time, and closed the door to my room quietly behind me, careful not to wake dad, who, I knew, already had enough trouble sleeping without my puttering around in the middle of the night. There wasn't much of a point in getting under the covers of the bed my mother had made for me on my old fold-out couch, the green fabric of it fainter now than I ever remembered it being in high school; it unlikely ever expected to have me back. Having lived through almost a three-week re-acclimatization period after having returned home from Spain years go, I knew that, with the jet lag, I'd be up at 5 A.M. no matter what I tried to do. I considered unpacking, but that would mean I was staying.

Groggy and shaky, I sat through an awkward breakfast with my parents, where no one said much of anything. George's stab at suicide managed to make us strangers, at least for the day, but I suspected its effect would continue to widen in radius. Eventually, having demonstratively cleared my plate by disposing of its contents directly into the garbage pail before washing it, I insisted on walking to the bus, claiming that I needed to clear my head, which wasn't exactly a lie. Cold with the early morning spring chill and lack of rest, I waited inside a formerly translucent bus shelter and eventually boarded a weekend bus into the city.

I thought I was alone inside the stale vehicle until I noticed a teenage girl seated all the way in the back. Judging solely from remembering myself at her age, I guessed that she likely had as much of a plan as to what to do when she got there as I had. The difference between us was only about a decade.

I was this girl once upon a time. Slightly less put together, of course (there was never a scarf comprised of tiny skulls artfully looped around my neck, and I never had perfectly ombre highlights, either), but, at the very least, I was certainly seventeen once, so we had that much in common. I, too, spent my fair share of weekends going into the city aboard a New Jersey Transit bus, just like this girl probably did. Most often, it was without any justification, though I'd always tell my parents that it was all in the name of research on a paper for one A.P. class or another. I sure had enough of those to pick from. Sometimes Jessica would come with me, but, more often than not, I was on my own, always staring straight ahead, refusing to acknowledge the scenery around me. With every toll my bus would waddle through, the purple letters of EZ Pass bright overhead, the faster my heart would beat. I was never sure if the nerves of not knowing my way around Manhattan were to blame or whether it was just something I ate before I'd left the house. Like a gypsy, I'd ride the bus whenever I could, simultaneously aimless and full of unarticulated purpose.

"Did you know I was just driving by?" I asked when I picked up my phone on the first ring. I briefly turned to check on the teen girl sitting behind me to make sure that she saw that I was indeed talking on the phone and not to myself; or worse—to her.

"What do you mean?"

Jamie sounded like he was still in bed. I imagined him to be warm, his straw-straight hair pasted lazily to his long face.

"I just passed through Staten Island. Aboard an overheated bus," I explained, quieter. "Are you still at Abbott's?"

"Yeah. Can't sleep."

"Ditto. Is he up? Did you tell him anything?"

"You mean about what Ver said? The whole thing

with Paz and Sophie? No. Should I?"

Our last morning in London, Veronika certainly had left me with a whole lot of information but also, somehow managed to say nothing at all. Abbott was allegedly having an affair with Paz, and also, as of late, with Sophie. Allegedly. No one spoke to Sophie, no one spoke to Paz, but the accusations were out there, loud and substantial—he demands sexual favors in exchange for better grades. I wondered how many kids were already in the know.

"No, no. I think I have to speak to Paz first," I mumbled as I rubbed my forehead, as if all answers would reveal themselves if only I rubbed hard enough. My sinuses still felt heavy and foreign, but my fever, at least for the moment, seemed to have been forgotten at the Virgin Terminal at Heathrow.

"I agree. I mean, he can come across as a bit creepy, but this is serious shit. And Paz? You know what that girl is capable of." Jamie laughed and I flashed back to their close encounter in Paris—her manicured fingers inside his belt. "Anyway, are you coming by?" he yawned.

I closed my eyes. They were heavy, but I wasn't so sure that I would indeed be able to fall asleep were I given the opportunity.

"Can I decide later?"

Of course I could, he said. Anytime, he assured. I imagined his soft, long lips stretching wide in that seductive grin of his and wished off this bus immediately.

"Helen? Are you still there? I was thinking to go look at some rooms, apartments. You're welcome to come with," Jamie proposed, patiently, slowly, as if talking to a child. "Helen? Are you—"

"Hospital. I should probably go to the hospital," I muttered, surprising myself. I opened my eyes and scrunched up my face in not so much disgust as disbelief-I swore I'd never go back. This was the furthest I'd ever gotten. I'd even had me a chaser, as Jessica had so eloquently put it. But it was also an urge that burned with the excitement of its realization; there was nothing I wanted more, it seemed.

"Are you sure?"

If he were jealous, it didn't read. It was a cautious, academic, or perhaps even artistic, poetic, empathetic curiosity.

"I'm not, no. But I have to, anyway."

Chapter Four: *Addiction*

The hospital was cold: the floor, the air around me, the entire establishment—frigid. Were I brave enough to touch a wall, I was sure I'd get frost on my fingers. There were plenty of hand-sanitizing stations around, so I suppose I could've tested my hypothesis in relative safety, but I didn't dare. Instead, I wadded ahead with the posture and stride of a penguin on ice, afraid to trip, or worse—lose the bed in my sights. I shivered in my coat and buttoned it all the way up as I approached the glass cubicle that contained George. Dr. and Mr. Kasun, I was informed by a friendly PA, had only just stepped away for coffee; it was the first time since Mr. Goran Kasun (or, as I knew him—George Kasun) was admitted that the two did not pee in shifts. She was pretty, that friendly PA—a little pug-nosed, but tall and slender, hair the color of chocolate, mouth small and pouty. Her name was ethnically ambiguous. When I blinked, I almost saw the same androgyny in her that made Jamie so stunning. I made it a point to try not to blink anymore.

"He should be fine…well, his liver took a huge hit, so he may need a transplant, but he'll walk out of here. Eventually, anyway," Reina (the physician assistant) told me before sliding the glass door open to reveal George himself. The swoosh of it took all the air out of my lungs with it, leaving me mute and breathless, my legs made of silly putty.

The wires, the beeping monitors…. The volume of it all seemed to swell by the second, and I felt my head begin to swim, sure that my knees would buckle if I dared to step forward.

"He's just asleep, not in a coma or anything," Reina rushed to explain. She must've heard my bag slide down my shoulder and hit the floor, as if chasing my jaw to see who'll be the first to make it there.

His veiny foot was dressed in a sock I'd brought over the night before. Dr. Kasun had met me downstairs when I came back with it (as well as a plastic bag full of other intimates), dizzy from my nap in her son's bed. When I'd asked to come up, she pensively shook her head, saying only that this wasn't the right time.

"I think I'd feel better if I saw him," I'd pleaded in a way that made me hate myself.

"It's not about you, dear Helen," the good doctor had sighed, nodding as if to implore me to understand, even though she had to know that I could not.

Briefly considering sitting down on the only armchair in the room, I remained upright at the foot of the bed, fidgeting with the buttons on my coat. The chair was occupied by Dr. Kasun's jacket, anyway, and I'd probably dislodged enough in that woman's life already.

I fixed the blanket to cover the familiar black sock and walked around to the window to draw the shades. The sun seemed too bright on George's face, and with all those wires, that fork shoving oxygen up his nostrils, he could not have been comfortable as it was. It was the least I could do. My body attempted to sweat but couldn't help but shiver. Surely this incongruous atmosphere wasn't good for the patients—all fifteen of them, as I'd counted on my way in, hoping my relation (or lack thereof) wouldn't be questioned by any of the uniformed staff.

The smell of the place, the Lysol, the ammonia—it was potent. Had I eaten breakfast that morning, I'd be afraid of retching. What if I'd never moved out, never gone to Europe, would George still need a new liver? Had I never seen Jamie Sola at that bus stop in the rain—would he?

My hands shaky inside my pockets, I slowly brought my eyes up to George's face. If only a little pale, he looked just the way he did on my computer screen, in my Skype window, a little over ten days ago—same wide forehead, same pimples on his chin, same sparse eyelashes on his eyelids, same shattered lips. That was the last time I saw his face. I flashed right back to my place on my and Jamie's bed in our hotel room in Paris, and the trip gave me a head rush.

George's muscular body was well hidden under that standard, emasculating, hospital-grade gown, while his short-cropped hair lay limp on a starchy pillow. Remove the medical accessories and not much appeared out of the ordinary. Perhaps, were I to lie next to him in that mechanically operated bed, it'd be like nothing ever happened.

Without thinking, my shoulders quivering as if I

were holding on to a live, exposed wire, I reached out my hand to touch his fingers. Their nails were painfully bitten down, and they were familiar, but I didn't dare make actual contact. I hovered—nothing more. I pretended to stroke them, remembering the way I'd petted them that one time I accompanied him to the E.R. after he got into an altercation with four equally oversized teenagers over something not a single party could remember afterwards. As the fingers on his right hand were being reset, I'd stroked the ones on his left. He'd sucked in his lips from the pain as he did his best not to squeeze my hand back. "Tears are okay for emotion, not pain," he'd always say. I smiled at the memory now.

What would I do if he woke up now? I wondered.

I felt my neck stretch of its own volition, my head lowering, as if, were there no witnesses dressed in scrubs of much plainer variety than any of the ones Jessica wore to work, I'd rest on this man's shoulder after all, embrace his thick waist, wrap my tired limbs around him, and beg for forgiveness. Catching myself just in time, I tried to shake the uncomfortable warmth making itself at home right atop my diaphragm; I shook my head hard enough for my ponytail to slap me in the face. I hoped it was just the jet lag talking.

"I just saw him lying there and all these memories came flooding back. I felt all gooey-legged and soft-bellied, you know what I mean?"

"It's pity, not love," Jessica dismissed. I sat on the

steps of the hospital, shell-shocked, having just been asked by Dr. Kasun to "leave at once," before she explained that she didn't think it'd be a good idea for George to see me there when he woke up. The woman squeezed my shoulder and nudged me softly toward the door when I wouldn't comply.

"Where is your Turk?" Jess asked.

"At Abbott's."

"Okay, I don't know who that is, but go there, Helen, what the hell?" she shrieked. "Don't you dare go back to George because you feel sorry for him—"

"I don't feel sorry for him! I think I—"

"Don't you dare finish that sentence! You don't love him. Did you love him two weeks ago?" I didn't say anything in response, just sucked on the overly sweet orange juice I'd picked up in the lobby on my way out; it was undoubtedly made exclusively from concentrate. "See? So you don't love him now, either," this helped Jess conclude. "Please, you saw him in that ass-less gown, color drained from his face, no dignity to be accounted for, and you felt bad. It's okay. It's natural. You're not a terrible person—you empathize. But it's an addiction—you want to feel something for him, which is only logical considering how much time you wasted on him. Your brain wants to justify it all." On her end, I heard kids shriek. She was likely at a playground with her sons. We were finally in the same time zone. I wanted to ask where

Max, her husband, was, but I knew she'd only say that I was changing the subject, which I suppose I was desperate to do. "But don't confuse what you're feeling with love, Helen. Please, I beg of you."

I finished the last of my juice, the paper carton crumpling in my grip. "But I caused this…," I whispered.

"Not everything's about you, Helen. He took a bottle or two of Tylenol because…I don't know why, but it's not because of you. Maybe he hates himself, maybe even you, but he's an adult and responsible for himself. You're responsible only for you, so please just go get laid and then tell me all about it in disgusting detail." I wished Jessica and I were in physical proximity to each other; I'd love a hug, the feel of her ample bosom on my own small set.

"I can't go where he is," I finally moaned.

"Why not?"

"Because Abbott is potentially screwing half the school and I don't really want to see him before I get to speak to the original source of these rumors—hear it from the horse's mouth, so to speak."

"Abbott is that older teacher you're close to over there, right? In any case, why is the Turk quarantined because of this Abbott man?"

I laughed. It felt wrong with the hospital behind me.

Chapter Five: *Technicolor*

Nuzzling, hiding in each other's flesh, our clothes only partly shed, we tried to muffle our own grunts. With our limbs contorted and sharp edges of the desk painfully wedged against various exposed slivers of skin, my mind only periodically wandered as I tried to remember whether or not I'd locked the door after Veronika. She'd stopped by to simultaneously inquire about "Mr. Sola" (like a little broken mechanical parrot) and how my "fiancé" was doing, but I had no answers I wanted to share with a student, even my Veronika. Instead, buying time, as well as some vague air of authority, I'd asked again, if she was sure about college.

My scrawny little protégé had rolled her olive eyes at me.

"Oh, Ms. Levit, who cares? I can still play, and I will still play. So I won't go to college for music performance—so what? So who cares if I won't play professionally for a living? I will actually get a practical education, instead. I am good at school, after all. I'm not giving up guitar altogether or anything." In a school of conceited prodigies, Veronika was a rare flower I'd tended to for almost four years. Her blasé attitude was as refreshing as it was sobering. But going to a city college to study accounting in order to stay in her homophobic parents' graces could not be worth giving up her entire self. I certainly hoped I'd been a better teacher than that. The whole thing left me with an uncomfortable heartburn. I'd sat dumbfounded with jet lag, unable to verbalize much of anything to contradict Veronika. I watched my yogurt curdle in its round container in front of me, the thought of chewing or swallowing revolting, before bringing my eyes back up to her. The girl looked mostly unchanged since our last conversation on my unmade bed in London: same heavy mop of hair in need of some deep conditioning, same ill-fitting clothes. "Don't do anything I wouldn't do!" she'd winked when she saw Jamie approach my doorway. Before I could say anything, she was gone and my door clicked shut behind her.

It was an impulse—a transparent and desperate attempt at spontaneity, this whole Jamie and me on my desk business. One flick of those lush eyelashes contouring those almond-shaped eyes and my mouth drew to his as if he were hiding a magnet under his tongue while mine was sporting a piercing. I latched on to him for dear life as he airlifted me to the table, his breath warm, sweet, and so imminent. The feel of him against me egged me on, though my eyes remained open the entire time for fear of George reclaiming his old spot in Jamie's place on top of me. There simply was no way of knowing how the universe would treat my recent musings, I feared.

On my way in to work, my hour and a half aboard that suffocating bus was spent largely trying to remember the exact lines of Jamie's tattoo; it was a welcome distraction from George and his wires, but it was also a handy way to stay awake. Nowadays, I would have to wake up at five in the morning every day in order to make it in by eight, I knew. I needed enough material to keep my mind from wandering. This much unaccounted for time was a dangerous thing in my state. Sleepy and nauseous, I would, from here on out, have to sit through a force-fed breakfast of ingredients much too fried for the dark of the early spring morning (and served to the soundtrack of my mother's sphygmomanometer cuff) before walking to the bus stop. Eventually, surely I would succumb to being temped to miss my Upper West Side apartment; over there I had to wake up no earlier than seven (six thirty at the very earliest, on Regents proctoring days) for the same call time at work. And breakfast was a street bagel and coffee by the school steps.

"I missed you," I conceded too quickly when Jamie and I finally disassembled, mere minutes after we'd first began clawing at each other. Though I looked directly at him, I avoided locking eyes with him.

"You? At least you didn't have to share a shower with Abbott all weekend," Jamie rolled his eyes as he buckled his belt. He watched as I struggled with the miniature buttons on my blouse with an amused twinkle in his eye. "You missed one," he pointed to my still exposed midriff. I hurried to fix my mistake.

"Oh God, not you too!" I laughed as he rolled and re-rolled his sleeves to expose the roses on his left arm. "I found myself literally running up the stairs earlier just to avoid having to make small talk with the man with all this junk I now have in my head. The image of you showering with him may just be the last straw for my fragile psyche."

"Okay, we didn't have to share the shower, per se,

but there is only one bathroom at his place so there is a fair amount of cohabitation. You should remember as much from having to share a room with me in Paris."

Those lips, those vines…. Jess had a point—this was what my temporary lapse in judgment needed—this beautiful distraction.

"So where was Stephanie with all this shower sharing business going on?"

"Oh dear God, that woman's lipstick is all over the only hand towel Abbott seems to own over there. What in the world is their deal?" Jamie groaned as he plopped down in my visitor's chair and rested his heels on my (now admittedly much messier than before) desk.

"There's much we don't know about Abbott, it appears."

"You can say that again! I mean, I only had to watch them suck face before I left yesterday morning, because when I came back at night, he was out. Guess he took her home, and who knows what else after. He gave me a key out of some bucket, where I presume he keeps more copies."

My fingers grew cold and my ears began to burn.

"So you went apartment hunting, after all?" I asked breathlessly, sitting myself down.

"'Hunting' is too big a word for what I did. I

checked out a couple of rooms my buddies had leads on, nothing special. And none of my friends have a free couch at the moment, or so they tell me, so I'm stuck at Abbott's for the time being. Thanks for setting that up, by the way."

"I didn't, really. Another minute and he would've offered."

"Abbott is your dude, so you asking definitely helped. Anyway, you were invited along on this apartment search of an expedition. Still are, as a matter of fact," he said with a smile so intent on reading frank, it seemed almost smug.

I looked up at him from behind the few strands of my hair that had managed to fall loose to hang in front of my face during all the commotion. His bright eyes illuminated the rest of his face in an improbable way, making everything sharper—his nose, his plush, slightly downward-turned lips full of almost girlish pigment. Everything was indeed Technicolor when he was around.

"I know I was— am, thanks. It's all crazy right now. Maybe I can…you know, help you figure something else out until I can properly join you? In looking for a new place, I mean," I sputtered, mesmerized by the depth of his hair color—it really was crow black, his olive skin looking almost alabaster by contrast. "Maybe I can ask my brother to house you for a bit?" I muttered before I could properly think that proposition through. "Or maybe you can stay with me at my parents' house?" I plowed on, recklessly, stammering, at once busying myself with restacking papers we'd dislodged before. "It's just that between moving in with my parents and—"

I cut myself off. I'd only made it back to New Jersey late last night, and was yet to unpack so much as a box. That was hardly "moving in." The truth was that, after being ousted from the ICU by my former future mother-in-law, I'd spent a significant chunk of my Sunday afternoon on those hospital steps listening to Jessica chastise me, and the other chunk of it on the steps of my old walkup, my keys already safely back in Dr. Kasun's pocket. I'd listened, pointlessly, for my bike's bell in the distance, and periodically looked up (equally pointlessly) to my old windows, the leafy tree above me now truly lush. Maybe having been with Jamie now (and in such a hungry, desperate manner) would help, because last night, all I did was mentally de- and re-construct the soundness of my reasons for leaving George in the first place, for leaving that decrepit walkup full of various perpetual odors that could never be aired out. My phone would periodically let out a grunt as it'd vibrate against the limestone steps, next to me, but I ignored every single incessant call from Abbott. He left messages, but I couldn't bring myself to check those, either. I knew I was expected to look at him with a different set of goggles now, but I hadn't had the time to acquire those, so when he suddenly appeared before me, as if out of thin air and holding a tray of coffee in his right hand, I panicked and ran further down the block. More speed-walked than ran, really. I heard him call out my name, repeatedly, his Scottish accent ringing sharp and reaching far, but my neck wouldn't turn no matter how hard I willed it to, my legs rounding one corner and then another. Flushed with shame, I kept picking up speed. For a split second, I wondered how he ever knew where to find me, but then I remembered that he was the one who helped me haul the last of my belongings out of this apartment. When I'd eventually found myself in midtown, I reluctantly boarded that uncomfortably warm interstate bus. My mother had insisted on sending my dad to pick me up at the Park & Ride this time.

I didn't tell Jamie any of this, although, given Abbott's track record on keeping my secrets, I suspected he would soon know one way or the other. Instead, I leaned back in my chair and watched as Jamie played with the ring that was still on his finger, turning it over and over as if it were oiled. I wondered how long it'd continue to grace his hand.

Chapter Six: *Turbulence*

The elevator jolted and banged to a halt at the precise moment my phone let out a ring, as if the two were planned and coordinated events. I doubted it could be Jess, given that not an hour ago she called me from her delivery room upstairs, panting in slightly premature labor (her husband was apparently stuck in a conveniently timed meeting). I was pretty sure that if I focused hard enough, I would be able to hear her screaming not two floors above where I was now apparently going to be stuck. As the cabin jerked again, the sensation of it flipping my stomach, akin to turbulence, I pulled hard at the alarm knob, startled by the bell it sounded at my command.

"I can't talk right now," I hissed into the phone, hoping that Javier could hear me. I was suddenly hot with the realization that I was in a confined space with Dr. Kasun (as well as a man in a likely backless gown, strapped to a gurney, accompanied by a short, balding aide at his side).

"Jessica is in labor," Javier reported before I could hang up. His English has always been much better than my Spanish would ever be.

"I know, Javier, I'm on my way there right now. I'm stuck in the elevator!" I whispered, turning stupidly, to face a corner as if that would render me inaudible to the doctor.

I wrestled my way out of my coat and shoved my

scarf into its sleeve before turning back around to smile obediently in George's mother's direction. My sinuses still recovering, I had the urge to sniffle but restrained myself for fear of displaying poor manners (though now, post our near-familial acquaintance, I knew that it would hardly matter one way or the other). Three stacks of term papers weighed heavy on my shoulder—Sage's, Ofir's, Jordan's, Riley's, everybody's. Escaping the school building so as not to run into Abbott at the security desk with my bag this bulky was no easy feat.

"Helen, you know that I've never treated you like anything other than a daughter, but George is going through a significant amount of hardship right now, and I think, given your history, it'd be best if you could exhibit enough self-restraint to stay away for the time being."

The knowledge that the cabin was still not moving (despite the staccato distress signal that its speaker was now emitting) was making me sweat profusely. I stammered, stumped for an appropriate response.

"But—"

"Are you planning on getting back together?"

"I don't k—"

"Then please have some self-respect and don't make me say any of this again."

Our eyes were locked on each other's: my dirty brown on her eerily bottomless gray, neither blinking. The volumes of our voices were well controlled; I'd like to think that that bit wasn't just on the account of our captive audience, though that was surely a factor.

"I wasn't—"

"You weren't what?"

"I'm not here to see him."

"You are, Helen. I saw you by the ICU earlier. I had to chase you in here, for goodness' sake. Let's not get silly here."

She was right. Like the coward that I was, instead of rushing to my laboring friend's side, I'd stopped by the ICU and stood at its doors like a homeless puppy waiting for a bone, not daring to step foot onto its actual territory-proper for fear of being shooed away. It was a pull I could neither rationalize nor fight. Reina spotted me and waved, but she didn't approach me, either, likely already chastised for having briefed me on George's condition at all.

I stood leering, various images of us flashing before me. Like our Groupon trip to the New York Trapeze School, where he could've very well made fun of my inaptitude but instead gave me practical and patient tips until I was able to let go and do that crazy grip change. Or the time we were the only ones at the bumper cars arcade in Coney Island. Or my first Uncle Luigi's in Park Slope. I feared that I would continue to do this (the creepy lurking and reminiscing) every day for the rest of my life now, or at least until George would be moved. He did always say that I was a slow learner. I imagined I'd continue to stand there, careful to exhale to the side, afraid that otherwise the automatic doors would pick up my presence and open for me against their own judgment. What I needed was to breathe in Jamie—deodorant with the sweet add-ons of sweat. I needed him now more than those few weeks ago when the fantasy of him alone allowed me to finally leave George.

"I thought you said we can be friends," I practically whined, bitter and childish, to Dr. Kasun, my phone again ringing in my pocket. The man wearing a pair of wrinkly blue scrubs smirked (while his charge seemed to begin to drool). I did my best not to scowl in his direction.

I had a clear memory of this: she said this to me in her office, the day of my flight to Europe. This, of course, was before I knew that Jamie was married, and before I knew that that marriage was no more. Before I gave George hope at reconciliation by moaning compliantly into the phone, all the while fantasizing about Jamie. Before George had tried to end his life by way of Acetaminophen, and before I found myself helplessly chained to this fact.

"We are friends, Helen. There is no reason why we can't be cordial. I'd said as much to you before my son tried to kill himself, but I still mean it now, you have to believe me. I wish you nothing but the best, but I have to protect my son, whatever his wisdom, or lack thereof, when it comes to decision-making. So as a mother, and a friend, I am asking you to please make good on your promise and stay out of my son's life. I know you aren't here to stay, so let's not even go down that rabbit hole." She was close to me now, her cream cheese breath sour. Before I knew it, my forearms were in her wiry grip. "It can't be good for him, this taunting, you understand? When he's better, should you still be so inclined, and if he would like to reach out…but that is his decision. I have to put my foot down, right here, right now. I have to protect what's mine and can't fend for itself, okay, Helen?"

Her eyes, I could see now, were glistening; her hands, I could feel now, were trembling. Maybe they were trying to rattle me awake.

My phone let out another shrill ring.

"Saved by the bell. Please get that, Helen," Dr. Kasun instructed in no uncertain tone.

I complied, cringing at the photo materializing on my screen.

"You're stuck in the elevator? Are you okay?" I heard that familiar concern on the other line—that modest but assured delivery, those vowels unmistakably native to Seville, and immediately felt bad for dreading picking up in the first place.

"Javier, I'm fine, but yes, I'm still in the elevator," I mumbled as discreetly as I could, disoriented under Dr. Kasun's bottomless eyes, growing more breathless with each second I found myself staring into them, drowning. I fumbled to end the call, my eyes still inside hers. "I'll call you back."

"You lived with a Javier before you got together with George, right?"

Trying to make out the voices outside (voices that presumably were working on getting us out), I stalled as I struggled to string my words together, as if it were a foreign language that was required of me, like in Javier's case.

"Javier's parents housed me during my summer semester in Seville. And yes, that was a couple of months before George and I got together," I clarified, growing inexplicably hot. It's been mere minutes, I tried to tell myself; we were hardly running out of air. My palms sweating, I brought my fingers to my neck to scratch it, hoping I could graze my chin to check for any stray hairs nonchalantly enough not to be noticed. Any visible imperfection wouldn't go in my favor now. But, my manicure far from fresh, layers and chunks of that translucent, pale pink missing, I hid my hands away as soon as I caught a glimpse of them.

"I see. I thought his name was Hector for some reason," Dr. Kasun eventually concluded, though her eyes didn't give away whether or not she believed me or even cared. I could feel the man-nurse's close attention, though; he'd be retelling this story to his perennially bored looking co-workers for the rest of the day. I was thankful that his charge now appeared to be completely out, his neck uncomfortably bent, hanging off to the side. "Well, you didn't have to hang up on my account. Take the call, talk to him. No one's cheating on anybody now."

This sounded like a dare. I felt my thumb hover over the "call back" button.

Chapter Seven: *Could Do Worse*

Unfolded, with a crease down the middle, between its two mattresses, my old couch looked more like an open book than a bed. My sheets traditionally ironed (in accordance with some antiquated Soviet mandate) by my occasionally wheezing mother, I felt preemptively guilty for every wrinkle that I knew my clumsy body would impose on it should I lie down, apparently unable to stay still even in my sleep. My socked feet in front of me, my scrubbed clean hands still damp, tired, I sat just beside it, resting my head against its side. I could do worse than my old room, I knew, but I couldn't help but squirm on the cold parquet underneath my buttocks, anyway.

I reached for my bag and wrestled my three Red-Welds out of it—three sections of Government Participation mid-term papers. Had I taken them with me to Europe, I could've been done grading them by the time we landed in Paris, but, high on the charcoal of Jamie's eyes, there was simply no way I could even think about work back then. Instead, all these single-sided, double-spaced pages had been patiently waiting for me on my desk at school, and my students now pouted over not getting their grades on Monday after spring break, as they had anticipated. Not all of them had come along, after all, so not all were placated by all the rumors swirling around the place. They had a point—they needed these back in order to eventually develop them into legitimate term papers due in only a matter of weeks. If I wanted them to do well, a few had muttered on their way out of class, it would only be fair if I afforded them maximum possible time. These were seniors, and expecting them to care through the very end of June was an exercise in self-deceit. I had to hurry up while at least some were still plugged in.

Aisha's paper on evolution of democracy lay on top. I'd finished grading that one on the bus—B+. I'd also finished Liam's (B-), and Andrew's (C+). Perhaps there were advantages to long commutes that did not involve me pedaling. Fifty-three to go, I sighed to myself as I unbuckled my pants to be able to refold myself in a manner slightly less convoluted and uncomfortable. I still had my small desk nuzzled over there in the corner—a relic from my high school days—but it wasn't the small red dining room table I'd grown so used to at George's. I stayed on the floor.

Bending at the waist, closer to Riley's paper on civil disobedience sprawled before me, my cigarette pants straining at the seams, I tried to remember my first home outside these faded green walls. Never having attended sleep-away camp, it would have to be my first dorm room at American: thirteen by twelve, a cross between a cruise ship stateroom and a prison cell. I had to share it with a third year pre-med student from Minnesota, and she claimed top bunk, relying on seniority as justification. Given that within days of the move-in date she took to doing her boyfriend on that same top bunk with regimented regularity (sometimes even before I could escape the confines of my duvet to tip-toe out of the room and into the common area outside), I'd soon stopped questioning her logic. Unable to fess up to my banishment to the hallway couch to my mother during our nightly phone check-ins for fear of hearing the dreaded "I told you so," I'd always pretended that we had guests in our room to explain the noise. Of course, with this information, my mother wound up thinking that I was popular, thus regularly voicing her preemptive concerns over my GPA. That was probably a good example of a worse place to lay my head than this, I told myself.

There'd be two more dorm rooms between that salmon-colored cubicle and George's walkup. And between those, there was the guest room at the Aiza's home.

It was pleasant, that room: small and dainty, but with a high ceiling and my own balcony that opened into the courtyard. The courtyard housed a fountain that I'd never once seen spout actual water. I shared a wall with Javier, headboard to headboard, our twin beds as if reflections of each other, and on those nights we weren't in each other's rooms watching movies on his outdated twenty-inch television set, we sometimes challenged each other to a tap-off through that wall, rattling out sequences and, without exchanging a word, daring the other to repeat them. Or we'd talk through the same wall, sometimes, until Señora Aiza would stomp down the hall and, like children, we'd immediately cease and, unbeknownst to each other, proceed to hide our heads underneath our respective blankets, feigning sleep and stifling giggles.

I'd always wanted to do my best and speak Spanish when at the Aiza's (such was the alleged objective of the trip, the rationalization for going into further debt for the sake of time abroad for college credit, after all), but other than Javier, everyone in the house graciously slowed down their speech to an almost screeching halt around me, and soon enough, whenever I'd dine with my host family, we'd all resort to English. Javier, however, forever patient but resilient, always insisted on Spanish—that sing-songish way that Andalusians speak. He'd wait for me to leaf through my dictionary to Google idioms, but he rarely wavered. In later years, he would eventually give up, lapsing into his own effortless English post-telephone greetings more often than not, but back in Seville, it was exclusively Spanish for us. Still, Señora Aiza would be none the wiser when some of our movie nights would turn into naked fumbles under one set of her sheets or another. Javier's bed smelled like vanilla, while my room smelled of lavender (likely due to the generous portion of potpourri that Señora Aiza insisted on stashing in my tiny bathroom, like some unspoken, passive-aggressive hint as to some offensive odor she would like to exorcise). The smell was so strong, and the heat outside so oppressive, that, prone to migraines, I actually preferred Javier's bed to mine. For the same reason, I also often kept the doors to my balcony open against multiple instructions to the contrary from my hosts; they weren't burglarized during my stay, but I'd been warned of the danger and accosted regularly (in Spanish)—an educational experience of sorts.

When in Javier's room, even if he was not at home, I liked to bury my face in his sheets and hug his pillow, immediately connecting to my first night in that apartment, when his kindness had descended on me in a degree I'd previously been unaccustomed to accepting:

when, tired and scared, I'd dissolved into toddler-like sniffles and everyone laughed, Javier did not. And when I finally braved the household outside the bathroom where I'd spent the entire evening heaving an embarrassing amount of tears, without any words, he proceeded to wipe my mascara-streaked face with his thumbs, occasionally tucking my unruly hair behind my ears, his puppy-dog eyes as round and warm as the rest of him. His pouty lips promised the same safety in them, and I dove in mid-hysterical gulp for air, part jet-lagged, part terrified of the distance I'd put between myself and everything I'd ever known in a matter of two flights, and part downright hot. My ears having not yet adjusted, I understood very little of what he said to me when we'd temporarily parted, but it didn't matter, because in a matter of seconds, we were one again, my fingers looking for a way inside his pants. It was my first time, but the buzz of a drastic time change made it not as memorable as it should've theoretically been. He, too, smelled of vanilla.

George's apartment smelled like talc when you first walked in. At least it did when I'd first walked in those many moons ago. Baby powder, that's what I first thought of when he'd turned the key in the lock and nudged the door open with too much unnecessary force (likely displayed only because he wanted to show off his flexed bicep). The trip was meant to show me where he saw us living within a year—when I'd graduate from college. After a sweltering summer in Spain, and having to live in yet another dorm room that lacked proper air-conditioning all through an unseasonably hot autumn, walking into a living room so heavily shaded by a tree so tall and leafy was a relief. Its leaves were just beginning to morph their color and the sun was just beginning to set. The patterns that the combination painted on the floor beneath my feet, and above my head, were exquisite. The warm orange glow nudged me in the direction of acquiescence before he formally asked. Javier, despite his regular calls and e-mails, was many miles away by then, unlikely to ever become more than a truly authentic summer fling. And, come May, I knew I was due back home—back in my parents' home on a bank of a pond-come-shallow lake separating the development from a picturesque cemetery. And if I were to live there, I knew I'd need to spend hours aboard one of my high school weekend buses every day to get to graduate school, all the while trying to keep motion sickness at bay whilst reading for class in rush hour traffic. It was but a logical decision.

I'd wiped the sweat off my brow, patted down the trickle of perspiration between my breasts with the cotton of my t-shirt, and kissed George when he finally asked what I thought, immediately high on the cloud of cologne that seemed to envelop him. To my surprise, there was a definite aftertaste of lube to his tongue, but nothing could put me off just then. It was a small, but not a bad place to live. I could do worse, I'd quickly decided. He kissed me back, sliding his calloused hands inside my jeans' back pockets with the agility I wasn't necessarily expecting but did not mind. Soon we were writhing on the shaggy area rug by his parents' old couch—our first time. Thanksgiving was weeks away and, once Dr. and Mr. Kasun gave their seal of approval over some turkey carving, I was set to move in before next summer would even get the chance to properly commence. A lot had changed for me in that one year.

"But I thought we were going to go to Morocco together," Javier had remarked with particular lament when I'd excitedly reported my new living situation to him. I knew he wasn't expecting a response, not really, so, feigning a dropped call, I hadn't said anything at all, thus beginning to gently but persistently shepherd him into a presence in my life that was precious but sexless.

Raily got a B+, which was consistent with her ability and track record. Ofir—a C+, Megan—a B. A C+ was low for Ofir, but I figured, now that he was insisting on throwing away his future in favor of strapping on a uniform and a rifle, what did it matter?

"Why are you sitting on the floor with your pants off?" I heard my mother ask and looked up from my slowly dwindling stack of to-be-graded papers (at least for Section One). She was at my door, which was now open even though I did not remember hearing a knock. She stood expectant for a moment before waving her hands in a gesture of exasperation at my distractedness and walking away toward her own bedroom. I could hear my father take to the bathroom, sure that he was armed with an iPad.

My pants were indeed off, I realized, finally taking myself in. I was apparently using the plush piece of oval that was the foot rug I'd picked on a trip to K-Mart with my dad in junior high as a throw. I must've taken my pants off somewhere between Veronika's paper (a predictable

A+) and Paz's (a similarly predictable B-), to continue to pore over the pages laid out on the floor in front of me while expanding less effort and experiencing less pain. My sweater was still on. I missed not having to explain these things.

Chapter Eight: *Statutory Rape*

I ducked into an elevator reserved for students with disabilities to again avoid Abbott. He'd raised his hand to wave in my direction, his smile as white and childish as usual, his thermos of coffee already in hand, but I jerked my eyes down, hopping inside the cabin with such momentum that I almost knocked Jacob off his feet—an unlucky freshman dancer who happened to re-fracture his freshly healed foot within weeks of getting out of his original cast. It was yet to be determined if he'd dance again. He'd stay at the school, of course, but would it be worth it for him to travel here all the way from Riverdale for regular curriculum? Time would tell. The shy boy shuffled away from me on his crutches, his sideways look of deep distrust.

"Sorry, dude," I tried, emulating what I thought would sound relatable to a teenager. "I'll be grading your class' papers later this week, but I'll be sure to do yours first and add a few bonus points just for this." I smiled earnestly but felt compelled to clarify that this was merely my attempt at humor when Pat raised a curious eyebrow at me. Pat was the school's beloved elevator monitor, though really he was just a young man who'd graduated two years before I'd started teaching and never really found a reason good enough to move on. I liked Pat.

I stumbled out of the elevator last, making sure to give Jacob all the room he and his crutches needed, and staggered towards my office with my bag too heavy for my heels. Intent on finding some liberation in the absence of my bike instead of mourning it, dressing whilst bleary eyed in the morning hour previously unknown to me, I'd decided to try wearing heels too ambitious for my frame to work. By the time I rounded yet another corner of one of the many of the school's starkly lit hallways and could see my office door, I was practically visualizing kicking off my shoes to sit barefoot for the ten minutes I still had before my first period class. The soles of my feet could practically taste the sweet deliverance they were about to be granted when I saw Paz in my visitor's chair.

"What the—"

"Oh, hi, Ms. Levit," Paz purred as she turned in my direction and crossed her legs, simultaneously. Her "liquid" leggings looked indeed liquid on her shapely thighs and her hair was in a perfect fishtail on her shoulder—all at barely eight in the morning. "Mr. Goldwyn let me in, hope you don't mind," she explained before turning briefly back to Mr. Goldwyn—my officemate and a recently divorced Advanced Placement European History teacher. The man practically swooned under her gaze. His full name was Edwin Goldwyn—a name that screamed strictly "elf," which, judging by his height and musculature, he was most certainly not, but this still afforded the kids quite a bit of jokes.

I took two wide, efficient steps to my desk to take the load off my shoulder; there was no break in sight for my feet.

"Ooh, the most beautiful man this place has ever

known is here! No offense, Mr. Goldwyn! How are you, Sola?" Paz suddenly called over my shoulder. "Haven't seen you since Paris, and I was a wee bit under the influence that night, so I do hope you forgive me any excesses. I've been meaning to ask you—were my hands too cold that night? Remember, in that hallway outside the club?" I saw her wink and felt a whirlwind take root in my belly; it was soon shooting its way directly up to my chest, only to leave me nauseous. In an instant, without needing to close my eyes, I flashed back to that moment: in my mind's eye, I again watched as Paz grabbed ahold of Jamie's belt and slipped her fingers inside his pants. The memory gave my shoulders a shudder. "Come on in, Mr. Sola! Join us."

If only to escape Paz's eyes and not let her see my cheeks begin to redden, I spun on my toe (though it seemed on fire) to look to Jamie. Then, in spite of my better judgment, I stepped out of my shoes altogether, walked over to the door, and gave him an unchaste peck on the lips, which, with eyes open, he reciprocated. It was a human equivalent of marking territory, I acknowledged mutely.

"All right, all right, Ms. Levit, we got it—paws off! I'll try to remember. Jesus, those Russian women, I tell ya!" She was still laughing when I turned back around. The man with a name of an elf wallowed in amusement at the spectacle.

"I have a first period guitar section, talk to you later?" Jamie whispered to me, ignoring Paz entirely. I nodded feverishly, giving him a hug too incongruously platonic in nature with that kiss.

"Is Abbott okay?" I asked quietly, jerking him back by his sleeve when he began to walk away.

"I guess so. I didn't stay there last night."

A chill pulled at the skin of my scalp.

"Where did you stay?" I almost mouthed, not sure if anything at all could be heard. Wisdom skipped by my door, hand in hand with Aisha. "Hi, Ms. Levit!" she shrieked. I waved a hello in what felt like slow motion.

"Don't worry, I wasn't with my neither underage nor Argentinian groupie ex-wife," he whispered into the top of my head. I could feel his smile, his lips stretching against my hair.

When he was out of my field of vision, mere seconds later, I released a breath I did not know I'd been holding.

"What do you want, Paz?" I barked when I finally turned to brave the girl for good. There was no reason to be afraid of a teenager, I reminded myself.

"My paper, Ms. Levit," she declared matter-of-factly, her gum popping.

"You'll get it in your fifth period government class, with everyone else." I walked around my desk, confidently, and demonstratively lowered my Redwelds into my drawer. "Mr. Goldwyn, don't you have first period A.P. Euro to teach?" I called to wake Edwin from his stupor, seeing that the man was frozen in a stare locked somewhere around the curve of Paz's sizable breasts. I was afraid drool would begin to accumulate in the corner of his mouth.

"I do, Ms. Levit. How kind of you to remember! It's right next door to your first period honors Euro, so I'll wait for you, if you don't mind," he answered without missing a beat, his eyes unmoving. This was typical behavior around Paz. Jamie seemed to be the only man immune. I suspected Edwin Goldwyn would rather remain seated for the time being.

I rolled my eyes as I walked back around my table to lean on its edge next to Paz. My shoes stood where I'd left them, marking the spot where Jamie stood so recently, empty, waiting to be filled.

"Paz, you'll get your paper in a couple of hours, like everyone else in your class—"

"Ms. Levit, I envy your stout refusal to show favoritism, but I have an audition at two. It's a first callback. Got it when Abbott shipped me home—one of his many gifts to me, one may say. I really need to be out of here by noon—"

"That's your problem, Paz, not mine. If you know that you're done with your last class at two o'clock, you shouldn't schedule—"

"Yes, yes, responsibility and all that. But I'm not quite Meryl Streep just yet, so I just have to make things happen when I can." She sounded vaguely annoyed, but I wasn't sure if it had to do with me or the fact that she was "not quite Meryl Streep just yet."

Under the overgrown elf's arched brow, I suddenly got an idea.

"What's your first period?"

"I'm repeating sequential three math first period."

"And after that?"

"Lunch."

"At nine in the morning?"

"Imagine my surprise when I got my program card! My guidance counselor is a genius."

I crossed my arms, feeling my chest tingle with anticipation.

"Make you a deal…come by next period and we'll talk," I said as authoritatively as I could.

"You're off then, too? Marvelous. It's a deal!" Paz squealed, mockingly, sprinkling just a couple of gratuitous claps for effect as she jumped to her feet. She was sporting the same cobalt blue platform sneakers she wore the day I'd escorted her to the airport back in Europe, cutting her trip short just a day before London. "I'll bring coffee."

"Well, girls, looks like I'm going to have to miss that meeting, because some of us don't get an hour off until eleven. Shucks." Edwin coughed through some likely imaginary phlegm. Then, he gathered his papers and visibly adjusted himself. "Ready to go, Ms. Levit? Two flights up in about forty seconds. Should I grab your shoes for you, or you got it?"

~ ~ ~

The pain the balls of my feet were feeling paled in comparison to the ache of anticipation of my impending conversation with Paz. I didn't expect her to protest her grade—not when she was already on her way to Yale School of Drama come August; she was far from failing, so I doubted that even the sport of it would tempt her to waste my time at this late a stage. I rattled through my forty-five minute period dedicated to a few undoubtedly titillating bullet-points on the subject of the various challenges facing the European Union and mad-dashed out of the fourth-floor classroom before anyone could stop me to ask about their own papers (sophomores were on the bottom of my stack, like the middle children that they were).

"'B-?' Not too shabby. Thanks, Ms. Levit!" Paz cheered, snatching her paper from my trembling grasp to begin her feline procession to and out of my door.

"Not to fast, Ms. Terranova," I called, consciously steadying my voice.

"Okay, okay, no need to shout," she teased, compliantly backing up and easing into the same visitor's chair her perfectly rounded behind had occupied not an hour ago. The door locked behind her before I could get over there to close it myself. Boundaries be damned. "I'm sorry I forgot the coffee."

My feet slithered out of the confines of my shoes (into which I'd reluctantly slipped again before commencing with my sophomores). The linoleum tile was cold under my toes, which was a nice contrast to the rest of my body. I let this girl get too deep under my skin and she was clearly setting me ablaze from within. June couldn't come fast enough. I'd miss some, but I wouldn't miss all.

"Spill it."

"Spill what?"

Her white tunic hugging her figure just right (not swallowing her whole like a potato sack, nor restricting her like a corset too small, like it would me), she fixed the sleeves of her burgundy blazer with effortless precision.

"Look, I don't know what I was thinking saying those things about Sola. Let's get him in here and I'll apologize. Deal?" Her eyes, after resting in her lap for a while, were strong and defiant on mine. They were so dark, I couldn't make out their pupils.

"What would make you want to do such a thing in the first place?" I asked as my heart swelled. My mind was trying really hard not to paint pictures of Abbott in anything less than a cashmere sweater and a pair of jeans.

She studied me for a length of time that felt uncomfortably long. It'd feel like a betrayal to consult the clock above her head, so I just folded my arms and waited. Humoring this girl behind closed doors was a dangerous thing to do.

"I was only saying those things to make Abbott jealous. Hadn't Veronika run to you like the second Sophie grew some balls and tried to implement her little plan?"

"Plan?"

"Ms. Levit, look— I'm not sure what you want to do with any of this, but I'm graduating in June, period. I don't need any of this anymore, so I better just ge—"

"If you don't want me to go to the principal and let her figure it all out for herself, you'll tell me what's going on." The assuredness in my voice took even me my surprise. I was too familiar with myself to think that I was at all convincing to my adversary. I don't know when I'd decided that that's what she was.

"What, and get your pal Abbott in trouble? Get him fired with a fantastical scandal, his legacy lost? I don't think you'd do that, Sweet Levit! Nice try, but I just don't buy it," Paz groaned, not buying it, indeed. She crossed her legs and the shine of her leggings picked up the light of the halogens above, making her thigh appear fuller than it was.

I leaned back, away from the girl, naïve to think that I was safe from her dark, solid gaze back there.

"Veronika—"

"Has she told you she's agreeing to waste all those callouses on her fingers just to barter with her parents? As if her doing corporate tax work is somehow going to make her less gay."

I squinted, keeping an ear out for some compassion in her voice.

"Yes, it's messed up, I agree," I sighed, leaning forward on my elbows, my cleavage feeling competitive. "You kids are my first batch—the first class I got to see enter in ninth grade and graduate. Help me understand what you're going through."

Though Paz wasn't Jewish either, perhaps her Latin roots were more inclined to respond to guilt than Veronika's Slavic ones, I hoped. She squirmed in her seat. I wasn't sure if this was because observing my mom perfect this artform for decades had finally made me good at it or because Paz needed to go run some lines and getting me off her case would only help her get there faster.

"Okay, what do you want to know, spring chicken? And in what detail? So I fucked Abbott a few times, happy? Blew him in his office a couple of times, too.

You know that smell of gum that follows him around like some cartoon peppermint cloud? Well, not everything smells that way, capisce?"

I tried to swallow, discreetly, careful not to let my nostrils flare.

"Why?"

"Sweat, I presume—"

"Why did you do any and all of those things?"

I felt my neck begin to itch but willed my hands still.

"I suck at French, Ms. Levit. If I sucked at history half as much as I do at French, I'd volunteer to fuck you in your office…oh wow, is this why you refused to just give me my paper this morning and summoned me here now, instead? To tap into my desperation?" she laughed with gusto. "Veronika may be better with all the girl parts than I am, though, if we're being honest, but I'd go where I hear Sola has been," she added with a suggestive raised brow.

Interlacing my fingers in front of me, I stayed as motionless as a tiger bracing for battle (despite the taste of bile in the back of my throat).

"Who started it?"

"I did."

"You did?"

"I'm a liberated female, Ms. Levit. I think you've lectured on something called 'women's suffrage.'"

She uncrossed and re-crossed her legs, the lights overhead reflecting distractingly off her leggings, again.

"How did it start?"

"I was failing French this time last year. As you're aware, third year grades are very important for those pesky college applications, even for someone of my caliber. I went to talk to my dear teacher about it. He offered extra credit, but I pretended to drop a hairpin and dropped to my knees. The rest, as your kind would say, I suppose, is history." She sang the last part gaily.

My head began to sway of its own volition. The clock on the opposite wall seemed to tick louder. I finally dared to look at it; the long hand was slowly snaking its way to marking the end of the period. Periods I had free always seemed to fly faster than the ones I had to talk through. This one, it seemed, was in an even greater hurry.

"So he never propositioned?"

"Not per se. I'd have to clip articles from some French newspapers for extra credit—that was his fabulous idea to help my grade."

"And how did things progress from there? And where?"

"You mean, where we used to do it? We don't, anymore, if that's what you're asking. All the grades that matter had already been submitted, so I'm good, Abbott, thank you very much." She laughed as if the joke was all on him, which, I suppose it was. "And he wouldn't dare fail me now, for obvious reasons."

"Yeah…"

"So, anyway, the office, a few times at a hotel, whatever. I think he thought I was going to screw him in Paris, so I started hitting on Sola to piss him off, and then saying these things…. I don't know who else heard but honestly, it was only supposed to signal the end of an era for Abbott. Sola was collateral damage. He is too skinny for me, anyway. I need a man's shoulders to be wider than my own, if you don't mind my saying so."

"And Abbott's are?"

It was a knee-jerk reaction—defending the attractiveness of a man I did not need the likes of Paz to find attractive.

"Abbott's fairly slim, you're right, but screwing him got me from a likely 'D' to a believable 'B+' and then, eventually, an 'A-.' I have no interest in anything guitar related, so screwing Sola would do nothing for me. You, Ms. Levit, on the other hand, are blossoming before my very eyes. He's gotta be good! I think even your skin is clearer," she remarked, clinically. "Guess your engagement really is over, then. Sorry I gave you a hard time about it. Is that fiancé of yours still alive over there?"

Instinctively, I brought my hand to my face, my finger checking for strays along my jawline. I nodded, anxious to steer clear of the Kasuns for the time being, my ring finger still heavy with phantom weight. It was impossible to keep anything a secret in a building full of teenagers. I'd been hoping that the occasional whispers that I'd been hearing fizzle out whenever I'd come into a classroom were only in my head, but Paz made me reconsider.

"And Sophie?"

"What about Sophie?"

"Was there anything between them?"

"Sola and Sophie?"

"For goodness' sake, Paz, stop it! You know what I'm talking about."

"Fine, have no fun in your life. For the record, I don't spy on people, so how the hell should I know?! All I know is that she asked me about my grade improvement and asked me to tutor her. I did—taught her my technique. Not sure if she's attempted to implement it, but Veronika told me she's at least attempted to talk about it. Smart…create smoke without fire, scare the crap out of Abbott into giving you a better grade without having to gargle after. I've created a monster there!"

"He may get fired if this gets out!" I shrieked. I felt panic at the sound of my own voice carrying these words. My heart felt angular and awkward. I'd need to check with Jessica before figuring out if this was affection or pity.

"He's no innocent lamb. He could've told me to stand up instead of watching me unbuckle his belt a year ago."

Chapter Nine: *Unaccompanied*

That odor—the mixture of industrial cleaner and anti-septic—it was vicious. It made me miss being more congested. I never hated breathing as much as I did whenever I found myself by those automatic, sliding doors, careful not to exhale with too much force for fear of the sensor picking up my presence. Paz's melodic voice competed with various (albeit imagined) angular enunciations by Abbott inside my head, making me dizzy; though I had no way of knowing if their stories actually matched, somehow it felt wrong to contemplate them on an even basis.

Trying to inhale through my nose and exhale through my mouth, I squinted through multiple sets of glass doors to see if I could steal a peek at George. My feet now quiet inside the emergency pair of Uggs I had to buy across the street from the school before catching a bus to come further uptown and to this hospital, I lacked the few inches in height that I had that morning and could see nothing past Rayna's head at the nurse's station. Still I continued to try, wondering if he was awake, if he was sitting up or lying down…. I'd been afraid of this—the danger of George becoming predictably more attractive once on his deathbed. A ghost would always beat out its predecessor. I'd miss the acne scars soon, I'd feared, if I weren't careful.

Hospitals are full of incongruous notions. Each and every one smells simultaneously clean and diseased. They all look sparkling clean and yet no one ever wants to be the one to push the button for the elevator. You come here when you're sick and to make sure you never become sick; you come here to meet a new family member and also to say goodbye. Everyone, at a certain point of his or her life has had a grandmother die in one of these wastefully lit institutions and is not eager to revisit the memory. Nobody ever takes coming to the hospital lightly, no one is eager to visit. I wondered what that said about me.

Technically, I was there for Jessica—just two floors up. But the closest elevator bank also happened to be the one that would deposit me directly to the left of the entrance to the ICU were I to hop out before my intended floor. I could always claim convenience, I told myself as I planted my brand new soft soles on the shiny linoleum floor.

Jamie had offered to come with, keep me company, meet my friend, when I'd inadvertently told him that the hospital was where I was headed after school (explaining why I couldn't go look at a studio apartment in Astoria with him).

"Are you going to see your ex?"

"No, my friend."

"So definitely not your ex?"

This went on for a while.

"So why can't I come with you?"

I'd fingered the musical stand I'd been leaning on, waiting for my brain to string together the right amount of syllables that would result in an answer that was appropriate yet believable. The room smelled of magic markers and wood—soothing, comforting smells to my conditioned brain. His scribbles on the white board made zero sense to me: it looked vaguely binary, I remember thinking, but then there were also 2s, 3s, and 4s, written on different horizontal lines. By definition, there were too many digits for it to be binary.

"My friend's family situation is not ideal."

Jamie turned his back to me to begin to erase the blue writing on the board—Gs and Cs and Ams. He may as well have been teaching a foreign language in here, like Abbott.

"It'd be like I'm flaunting you or something," I'd continued, not really lying. Plus I shuddered to think what Dr. Kasun would say were she to spot us together; the bridges would not only be burned, then—they'd be detonated. I'd leaned my weight further on the music stand until I felt it begin to wobble.

"I'm cool on Abbott's couch—saves me some money. I don't need to go looking for an apartment on my own for now," I'd heard him say, his slim back still turned to me. His crow-black hair was gathered in a limp ponytail that did nothing for me.

"Just give me a couple of days," I'd muttered as

the stand behind me finally gave way, my hardly supportive heels failing me. Jamie turned around just in time to grab ahold of my elbow, successfully keeping me on my feet. Good thing, too, because my falling, I predicted, would've caused for quite a domino effect with all the guitars in Jamie's practice room. I planned to stall by relaying my conversation with Paz to him, but with his fingers tight around my elbow, my body still awkwardly bent from the near fall, I chose to instead stall by peering into his warm, brown eyes. We didn't talk.

The clinical white around me now hurt my eyes, making them water. This cold was persistent. Or maybe it was some sort of an allergic response, though I wasn't sure what was the trigger. Whatever this was, it was making my lids heavy.

My heels inside my bag (my bag lighter having been graciously rid of the senior set of papers), I leaned to one side, my shoulders painfully uneven, continuing to try in vain to catch a glimpse of George's cubicle. I squinted through the light but saw nothing except myriad monitors and IV poles. Still, I didn't dare take a step inside the ward.

"*Estoy pensando de ir a Marruecos este verano,*" Javier informed me as I slid down the wall to the side of the entrance to the ICU, squatting painfully. "You know, like we planned back then. I want to take a ferry to Morocco this summer, finally. For a few days." He called me just as I was about to call it quits and go see Jessica, hoping not to run into her husband, Max, along the way. Not that I wanted my best friend to be a single mother of three, but I didn't want her to live at a higher risk for STDs, either. He hadn't visited since the day his daughter was born, so the odds of a run-in were slim, I knew, but still, staking out George's futuristic Unit bought me time to rein in my hostility, just in case.

"I never wanted to go to Morocco," I said as I bit into my pinky nail. I'd have to get a new manicure one of these years, I thought to myself. The nail polish being the color labeled 'spermatazoid' by the manicurist or not, all this peeling was getting disgusting.

"Oh?"

"Yeah, sorry, but no, I never actually wanted to go. I'd only agreed then because I knew I was going to be leaving for home soon and would never have to follow through."

This was true. Rich in exoticism, Morocco seemed just cool enough, appropriate enough of a country to name as a destination for a desired weekend away while in south Europe (for an American student aged twenty with limited travel experience, anyway). It seemed it would secure me a certain status of both sophistication and cultural curiosity to last a short lifetime. This was a hedged bet, of course, given that I knew that of the few remaining weekends of my stay, all were already booked.

"Really?"

"Yup," I confirmed. "Sorry to disappoint."

"You couldn't."

"Oh yes, I could! I am!"

"Any place you would like to go, then?" Javier always was quick on his feet.

I shrugged, though he couldn't see me do it, cradling my chin in my cupped left hand; it helped with the urge to rub the naked skin on my formerly ringed finger.

"I don't know," I mumbled as a couple of teenagers, their faces stained with tears, stumbled by me, alerting the automatic doors. They'd probably just lost a grandma.

"Where are you, Helen?" Javier's tone read alarmed, but not upset—decidedly, stubbornly not disappointed.

I hesitated.

"The hospital."

"With Jessica?"

"Not yet," I reported, my behind finally landing on the floor, my thighs not strong enough to sustain such a static squat for that long a time. I knew I would now have to wash these pants as soon I'd finally get back to my parents' house. No matter the smell of cleaner, this place had to be crawling with disease. I'd need to scrub my hands with a boatload of hand sanitizer if I stood a chance at holding Jessica's daughter upstairs.

"What are you doing, Helen?"

"Nothing! Javier, I'm doing nothing," I shrieked. I owed him nothing, I reminded myself. Any comfort and hospitality he'd ever extended my way was heartily repaid at the time. "I'm literally sitting on the floor, doing nothing. I'm about to go up to see Jess, don't worry about it."

"No, Helen, what are you doing? I told you to respect my family and never to show up here again."

My stomach grew cold. Dr. Kasun. It wasn't Javier. Mr. Kasun stood at his wife's side, patient and pensive—forever mute, his ordinarily distant eyes now raging fire that engulfed the floor before reaching me, feet first.

"I—"

I scrambled to my feet, my phone escaping from its nook between my shoulder and my ear. It fell to the floor with a clank. For a moment, I hoped that that would be its final performance, but then I remembered Jamie—how would we get in touch if it broke? Hoping the gesture would be seamless, I snatched my phone off the floor.

"Helen, were those terms not as certain and concrete as I'd hoped? Because, if so, I apologize. Let's see if we can understand each other now—do not stalk my son's hospital bed!"

Her composure unnerved me: the evenness of her tone, the control of her voice's volume. Her peach cardigan pristinely buttoned up in a smooth, straight row, her flat chest appeared somehow even more powerful. Her straw hair was clean and shiny, and her hands were visibly moisturized.

I tried to get myself together, but every time I attempted to stand up, either my bag slid down my arm or my phone escaped my grasp again. I prayed that, in the commotion, either Javier or I would have the sense to disconnect the call.

"You can pick up with your boyfriend when you leave," Dr. Kasun added, handing me my phone (which I didn't even realize fell out of my fingers one last time). The call, as I now saw, was still active. The good doctor positioned herself in the ICU doorway, as if her narrow frame would protect it were I to take it by storm. I stumbled backward in the direction of the elevator bank, my eyes mostly on the floor. Grownups weren't meant to feel this meek, act so childish, be so helpless.

"I think I may want to go to Morocco this summer, too," I muttered into the phone as I pressed the "close doors" button inside the oversized elevator cabin. I was alone, unaccompanied this time. There was no half-naked man on a gurney (or his aide) to keep me company.

Chapter Ten: *Ingrate*

The bus was overheated, which was, of course, its usual deal during those in-between seasons. In the summer, it was usually freezing (so much so that my bladder always tended to shrink to the size of a raisin May through September). And in the winter, it was a furnace on wheels—the sensation of its radiator working to exhaustion only welcome when you first boarded after having waited outside in the cold anywhere between five and twenty minutes. But spring and fall were the hardest to anticipate, your seasonal dress code not always in sync with the depot's thermostat. I could feel a headache begin to take root at the base of my skull, the line above my eyebrows sore and heavy as well. The sun warmer than I remembered it being before my ten-day break from the tri-state area, I squinted against the glass of my window as I wiggled in my seat, struggling to take off my coat, the buttons of my shirt straining. I probably should've been doing this standing up.

Still cloudy with the remnants of jet lag, I rested my head against the headrest and closed my eyes. This was only day four back on American soil and I was already drained. It was as if my trip, contrary to what my family believed, wasn't a vacation, after all. My days now hours longer than ever before, stifling a yawn, I took to "Words with Friends" to reluctantly keep awake. I'd been neglectful since returning and yet, I suspected, Javier was still not disappointed. Forgetting where I was, I released that yawn with excessive theatrics.

Jessica, I saw, hadn't played since Monday. Not that I was expecting her to: between breastfeeding under strict instruction of the nurses who hinted at withholding pain medication when she dared to so much as think the word "formula," and Max, she clearly had enough going on without having to strategize at Words with Friends. Javier, on the other hand, was as fierce a competitor as ever. If anything, he seemed to be playing even more ruthlessly now. "Fellated" was the last word he played; fifty-three points—BAM! He was getting cheeky, likely having played the word before hearing my accosting at the hospital. I played "fat" for eight.

"I hope I didn't wake you, Helen," I heard Dr. Kasun's voice when I hesitantly clicked the green "accept call" button that materialized on my screen, muting my game.

"No," I croaked, after clearing my throat, somehow more eager to impress now more than ever before. What was it that Jessica had told me I was suffering from when I was in Paris? Stockholm syndrome? Abused-wife syndrome? "No, Dr. Kasun, I'm on my way to work now."

"I see. Are you currently living in New Jersey with your parents, as you had planned all along?" She sounded brightly awake and precisely caffeinated, like she usually did. I wasn't sure how much sleep George's parents were getting nowadays, but she didn't seem any different. She sounded the way she did the day I came to her office to return my keys to her apartment—the time I shrugged when she asked me if I loved her son.

"I am." I was still too hot and now getting warmer. "I am," I repeated as I unbuttoned my wool cardigan.

"Very well. That makes sense, I suppose. It's good to be surrounded by people who love us." I nodded as if she could see me, my heart swollen and awkward inside. The heat made my head feel even stuffier than it legitimately was. It swam. "The commute is probably unbearable though, right?"

My bus jerked with a patch of traffic, right on cue.

"It's a little long. And I miss the exercise of my bike."

The heat and the bobble of the occasional short-distance breaking were beginning to make me nauseous. The sound of Dr. Kasun sipping her coffee with intermittent slurps only intensified the sensation of acid penetrating my throat.

"Helen, look, I'm sorry I've been such a bitch lately. I'm sure you are already cutting me some slack for my histrionics, given the context, but still—I owe you an apology."

Much like everything else this woman ever said, this, too, sounded certain and effortless. Even native speakers, I was sure, did not possess such command of the English language.

"Sure," I croaked again, my mouth dry. There was no time for breakfast, or coffee anymore, no matter how much my mother tried to coax me into having fried eggs and tomato juice before I set out for my walk to the Park & Ride (refusing her daily offers of having dad drive me). "I get it, Dr. Kasun. I understand, I'm so—" I bit my tongue so as to at least try to stop apologizing.

"Thank you, Helen. I appreciate that. Now, here's something that may compensate for my rudeness. I don't know how much you really know about George's condition, but his liver took a significant hit after—"

"Dr. Kasun, I'm so sorry!" I pleaded before I was promptly and vehemently shooshed by a woman sitting behind me. "Some of us are trying to rest," she emphatically hissed before gathering her belongings in a huff and stomping to the back row.

"Helen, we've talked about this. You didn't do this. Now, listen to me. George may or may not need a liver transplant. We're still trying to figure it all out. Plus, there's a psychiatric matter of the attempted suicide. Regardless of what will happen and when, George will not be returning to the apartment any time soon. Once ready to be discharged, he's moving back in with us in Scarsdale. That being said, I'm not quite ready to rent out that walkup apartment to strangers, either, like the rest of the units, so if you want, you can move back in. We'll collect more of George's things, of course, but the furniture can stay. And, as before, I wouldn't charge you anything. Consider it a family discount," she tried to snicker. "Well, an almost-family discount, anyway."

"Yes!" I screamed, forgetting the menacing plea of the woman trying to nap in the back. I turned over my shoulder to check on her and was immediately grateful that looks couldn't kill. "Yes, thank you!" I repeated, quieter. I almost offered to pay, but I knew I couldn't afford anywhere near the place's market price unless… "Would you mind if I had a roommate? Together we could pay, so it wouldn't be a total loss for you."

Dr. Kasun scoffed.

"You don't have to be so mercantile. Is that a Soviet thing? A Jewish thing? George told me about your little quirks. There are things more important than money."

My neck ablaze, I backpedaled.

"Of course! I just meant I'd feel better if I could pay you something. And, if I could have a roommate move in with me, we could pay you more—closer to what the place is actually worth in rent," I rushed to explain as the bus inched on its way closer to New York, traffic thickening.

"I suppose I don't care, so long as the person is clean and tidy and won't cause me any problems with the other tenants," she reasoned. "But of course you don't have to pay me, regardless."

Elated to the point of glee, I was a giggle away

from cheering akin to a trained sea lion taught to clap his flippers on command at a local aquarium.

"But it's a one bedroom. Aren't you too old to be bunking?" Dr. Kasun asked after a beat, though I could barely hear her over my excited brain mapping out my move back to the city. I could get another bike now, I thought, and ride to school. I couldn't wait to tell Jamie.

"What?"

"Would this roommate of yours be okay sharing the one bedroom or sleep in the living room?" she repeated.

"Oh, I guess. I'm sure he won't mind," I spat out excitedly.

"He?"

Crap.

"Yeah…a coworker," I stammered, now decidedly on fire and unambiguously nauseous. As I tried to wrestle my way out of my cardigan, the bus jerked at a tollbooth and I hit my head on the seat ahead. So much was surely cosmically deserved.

"So this is not that Javier?"

"Oh no, no. Javier is just an old friend from my summer in Spain," I rushed to quasi-explain. "This is a co-worker. We just chaperoned a trip together—"

One could practically hear all the air getting sucked out of whatever room that Dr. Kasun was occupying at the moment. Another second and I was sure she'd pull me in through the telephone.

"So that's why you left my son? That's why you rushed to chaperone that trip?"

In reality, her tone didn't differ much from the one she probably employed when interviewing her patients—it was of your common, staccato, interrogatory variety, one that made you suspect that she already had a preferred, anticipated response in mind. It infantilized and belittled.

"No-I—no, Dr. Kasun, I was leaving George, anyway. We both signed up last minute—"

Stutters and overly detailed clarifications—that's what I'd become reduced to. As my bus waited at that same tollbooth to gain us access to the city, I could see the prospect of getting back inside that walkup disappear.

"You really are an ingrate, Helen—"

"Dr. Kasun, I swear that was never my intention—"

Now it was beginning to take shape of a confession. Quit while you're ahead, I could've told myself, but I wasn't ahead.

"So it wasn't your intention to bring a new

boyfriend into an apartment in my building? Free of charge? While my son's life is still in danger because he actually considered ending it over your highness?"

Now her voice was losing its academic cool and gaining a tremor I'd heard back inside that elevator. This was a different register. I squeezed my eyes shut, wishing I could get off this bus if only for some air.

"You've said yourself this wasn't my fault," I tried, knowing full well that I'd long ago overstayed my welcome in this conversation.

"That was back when I'd hoped we could maintain some civil decorum between us. That was before you asked if you could move your new boyfriend into my apartment!" the woman screamed for, what sounded like, the first time in her life. I'd never heard her accent before, but now its traces were more than audible—they were prominent.

How many boyfriends was this woman intent on assigning me?

"He's not m—"

"Honestly, it doesn't even matter, Helen! You've made it perfectly clear that you don't love my son. You're done with him now—I get that. We all get that! You played us all for years, but it's all fine. Own it, for God's sake! You're free to busy yourself with whomever you want, just don't do it at a place I own." Not an unfair point, I nodded to myself, having unbuttoned my shirt one button too many, my bra showing. I looked down to check its color. Purple. Odds were, my underwear didn't match. It never did. "And yes, you are to blame for this. Absolutely! I've looked through his phone—he'd warned you! He'd texted you his intentions! You didn't deem it important enough to at least warn me of his plans? That's how much you care?"

"I didn't think he was serious! I'd heard him say these things before and nothing—"

"Apologist! An ingrate and an apologist, Helen—that's what you are! I used to think you were a decent person, just maybe not a good match for my son—"

"I am!"

"Oh, stop it, Helen! Seriously now, if I spot you by the ICU…no, scratch that, by the hospital, I'm getting an order of protection." She was back to cool again; so cool that I was no longer hot. I twisted in my seat to look for my scarf; it was snaked around in my seat, on top of my coat. I looped it twice around my throat. "And it goes without saying that my offer is hereby rescinded, all right, my dear?"

I wasn't expected to answer this—the doctor ended the call before I could throw my scarf around my neck just one extra loop for good measure.

Chapter Eleven: *Ceremonial*

Abbott's door was closed when I knocked on it during his lunch period. After my last phone conversation with my former almost mother-in-law, I couldn't bring myself to do much of anything other than to rake my fork through my salad back and forth at my desk, anyway. Even Veronika left me alone for the day, it seemed. She was not in class in what felt like the first time in her tenure at the school, thus making it more rare than a certain type of an eclipse. I'd texted Jamie to ask if she was in his workshop, but he hadn't replied, either. Clearly, the universe was seeking action of me by leaving me alone with myself, so I again thrust my feet into the overly ambitious heels I'd decided to try out one last time and stumbled downstairs less than elegantly, my posture unlikely to read much by way of moral (or any other) authority, I feared. But this conversation had to take place sooner or later. I knew I wouldn't be able to keep running away from Abbott forever, especially if I kept insisting on test-driving those shoes. En route, I caught a peek of Sophie in the strings' practice room, swaying elegantly with her cello. At least I now knew she wasn't behind that closed door inside Abbott's office, like she was the day I came to sign up for that damned trip to begin with. As I waited for Abbott to answer my timid knocking, I felt my heart spiral inside, not quite making the turns, grazing its cage. I tried in vain to stop shivering.

"Ah, such a spring chicken at my door. To what do I owe this pleasure? How's Georgie-boy?"

"Let's not pretend you care about George."

"But I do, sweet Levit! You're my friend. Now, I may be paranoid, but I'm pretty sure you've been avoiding me since we parted ways at the airport, and I'm beginning to take it personally. Are you jealous that your new boy toy has been staying with me and not you, is that it? Though I have to tell you, in strict secrecy, that he wasn't to be found on my couch last night, either—"

"Did you fuck Paz?" I was careful to let the door click shut before I allowed my lips to part and let these words out of the confines of my mouth.

You could see a small ripple of surprise make its way from Abbott's forehead down through his shoulders. His brow wrinkled but fought to straighten back out before I could be sure if it ever really fell out of formation.

"Look—"

"And Sophie?"

"What? No!"

I walked over to his desk and sat behind it. It wasn't so much in the effort to exude any power as much as to simply take the pressure off the balls of my feet.

"From the beginning, please," I instructed anyway, my chest suddenly seizing. It was a struggle not to cough.

"I—What are you looking for here, Levit?"

Abbott sighed, plopping down in his own visitor's chair.

The overhead lights in his windowless office buzzed as we sat in silence the way they would in my room. Though I knew it was impossible, it sounded like someone was turning the volume intolerably up. With my arms crossed tightly across my chest, my Fair Isle sweater itched wildly where I seemed to be deliberately pressing it to my breasts. Before I could decide if I should go ahead and scratch the burn, the phone in my grip vibrated against my arm.

<Sorry. A gig came up last minute. Just for the day. Got a sub. Call you later.>

That was the first text message from Jamie that I'd ever received. His texts, I could already see, were different from George's, or even Javier's. Though I did not yet have a sample with which I could do a thorough comparative study, I could tell that Jamie's texts were going to be simple declarations of fact, no more, no less. I expected more from an artist.

<Not sure re Ver.>

"Heard Jamie left for the day," Abbott stated, plainly, as if reading my mind (or my screen). "Musicians…."

I said nothing, just tucked my phone away, averting my eyes, focusing somewhere in the vicinity of the wastebasket.

"I never laid a hand on Sophie, Levit, I swear to God," Abbott said when he eventually spoke again.

"But Paz—"

"Please, sweet Levit, let's be frank here—given the opportunity, wouldn't you fuck Paz?"

His Scottish accent seemed more acute whenever he appeared excited—good excited or bad excited. I shuddered to think what Paz must've heard whispered in her ear adorned with those many piercings.

"I doubt that."

"Well, teacher of the year, you're screwing Jamie," Abbott almost pouted. "How many times now?"

I'd almost managed to forget about winning that stupid teacher of the year thing. As if anyone needed that much time to write an acceptance speech that was unlikely to consist of anything other than clichés that all the students surely had all heard before. Abbott's were, every damn year.

"Once," I muttered, in spite of myself, my ears ablaze. "Well, twice…I guess…. But Jamie is 33 years old and not a student. Not at all a valid comparison."

"Well, Paz is an adult—"

"As of how many months ago?!" I shrieked.

Abbott shuffled in his seat. He took off his glasses and wiped them on his silk sweater, his gaze in his lap.

"Well, seventeen is the age of consent…ugh, I know, Levit, I know! You don't have to say anything. I messed up," he groaned, his eyes even lower than before—on his shoes. His glasses were back on his sizable nose. "I swear nothing like that had ever happened to me before. I look down one day and there's this beautiful creature kneeling in front of me—"

"Oh my God, Abbott, shut up, I beg of you!"

"But you wanted to know!"

"Not the blow by blow…no pun intended," I grumbled, my hands rushing to cover my blushing face.

The yelp of Abbott's laughter startled me. When I looked up from behind my fingers, he was laughing so hard, tears were streaming down his face.

"I'm just such an idiot. That little bitch had me so good, too—I was actually beginning to think she gave a shit about me. I even volunteered to do this damn trip thing as an excuse to be with her," he admitted, bringing his eyes slowly back up to meet mine. "A rather convoluted and involved plan—all for her! I even put up the money."

Pity. I was pretty sure it was pity I'd been feeling for Abbott nowadays. I wished I were that sure about George.

"Why did you bring Stephanie, then?" I asked in an unnecessary whisper.

"She's a friend from a while back. Recently divorced. Figured two birds and all—a chaperone and a deflector, so to speak. This Paz thing was going too fast, I figured an illusion of a girlfriend wouldn't hurt."

"For real? 'Cause I'd heard rumors of noises coming out of your room that could've potentially scared the few virgins among those kids."

"Okay, she's definitely a consenting adult! Why can't we?"

Touché, I thought. Who was I to judge when the second the object of my affection returns it, I wax poetic about the man who wasted a whole lot of Tylenol to prove that it was as easy as snapping a leash to get me back at his feet.

"And then?"

"And then Paz got drunk with you guys and started spouting those things about Jamie. I knew it was bollocks, of course, but it couldn't mean anything good—soon she'd start talking for real. I may be a numpty—"

"A what?"

"Like an idiot. I hadn't lost all of my 'Scottishness,' I suppose. Anyway, I'm not a complete idiot. And then she leaves and Sophie starts cozying up to me in all the familiar ways. So, you know, again, basic arithmetic, putting the two and two together—she was definitely talking, at least to Sophie. Anyway, she is now getting her 'A-' or whatever, and we're calling it a day."

"Which one?"

"The both of them, I guess. To be safe."

The mechanical shrill of our school bell rang through the speaker mounted in the corner by the door. It's been painted over so many times, the layers of the pale pink paint on it looked three dimensional.

"Why would you even think she cared to begin with?"

Abbott chewed on his lips.

"Levit, she could've called it a day after that first time. Like she didn't understand that would I even consider, for a split second, giving her anything below a B+, she could very legitimately destroy me. Give me a break! None of it had to continue if she didn't want to. One time was enough to have me by the balls."

He looked smaller than he ever had before, sitting there in his hard surfaced visitor's chair. But, even with his shoulders slouched, his legs crossed, his eyes still remained hopeful, like those of a child. As if some sort of equilibrium had to be maintained, the gray in his temples was brought out by the baby blue of his sweater. This man-child, my friend, my mentor, needed assurance, but I couldn't bring myself to give it.

"So, about Sophie?"

I was slow to stand up, my feet not ready.

"There was nothing going on with Sophie. Ever. Come on, Levit!"

"And the day you took her back to the hotel in London?"

"Jesus, Helen, I'm still me! This one…okay, fine, a couple dozen transgressions can't undo years of friendship. Am I right? I mean, am I wrong? Sophie had a migraine, or so she said, and I took her to her room. After she buried her head in her pillows and asked me to close the curtains, I went back to my own room to take a nap. I sort of had a lot on my mind, you know?"

"How do we get her to stop saying things…"

"Paz has clearly been coaching her. I told you, I figured that out back in London. So before Paz coaches anyone else, I gotta pack in, so to speak."

"What do you mean?" I asked with my voice small, my throat tight. I was next to him when he took my hand and gave my fingers a squeeze before standing up to meet my height. A cloud of mint of his gum rose with him.

"I'm going to retire. I've already told the principal everything. Figured it'd be better if it came from me, first, especially before this Sophie thing gets out of control. We agreed that if I go quietly, I don't have to lose much by way of reputation and pension. If our stories match, and Paz admits to coaching Sophie…and if Sophie doesn't turn out to be an even bigger conniving bitch than Paz, this should be it for me. Slap on the wrist versus a scandal—I could do worse. Paz was seventeen when it all started, and eighteen now, so it's not even really statutory rape…you know, it's all good…or as good as it can be. Oh, sweet Levit, please don't judge me."

My fingers reached for the door handle, anxious for the cool metal of it to finally be within my grasp.

"Have you seen Veronika in class or anything?" I asked, buying time before having to brave the hallway full of kids.

"She's not in French, Levit, so I wouldn't know anything about that. Besides, my classes have been rather loudly abuzz with poorly masked whispers, as well as some completely unmasked texting, as of late. I wouldn't notice her even if she were."

I nodded. Why couldn't I remember that she took Spanish?

"Do you need a lift or anything after school? I drove in today," I heard Abbott call just as I turned the knob. He sounded like he needed me to say yes.

"No, thanks. I'm going uptown, so really out of your way," I answered without turning back.

"Ah, George." This wasn't a question. He suspected he knew the answer. "The hospital."

~ ~ ~

A private maternity suite was something that sounded much more impressive than it actually was. As I helped Jessica fold her few belongings into her weekender bag, I couldn't help but inch my way out into the brightly lit hallway at every single momentary opportunity I got. And it wasn't just so as to make sure that Dr. Kasun was not searching the premises for my presence—I needed breathing room. I'd come up here every day since Jess' little Deena was born a wee bit earlier than expected but, lost in my own head, somehow I'd never paid attention to just how much like a closet this room looked. Its sole grimy window overlooked a narrow alley and the neighboring windows mere feet away. There was little natural light to speak of. The space itself was no larger than my freshman year dorm room, really, and the bathroom, though private, was predictably institutional, with unambiguous railings covering every available surface. This was supposed to be costing her over three hundred dollars a night, but I hoped some professional courtesy was extended.

Abbott's words buzzed endlessly in my head, competing with Paz's for airtime.

"Is he not coming?" I asked Jessica, idiotically, as I passed her a pair of fuscia pink overalls for her baby girl. After two boys, this little one was going to be decked out like a Christmas tree at every occasion, I feared; she already had a headband with a bow larger than her head installed on her bald skull.

"Well, do you see him here?" Jessica snapped, dressing the child a little too aggressively from where I was standing.

"A meeting?"

"You can start calling it for what it is," she sneered, pulling Deena's arms through the sleeves of her coveralls in a huff.

"I really didn't mean to—" I began but abandoned the thought. It didn't matter if I were trying to allude to Max's infidelity or simply reminding her of his absence. I was there to help her collect her belongings and help her father pack the two of them into his aging Corolla. That's it. I hurried to dismantle a batch of balloons from the side-table and shoved a pile of newborn diapers into a plastic bag, trying not to think about the possibility of running into Dr. Kasun on my way down. A car seat in my hand would surely prove to her that I wasn't there to taunt her or her brood. I wished Abbott could know that, too.

"He always said he wanted us to have a girl and have her look just like me," I could hear Jessica suddenly whisper behind my back as I stood bent over her bed, folding and refolding a baby blanket. One could discern that her tears were imminent. "Well, here she is, but he's not here. I guess she's too late."

"That's a lot of pressure for someone weighing in just under eight pounds," I chuckled, trying to keep the mood light. Abbott and Paz suddenly seemed silly; Jamie and I—sillier still. My mother always said that problems were relative to one's own existence, but it felt wrong to contemplate my life of options next to the bloated Jessica and a translucent newborn splayed across a hospital bed.

"You remember—we dated only about six months. He proposed that New Year's Eve, saying that he'd seen all he needed to see—that I was what he's been looking for. It was so much like a goddamn fairytale, I should've known it was too good to be true." And now she was crying: it was that silent ugly cry that stretches and streaks your face, rendering you mute. Her daughter lay prostrated next to her, helpless. She was awake and alert but calm and quiet, looking up to the wall too clinical to be of interest, seemingly intent on avoiding observing the spectacle that was her mother (not that she was even capable of seeing that far). I sympathized.

"How long was it from 'proposal to wedding,' I don't remember?" I asked quietly, figuring that keeping this conversation upbeat was better than the sound of dead air.

"Also about six months," Jessica sniffled.

"So, a year from the first date to the wedding?"

"Aha. But I know what you're trying to say and

it's bullshit. We were happy.... I mean, we fight, but who doesn't?"

"Right," I said under my breath.

Jessica shuffled her still oversized body on the mattress, rattling baby Deena. She looked a bit like a deflated balloon (and was obviously aware of the fact, judging from the way she kept tugging at her sweater).

This was unnatural. Jessica was the infallible one, with a set of broad shoulders to match the strength her voice usually delivered. The tremble in her delivery now, particularly when matched with the visual of her swollen face and temporarily misshapen figure, wasn't compatible with anything I'd experienced during our lengthy acquaintance. The reputation and the image before my eyes were incongruous.

"He even asked my dad for my hand in marriage, remember? He went to talk to my father and only then asked me! Who does that nowadays? So chivalrous, so ceremonial," she cried, her tone unambiguously admirable of the charms of the man who was unambiguously in the process of leaving her with three children, including one born only days ago (and who indeed looked like her mother, just like he had allegedly wanted).

"Maybe that was a sign—he asked you second," I offered. Jessica just buried her fingers in her hair in response.

George never asked my father for my hand in

marriage; he asked his mother for permission to get married, instead. Jobless for all intents and purposes, and living rent-free, George was heavily reliant on the generosity of his parents. We both were, to be fair. No major agreements were ever to be entered into without their blessing, including so much as switching Internet providers. In Washington Square Park, on Valentine's Day many years ago, when he'd handed me a ring, his smile as full of teeth as it got, his green eyes all teary, he said, "My parents are thrilled." There was no question, no declaration of love. I could see my breath as I accepted.

"Oh, you guys discussed this?" I'd asked, twisting the band around my finger, the fit of it a little tight, even in the frigid cold.

"Of course! We went over a budget and everything," he'd cried, oblivious, his shearling unbuttoned and wide open. "See, three stones: one for the past, one for the present, and one for the future."

"Which one is for the present?" I'd smiled, surprised by the cold whirl of fury that at once began to gyrate wildly inside my navel at the mere mention of a discussion of a budget for my wedding ring; it was angry and painful, and it made me colder than the wind.

"The middle one, silly!" he'd explained, patting me on the head with his gloved hand as if I were a puppy. "See, it's the biggest of the three!" he'd explained as he pointed to the murky middle stone, kissing the top of my head for good measure, in case the petting didn't take. I guess the takeaway message was that the future could only get smaller, to match the past.

"My dad has his ideas for our wedding already! He can marry us, you know, but I'd rather do some research—have a real, authentic ceremony somewhere," George had rattled on excitedly, a project on his hands now. I, on the other hand, had mutely continued to try to inch my new ring up and down my finger. The fit was indeed snug. It didn't look like it was going anywhere. Eventually, once I'd lost a couple of pounds on account of my then-new-bike, it loosened up.

Chapter Twelve: *Vision*

I poked around my salad with my plastic fork, trying to resist rubbing my eyes in between reluctant bites. I couldn't believe that I'd ever been ungrateful enough to complain about the eight hours of sleep a night that I'd been able to get when I lived on the Upper West Side. Now, it was barely six.

"So what do you think, Ms. Levit?" Ofir's throaty voice brought me out of my open-eyed slumber.

What a handsome boy he was. No wonder the entire dance department, gay or straight, was swooning over him. If he was indeed serious about moving back to Israel, I'm sure he'd have major political sway there, too. One flutter of his long lashes and the stoutest Holocaust denier would inevitably turn into the stoutest supporter of the State of Israel. I'd seen it happen during our classroom attempts at scholarly debates over the effectiveness of the Oslo accords; Ofir hardly had to say a word before his opponents would predictably fold, stammering like the foolish teenage girls that they were.

"About?"

"My paper!"

For eighteen, he looked too tired—-like Jamie. It was probably his distaste for shaving—again, like Jamie. Unless he was performing, Ofir's face sported a handsome stubble; this, expectedly, left him looking older, but such, I suppose was partly his intent. Maybe Jamie's, as well.

"Frankly, I wasn't expecting you to care, given your allusions back in Paris."

"Okay, look, no matter my plans, my parents are first and foremost Jews, which means I still have to do relatively well in school."

I laughed at the boy's feigned nonchalance. Maybe Veronika wasn't the only relatable one.

"So you want to continue with comparing direct and representative democracy for your final paper?" Unprofessionally, I forked too much lettuce into my mouth before he could answer.

"Right. I want to focus on the differences between the United States and Israel, where democracy is much more real than here—actually representative."

"Ah, but one hundred and twenty opinions hardly make for a productive society," I remarked with my mouth full.

"Well, maybe my paper will convince you otherwise," my Ofir argued with a wink.

My sweet, sweet Ofir.

"So, you were serious then?" I asked after heartily gulping down whatever was left of my ginger ale.

"I'm very serious about getting at least an A- in this class before I graduate. For my parents' sake." What was it with these kids and pleasing their parents?

"And about not dancing?"

My office door was wide open. Jamie was supposed to stop by before next period. I listened out for his footsteps up the hall, the rubber of his tennis shoes always sloshy on those tiles, but there were none. Veronika hadn't stopped by, either.

"Maybe."

"You're going back to Israel to serve in the army?"

"Yes, Ms. Levit, I am." He flashed that pearly white smile at me, folding his muscular but lean arms across his chest. "I'll have a year to decide if I want to when I move back because I left when I was a kid. I'll have to check with the Consulate about all the specifics."

"And your parents kn—"

"Yes, Ms. Levit, my parents know."

"And they are letting you?"

Legend has it, my parents' big move was motivated by their desire to protect Vlad from military service. It was this thought, allegedly, that kept my mother alive and fighting while she lay recovering from a heart attack in the suburbs of Rome. They refused to go to Israel solely to avoid the army.

"They don't really have a choice—I'm an adult. What's dancing next to duty? They understand it—they served, too, in their time—"

"Didn't two soldiers just go missing in action up north over there this week?" I interrupted, feeling my heart pick up speed. Jamie was right about what he said back in Europe—I was too invested with these kids.

"Ms. Levit—that's exactly why more of us have to return home. We have to protect it! We can't all be afraid. Are you, like, the only Jew hailing from Russia with no family in Israel?"

"A rare breed."

"Oh, wait, was your family like one of those 'Grain Jews' you told us about in class like two years ago? I guess most Soviet Jews only agreed to go to Israel once America stopped bailing you guys out with grain or whatever, huh? Were you guys really traded in for grain, though?" He rustled his own spiky hair and leaned in toward me, his elbows on his knees.

"Well, not us in particular. And I wasn't even born yet! But I'm so glad that at least some of what I say in class actually gets retained, with or without context," I pretended to gasp as I tossed the remains of my salad into the trash.

"Don't you think it's humiliating—to be that dependent on someone's mercy like that? To wait for a handout—a shelter? Especially when you have a home out there that'll take you in regardless?" Saying nothing, I felt my hands begin to tremble while Ofir continued, "I mean, it feels unsavory. Almost ungrateful—you know, to be taking something like that for granted."

The dressing from my salad seemed to come back into my throat. I couldn't say anything even if I wanted to. I had no case to state.

~ ~ ~

My sweatpants already stretched unflatteringly around my knees, I sat in a beautifully executed lotus atop my parents' kitchen bench. I caught myself thinking of George once advising me on proper posture but chased the thought away. There was no use now, no going back. I'd started this, but he finished it.

"Are you tired?" my father asked in English. He was sitting across from me with a folded over newspaper in his veiny grasp. Even without my lenses in, I could see the Cyrillic script. Over thirty years in New Jersey and they still refused to release their tentacles off the country they allegedly despised.

"A bit. Living here adds over an hour to my commute." I tried to suppress a yawn, but it escaped anyway.

"Well, sure, but at least it's quiet here. I don't know how you were ever able to sleep at all over there in Manhattan." That was my mother, speaking Russian at the stove, one hand perennially supporting her lower back (just in case her verbal complaints as to its ache wouldn't be trusted). She dumped stuffed cabbage leaves onto a serving dish and spun around to face the table. No matter the calm (or the storm) she ever found herself in, the woman always managed to look just a hair disheveled. It was as charming as it was infuriating, depending on your mood; right now, I wished she'd combed her hair after her nap on the couch (for which her blood pressure monitor was banished to the floor, if only for thirty minutes). I didn't answer. Instead, I thought back to Ofir. He'd look handsome in any uniform, but I wondered if his parents would ever be able to sleep soundly again.

Following our tepid debate as to his future, I bored myself to near tears as I lectured my seniors on the types of defamatory speech. Veronika still wasn't in class, which was unnerving on its own but also meant that no one was willing to relieve me as the primary speaker for the entire class period. My father was right—I was tired.

Dad read the news out loud (a terrorist attack in Tunisia, the Russian ruble plummeting), and I saw no choice but to dig my flaking nails into my hair, hanging my head in the palms of my hands, my mane now a curtain between me and my parents. Did Veronika feel like this? Where was Veronika?

"Helen, that's just unsanitary—your hair will get in your food. Do you have something to tie it up?" Mother. My sinuses still recovering, with my face down, they began to hurt, but I stayed put—my unsanitary hair down and all.

Jamie had indeed stopped by my office during our common lunch. Our recent involvement apparently a poorly hidden secret, Ofir vacated his seat as soon as his thin frame materialized in my doorway.

"I'm leaving the door open, Ms. Levit," he'd called before he disappeared into the stairwell, the tips of his hair now dyed bleach blonde. Apparently, such was his first order of business upon returning to New York. I suppose he needed to take such liberties while he still could; soon, he'd have to cut it all off for the Israel Defense Force. "Don't do anything I wouldn't do," he'd teased over his shoulder.

Jamie and I had sat in silence for a while, as if sizing each other up. My priorities once again a murky blur, one look in his almond eyes, at those buttery lips, and all else was far away, if not necessarily forgotten. If not for Ofir's allusion to the fact that perhaps we were heard the other day, I'd shut the door to my office and wrap my legs around the man's hips.

"Were you at Abbott's last night?" I'd asked after a careful weighing of words.

"Yes, ma'am. And that other night I was on a couch at a studio, no worries, Ms. Levit," he'd winked in response, melting me to the core.

"Any apartment leads?" I'd tried to plow on despite the flush to my cheeks. My office really could use a window.

"Haven't looked at all, actually. Been busy waiting around for you. I hear you're at that hospital a lot?" Jamie had narrowed his eyes to ask this, intent on peering through me.

"Abbott?"

"Abbott."

"Well, my friend did just have a baby there," I'd rushed to clarify, unsure what to do with my hands now that there was no fork to make them appear busy. Instead, I'd brought my fingers to my chin and stroked my skin in faux-nonchalance, looking for a stray hair to rip out with my overgrown nails.

"But your ex is still there as well, no?" Jamie had probed, his legs crossed, his arms on the skinny sides of my chair, his narrow chest proud. Heather gray was a tricky color for him to sport—it did nothing for his beautifully muddy complexion. The sleeves of his turtleneck folded up to his elbows, I had something to look at when I wanted to avoid the wedding band still on his finger—the sugar skull among the rose vines.

"He is, but I haven't seen him!" I had protested with underwhelming enthusiasm, not really lying. "And, anyway, my friend was discharged yesterday so I have no reason to go up there anymore, period." I swore to do my best not to, anyway.

"So you haven't?"

“Haven’t what?”

“Veronika tried to scare me, saying that maybe you have decided to take pity and go back to that guy. George is his name, right?”

There was no way for me to know if he was speaking out of jealousy or simple curiosity. That control over his diction was enviable.

“Yes, that is his name, and of course not! What about you—have you seen your ex?”

“Nope.”

“And the baby?” I’d probed.

“That’s not my baby.”

Right—it was that Korean drummer in a band whose name I was never given.

The rest of our meeting was spent nodding. I feared we were losing momentum.

“I’m going to start looking for a place in the city,” I announced to my parents, sweeping my hair up and over to the side, to rest on my shoulder draped in a yellowing, junior high gym t-shirt. It was over fifteen years old.

“I understand that you may want to, Helen, but what about the money? Can you afford that without going into any more debt?” my dad asked. Mercifully, he did this in English.

"There's a teacher at the school who's also looking. We can be roommates," I answered, careful to swallow my heart down to prevent it from jumping out of my throat when I opened my mouth.

"That's not a bad idea," my father remarked with a trace of surprise that only infuriated me.

"Helen, you have a perfectly good home here, don't take it for granted. No one is rushing you out, so just stay put and save up," my mother pitched in before I could question my father as to why he was so astonished by the fact that I could make a remotely sound decision. Waiting a beat too long, I decided against it.

"Actually, he also doesn't have anywhere to live now, so he's staying on a different teacher's couch. I was wondering if he can move in here while we look together? He can stay with me—in my room, or the basement." My face ablaze, I was speaking much too fast, hoping that my haste would aid in the reception and treatment of this proposal. My language of choice was a foul combination of English and Russian.

"Wait!" my mom shrieked, in Russian. "Is that the man Vlad told me about? He said there were two men with you at the airport, and that you'd asked about moving one in here back then—"

"The younger one."

"Oh that makes me feel much better," my mother mocked, sarcasm always her favorite linguistic choice. "So, let me see if I got this right: you break up with George and go away on this impulse of a trip, which, at least now makes some sense, given your new lover!" She loved that word—lover, especially in Russian. It stung my ear. "Helen, you can't keep collecting these men. Female anatomy is not like that of a man. You will never be able to wash all these men out of you. It's like a dingy glass—you can never truly get it to shine like new again. Think about that."

"Please don't say that—"

"Helen, you're old enough for me to call things for what they are," she cut me off. "So you go away with this man, and then your former fiancé tries to kill himself over you—"

"Well, that's not really fair. That was just an excuse. She's not responsible—" my father broke his silence to try to argue. My father and I rarely had much to discuss when alone with each other, our longest conversation ever being about his little faith in my being able to remain solvent while living away and alone during college. Given my current situation, I suppose he had reasons for all that doubt, so any amount of support coming from him meant doubly as much.

"And now you want to move your lover in here to live with us? What will people say? That's not exactly the vision I had for this family, I'm sorry!" Once there was talk of "the vision," there was no going back, I knew from recent experience.

"Vision?"

"Darling, I love you, but please tell me you are only pretending not to understand how this will look." Mrs. Levit was livid. "Why can't you be more like Jessica—married and three kids now! You haven't even been married once! Jessica never looked for some sort of an educational experience when searching for a partner—she looked for compatibility, and the odds of that are just greater when you look within your own!"

My mother used her fork to saw a stuffed cabbage leaf in half before she shoved a piece in her mouth.

"Educational experience?" my father asked for clarification as he soaked up some sauce on his plate with a slice of rye bread.

"Don't you remember—whenever I'd ask our daughter as to why she would rather go out with this Mexican or that Hindu, instead of, you know, a normal, Russian, Jewish kid from the neighborhood, she'd always reply, saying, 'I already know all I need to know about my culture, and I want to learn about someone else's.' As if marriage is one big exercise in cultural tolerance!"

My father chuckled merrily along.

"Well, I guess a prom date doesn't a marriage make," he remarked. He liked playing around with sentence structure, as if that'd be enough to make him as wise as Yoda.

"I'd agree with you if only she didn't insist on continuing down this route! And she's not getting any younger, mind you! So, what's this one's pedigree, Helen?" my mom laughed, in a better mood now that she was sharing this joke with dad.

I pushed my food around my plate, unsure why I'd even helped myself to the dinner table in the first place; I never ate this late.

"Turkish and Portuguese," I whispered, easing myself up from behind the kitchen nook.

"Oh God, that's just what this family needs!" I heard my mom shriek as I took to the stairs, two at a time.

STATEN ISLAND

Chapter Thirteen: *Self-Fulfillment*

My commute to work from Staten Island was markedly better than my commute in from New Jersey. And, if not better, it was, at the very least, shorter.

The three of us the strangest of Musketeers, Jamie, Abbott, and I filed into the Staten Island ferry along with a small crowd of fellow commuters, and immediately took to the outside deck, our coffees in hand. I could see Manhattan on the other side of the murky, soapy body of water shaken and stirred by our orange boat, so I knew I had to be moving in the right direction. I couldn't believe my brother approved.

"I may not understand what exactly your thought process is at this point of your life, but you're doing something. You're not going backwards, so that's progress, strictly technically speaking." It was a lot coming from Vlad.

Abbott had moved me that Friday, after school. Asking no questions, he rushed home to get his car and was back in no time to drive me to my parents' house in order to yet again pick up my boxed belongings. When I saw my brother's Hummer in the driveway, my chest seized as if my heart itself were cringing.

"Yes, yes, I know—I'm living like a nomad, just like you'd predicted," I'd preemptively jested when he stopped by my room to watch me pack the few items I'd managed to unpack over the course of the week.

Instead of laughing, Vlad had bit into the last of his apple before asking, "When did I say that?"

"When you were helping me move out of George's."

I watched as my brother threw the remains of his apple into the trash bin by my old desk and walked over to me. I felt his arm wrap around my shoulders, bringing with it an unfamiliar chill. Affection was foreign between us.

"I don't know if I'd meant it. I was probably tired or hungry or horny or something. I tend to say things I don't mean under those circumstances."

"You're not sure?" I hurriedly threw my clothes into the same suitcase that'd kept me company in Europe. "It's not like it was the only shitty thing you ever said to me in our life of acquaintance."

"Whatever. Listen, you're just stagnating here. Move on, do whatever the hell you want," he'd laughed as he picked up a sweater of mine and began to fold it. I almost forgot what my brother's laughter sounded like, but it was infectious when it was roared. "There can be no self-fulfillment here, or anywhere you don't actually want to be, for that matter. Take it from me. Sorry for the cosmic talk."

I'd looked over at him; our heights almost the same, there was no need to look up. With those same soft cheeks, same soft chin, same slicked back overgrown hair, same goatee as always, my brother looked as tired as he did that night he'd pretty much told me that I was nothing but a selfish brat.

"Got laid last night, bro?" I'd scoffed, immediately lost in this unfamiliar territory. This much kindness hadn't been extended since that time in my middle school's parking lot.

"Um, no, but thanks for your concern. Alla is away at a conference for the weekend, whatever that means. And will be every weekend for a month, apparently—it's like some course or some such. I really don't care. It's glorious!"

"You sure she's not just having an affair?"

"I am not, like, at all, sure! That's the best part—I can afford to harbor some hope."

"And the boys?"

"In-laws, baby!"

The promise of his wife's departure seemed to make my brother practically giddy. He'd even helped Abbott fill the car full to the brim with my belongings and then kept our mother comfortable as we drove away. Dad was upstairs, sleeping off the insomnia of the night before; I'd heard him pacing when I couldn't sleep, myself, after our conversation at dinner.

Now, bright and early on a Monday morning, I looked from Abbott to Jamie to assure myself that this was indeed a move in the right direction. As if taking cue from my needy little stare, first Abbott put his soft arm around my shoulders, and then Jamie wrapped his long fingers around the cup of my knee. Surely we must've looked like a strange polyandrous family, but I didn't dare move. I had to pick and stay on course. Focus. Mother was right—I was not getting any younger.

There was no free couch at Abbott's. At least there wasn't one in the living room, the way I'd imagined there'd be on my way over.

"Why didn't I realize that you have a two-bedroom when I came with you to stash my boxes?" I'd asked last Friday, still mostly high from the rare moment of intimacy with my brother. It was unnerving. Was someone dying and I was yet to get the memo?

Before I would see where I'd sleep that night, I'd

peeked into the bathroom to quickly wash my hands as dictated by decades of habit. The odor in the lobby and the stairwell was musty, and I felt the need to disinfect.

"I keep my bedroom door closed. I'm private like that, sue me," Abbott had pretended to explain as he wheeled my suitcase into the room adjacent to the one that indeed had its door closed. "That is my bedroom," he'd smirked as he gestured over his shoulder when I finally caught up. "And this is my office. You can stay here. Jamie's bag is still over there in the corner, but I guess you two can negotiate who, if anyone, should move out into the…well, I don't have a living room, really, so one of you would have to sleep on an inflated mattress in the dining room, should you so desire. Or the bathtub, I suppose. But I think you'll be fine in here together."

The room was bright, the sun completely unobstructed—no trees or buildings anywhere on the horizon, only a thin set of blinds. Beyond them, the river, and beyond that—the City, glistening almost menacingly from behind an occasional construction crane in the line of sight. Small as it was, the room was also over furnished (with a couch, an overstuffed bookshelf, a chest, a corner desk, and a TV set, it felt downright claustrophobic), but the majestic view was worth it. I could almost make out the ferry terminal down the hill before I returned my eyes to the interior. By the windowsill in the corner, next to the familiar looking duffel bag, was Jamie's guitar—it stood humbly leaning against the faded paint on the wall the color of old bruised peach, its hard shell case its armor.

"Thanks, Abbott," I had sighed, collapsing on the sheets that already smelled of Jamie. My week seeming more like one continuous day, I was tired way before any acceptable adult bedtime. I closed my eyes.

"Relax and feel yourself at home, sweet Levit," I'd heard Abbott say, reluctant to lift my lids and disturb the images of Jamie that this scent was just beginning to paint in my mind's eye.

I must've fallen asleep, because when I woke up, I could see Jamie trying to tiptoe quietly into the room, the soles of his shoes sticking on the parquet with every inch gained.

"Hi," he'd whispered, loudly, the light from the hallway quickly invading the now dark office-cum-guestroom at Abbott's, illuminating him in a way that made him seem like a figment of my imagination—as if his presence here were momentary, transitory. I was afraid that, were I to blink, he'd dissipate. "I'm sorry I woke you. Go back to sleep!"

What was to stop him from simply taking off and flying away any second, I'd thought, sleepily. I had no choice but to leap up from the bed and wrap my limbs around him, grounding him, weighing him down, giving him a reason to stay put.

We'd lapped thirstily that night. There it was—his intoxicating skin, there they were—his wondrous lips. His capable hands, his swift and limber fingers, found their way quickly inside my shirt (and my shaky ones found their way quickly inside his pants).

This had to be it. I was too tired to look any further.

~ ~ ~

I stretched my arms up and over my head, feeling my chiffon blouse escape from my belt.

"You're so limber, Ms. Levit," I heard Wisdom call behind me.

"Why, thanks, Wis!" I tried to match her delivery, but having a decade on her stood in the way; it sounded as if I were flat out mocking the girl.

Discreetly, I tucked my blouse back inside my pants, each leg of which was really just too wide unless you were wearing those faux-stripper heels. I wasn't about to wear those to work again, but with my ballet flats, I was tripping on all the fabric. It seemed there was no middle ground.

"She's right, Ms. Levit, you're looking great! It's like that trip did you wonders. Did you get back to our time yet? I'm still waking up at the crack of dawn." That was Sage, always a step behind her "bestie." It seemed paradoxical at times, how two girls who, too often, sounded like they were stuck in fourth grade were actually gifted and legitimately talented in their respective fields. Just last Friday, a couple of hours before I moved to

Staten Island, Wisdom had raised her hand in class and answered, "Hinduism" when my question was, "name a political theory advocating class war, resulting in a society in which all property is publicly owned and each individual's work is compensated according to his or her ability and need." When I'd corrected her—the answer I'd been looking for being "communism"—she tsked, "Well, I knew it was one of the 'isms.'"

Before I could turn around and face the girls, I heard a familiar voice behind my back.

"How are you, Ms. Levit!"

Paz.

Unable to summon a response of myself quickly enough, my shoulder blades tensing, I heard my other kids lower their voices until they were nothing but loud whispers. Now I had to turn around.

"Ah, good afternoon, Ms. Terranova. How was the audition?"

"It was great. I got the part. Watch me on ABC next fall." Paz shrugged, nonchalantly, before plopping into her seat, located directly behind Veronika, who was either running uncharacteristically late or was going to be out again.

"Ooh's" and "aah's" rushed out of the mouths of my seniors.

I did a double-take.

"What?"

"You asked about my audition, so I'm telling you—I got the part. It's for a pilot for ABC. Keep your fingers crossed for a full season, you guys."

So impeccable, this girl—that perfect chin, those perfect eyebrows. She looked decidedly older than her eighteen years, but then again, her experience level required it.

"Don't look so surprised, Ms. Levit. You'd been preaching 'self-fulfillment' since ninth grade! Well, here I am-—self-fulfilling." She crossed her legs and rearranged her t-shirt just so, her eyes never wavering.

Before I knew it, I was crouching at the girl's desk, finding myself whispering too loudly, myself.

"You have to speak to the principal."

"What for?" She was humoring me—she crossed her arms and leaned in half way to meet me; the distance between us was not what Abbott, in his heyday, would consider appropriate. "You smell like Sola—deodorant and sweat, if I remember correctly from our close encounter in that club," she whispered, emphatically. "It's exciting, isn't it? Doing it on a desk?"

Wanting to punch her in per porcelain-looking, perfect set of teeth, I moved back an inch, my face too hot not to be spewing physical flames.

"You have to set the record straight—you have to tell them that you were seventeen, that it was your idea, that you weren't pressured, what have you!" I hissed through my teeth.

"I will, as soon as I get my 'A-,' and so does Sophie."

"Your protégé?"

"Is that French, Ms. Levit? Because I'd missed quite a few lectures, as you may have probably gathered," she laughed. "You can use any terminology you want, Ms. Levit. It is what it is."

"Self-fulfillment and all?"

I rose to my feet. The girl's brown-eyed stare was still stout on mine. It chilled with its determination.

I may have been too loud-—Jordan looked up from the phone that was preemptively hidden in his lap underneath his desk. These kids had to know that we knew that that's where their phones stayed all day—nobody can justify looking down at their crotch and smiling and nodding; at least not with such frequency.

Chapter Fourteen: *Fantasy*

"Unless it's more of Paz-flavored bull, I don't think she's gone to the principal, yet," I muttered as I chewed and swallowed a hearty forkful of spaghetti that Abbott had cooked for us. My new life was off to a bangin' caloric start—this must've been the first real dinner I'd had in over a decade.

Sandwiched between the front door, the kitchen, and the bedrooms, Abbott's dining room was a large but dim space. If a living room was ever in the blueprints, I wasn't sure which corner was meant to be it, although the kitchen behind my back was as big, if not bigger, than the two bedrooms combined. I could not understand such planning. Unless you ran a catering business out of your home, what was the purpose of a kitchen that large, especially if it was at the expense of actual living space? Who would give up a place for a sofa for some spare counter space?

We sat opposite each other, Abbott and I. Jamie was out for the night, as he'd been the entire weekend. Waking up with him in the mornings was worth it, I tried to remind myself as I sulked with my wine glass in hand. He'd texted earlier, speaking enigmatically of another gig downtown—-session this, bass that. My phone was much quieter without George, in general.

"Well, that's just lovely, isn't it?"

"You haven't heard from Adams?"

"No, our darling principal hasn't called me for the final verdict just yet, which could be a good or a bad thing," Abbott scoffed dismissively, sucking in a string of spaghetti with an arguably inappropriate amount of gusto. "Question, Levit—-you speak Spanish, right?"

"Used to in college. I'm only remotely fluent when I speak to the son of my hosts from my summer semester in Seville—"

"You're only fluent when speaking with one person?"

"Is it that strange?"

"Well, that's not fluency, I'll tell you that much. Must be a special guy, is all I can say. A first or something, no?" Abbott embellished his shrug with a wink as I tried not to blush, surprised by the temptation of it.

"Why do you ask, anyway?"

"Paz's last name—what does it mean?"

I almost choked on my wine.

"Certainly, you could not have only studied French. What's your other language?"

"German."

I could see it.

"'Terranova' means nothing, really. I don't think it does, anyway. If 'terra' would be 'tierra'—it'd mean 'earth.' 'Nova'—no go? I don't know, dude," I shrugged, never having given Paz's last name a moment's thought. "Why are you asking me, anyway? You're the one who's been spending an unwise amount of time with the girl."

Abbott nodded in assent, saying nothing.

Our silence made the room appear darker, heavier somehow. With the kitchen and bedroom shades drawn, the sun low, the room took on an orange glow. It was reminiscent of what nostalgia may look like. I knew I had to say something—anything at all—before my heart grew too heavy for my tongue. I could already feel it tumbling awkwardly inside.

"So how's Stephanie?" I spoke when my phone screen lit up with only an update from Words with Friends (Javier played "quest").

"Still bow-legged."

"Right?!" I snorted my wine. "I thought it was just my bitchy self taking note back over there in Europe."

"Oh, no, no, she's definitely bow-legged," Abbott confirmed, gulping the remains of his wine, whole. "She loves that ginormous kitchen of mine back there, by the way," he added, as if reading my negativity.

"Uh-huh."

"Oh, what do you want from me, sweet Levit? What does Stephanie have to do with anything?"

His eyes were somewhere else. I couldn't follow them.

"Nothing," I protested. "You're the one who brought her on the trip, don't look at me!"

"Paz or Stephanie?"

"Both!"

"What can I say, spring chicken? She was the perfect…'beard,' as the kids say. And with a sex drive to rival that of a twenty year-old's."

"Was she aware of her 'beard' status?"

"As in, did she know I was having an affair with a student and needed her to act as a distraction? No, she did not."

Despite the calories, or maybe because of them, I grew lightheaded. After half a decade of acquaintance, two weeks seemed like an unnatural length of time in which to suddenly have to learn that many new layers to a person. I needed more time.

"What time is it?" I heard Abbott ask. The room was almost too dark for me to see his features. I imagined him sitting still, his posture proper, his glasses on the bridge of his nose, his hair swept up. Like before, like usual.

I clicked my phone on, likely lighting myself in a ghoulish way.

“Nine.”

His silverware clicked against his plate.

“Time for bed.”

“Really?”

Something shifted inside my belly. Somewhere between anxiety and anger, it burned hot and weighed heavy. My heart threw itself clumsily against my ribcage before Abbott could confirm with a simple, “Yes, really.” Warm with wine, I suspected that being alone would result in a wasteful amount of tears. I needed him to stay.

“It’s early! And how can you sleep with all this? You don’t know what she’ll say—she’s blackmailing you, for fuck’s sake!” I cried as I spun around in my chair, following Abbott into the kitchen with my eyes in the dark, my fingers desperate on the back of the chair. If there were enough light in the room, you’d see my whitened fingertips.

“What else can I do, Levit?” Abbott groaned as he flipped on the light switch where he was, his back to me at the kitchen sink.

“But how can you fall asleep with all this?” I was

practically pleading now, childish, frantic—too invested, too dependent.

"I close my lids and—"

"I'm serious, Abbott! I don't know how I'd ever sleep a wink with so much on my mind—the trouble you can be in—"

"How have you been sleeping lately, spring chicken?" Wiping his hands with a few crumpled sheets of paper towels, he turned to face me again, his glasses now on top of his head, his eyes unobstructed. He did look legitimately sleepy.

"What do you mean?" I hiccupped.

"Your fiancé of as long as I've known you just tried to kill himself on your account, and having warned you ahead of time, may I add. So I ask you—how do you sleep?"

When I blinked, dumbly, twice but didn't answer, he rubbed his face raw and let out a yawn.

"My point exactly—we all need sleep. It's the only thing in life that comes naturally to us. Even if you skip a night, remember that, eventually, you'll have no choice but to sleep. It's a comforting thought," he reasoned, patiently. "Anyway, feel free to stay up and wait for Jamie. He'll come back, at some point, I suppose. Not that it's any of my business, but he hasn't exactly been coming home at any godly hour even before you moved in, so don't take it personally."

I sucked in my lips until I tasted copper. Within minutes, Abbott shuffled over to the bathroom; within some more—he was inside his bedroom.

The chair underneath me squeaking with every shuffle, I felt vaguely nostalgic for a bed. Two weeks ago, I was engaged, I had a home I'd all but made my own; now, I shared a futon with a beautiful and very recently divorced man (though technically, their marriage was annulled, so perhaps I could amend my descriptions in the future) who was never even there when I fell asleep. And the futon belonged to Abbott….

I finished my wine, my legs soft and folded painfully under me, and reached for my phone. Hot between my thighs, I resisted trying Jamie again. Surely my loneliness and fear were transparent enough to be audible even through a cell phone speaker. Instead, when I saw the light that'd been seeping out from underneath Abbott's door slowly fade and finally die, my heavy finger pressed on Javier's picture.

"*¿No puedes dormir?*" he picked up saying, his voice dry and hoarse with the sleep I'd likely yanked from him.

"Something like that. You know me—I call you only when I can't sleep, apparently," I whispered, my near-empty wine glass cool against my forehead.

"*¿Cómo está Jessica?*"

"Jessica is fine. She's home with the baby…well, all three of her children."

"Her husband still not there?"

Ah, mercy at last—English!

"Is and isn't. Depending on the day. Allegedly, a ton of work, but he sells cell phones so I don't know how many late night meetings he can possibly be having to take on such a regular basis. It isn't exactly a round-the-clock job."

"I see."

They weren't friends per se, Jessica and Javier. They never were. Jessica had visited me in Seville that same fateful summer, and flirted mercilessly with Javier whenever she thought I was out of earshot (and even when she knew that I wasn't). Their continued contact made little sense to me, but, having left Javier inside the sunlit terminal back in Spain to board my plane to meet George, I never had much of a right to protest, either. What harm could there be with them playing Words with Friends, anyway?

"She kissed me once," Javier said, reading my thoughts from a distance of a continent. His voice now sounded more awake in the middle of the night in Europe than my own did at only about 10:00 P.M. Eastern Standard Time.

I hauled the remains of the wine against my throat

straight from the bottle before turning it upside down to make sure that it was indeed empty. Then I placed it back down on the glass surface of the table with a clink.

"So?" I felt my heart make an unexpected dive down my system.

"Just once, in Plaza de España. You were in class, and I was showing her around, like you'd asked me to do—"

"Javier, really, it was a thousand years ago. I don't really care—"

Abbott was a bad influence, because I don't remember ever drinking this much wine in one sitting before that sad little dinner of ours. The warmth of alcohol was making me sway. I swallowed, potentially audibly.

"But you do!" Javier exclaimed as if he'd stumbled upon a scientific breakthrough after decades of research. I imagined him sitting up abruptly in his old creaky bed, his walls painted dark burgundy, his sheets white.

"No, I don't!"

Now Abbott could be heard muttering angrily in his room; I was too loud.

"You do! You so do, Helen! This is literally the happiest I've been in years," he cheered, his voice as young as it was back when I knew him.

"Easy there, you'll wake your mother," I did my best to whisper, stifling a grin of my own. Between the carbs and the wine, something was happening inside my belly.

Javier laughed a laugh that sounded virgin—as if his diaphragm, his lungs, his vocal cords were not used to producing such jovial sounds. "Why does she hate you, anyway?"

I sighed too dramatically for the circumstances.

"I clogged the toilet in my bathroom…like, my third day there, too. I flushed something I wasn't supposed to—like a paper towel or something, nothing gross."

"So?"

"So, I didn't fess up—I just left it as it was and went to school and let her find out for herself. It was some stupid world economics class or something, I remember. I got an A, but mainly because I was one of the three people who even showed up on a regular basis."

Javier sounded good laughing. His throat having warmed up, the sound he was producing no longer sounded so foreign.

"So that was it?"

"Well, that, and I guess she must've heard us fooling around some nights. That could not have possibly helped my reputation any. I presume you guys hadn't taken in any more study abroad students after me?"

"No, you're right—we haven't. Are you still at your parents'?"

"I am," I lied effortlessly enough to take myself aback. I was finally learning something from my kids.

Removing the phone from my ear, I checked the time; it was almost eleven and Jamie still wasn't home.

And how was I ever going to pay for this call? We should've Skyped.

Chapter Fifteen: *Stupid American Pig*

I could hear the sound of Sophie's cello from down the hall. Everybody could. Her bow was, as usual, expertly dragged against the strings, producing sounds that were as sorrowful as they were bittersweet. The notes seemed to reach your heart before they ever reached your ears. Standing at the door to the practice room, I looked on for a long time before I dared to break the solitude that that solo surely required. Eventually, I negotiated with myself and counted to ten.

"Ms. Levit!" the girl exclaimed when she saw me, her bow mid-stroke and her hair wild and untamed. "How did you know I was in here?"

"Sophie, I could hear you all the way from the stairwell." I willed my unruly hands to steady. The door behind me thudded closed.

"I thought these rooms were soundproof," Sophie shrugged, removing the cello from between her legs to cradle it in the case at her feet.

"Not when you leave the door open."

I walked to the front of the room and sat down in the first seat off the center aisle, to the left, looking up at Sophie still up on that stage.

"Oops, I didn't realize."

"Ms. Stein's calculus class two doors down is very much entertained."

I crossed my legs and I interlaced my fingers over my knee.

"Want to come down here, Sophie?"

"No."

Sophie fingered her hair before turning back to her cello. The tenderness with which she tended to that inanimate object made me equal parts jealous and resentful.

"Okay, let's talk like this. Here goes…French—how's it going?"

"Oh, it's great now," she snickered, her little bird-like body shuddering almost imperceptivity, as if she were trying to suppress a sneeze. Her eyes remained stout on her instrument.

"And before?"

"Not so good."

"Are you under the impression that I'm here to play 'free word association' with you? Fine, we can do that. Let's go—Paz."

"Awesome."

"Am I meant to read between the lines here?"

Sophie straightened her short spine and placed her hands at her narrow, childish hips.

"What's this about, Ms. Levit?"

Though stages in these little practice rooms were of fairly insignificant elevation, with me sitting down, tucked all the way into my seat, even Sophie looked like a giant. The tall ceilings in the room did not help the impression.

"Has Abbott ever touched you?"

It was barely noticeable, but it was there—a flash of panic rippled across her delicate, miniature face, her smooth, narrow forehead, her silky complexion.

"Yeah," she said after a short cough meant to clear her throat.

"How?"

"With his hands!"

That panic seemed to have escaped the confines of her tight skin and was now audible.

"Where?"

"At his home!"

"And where is that?"

"Lower East Side," she sneered, only a brief but clear pause between my question and her answer.

"A-ha, wrong!" I cried, disappointed by her lack of prep. "He lives on Staten Island."

I was up on my feet now, growing quickly lightheaded. I didn't get the sleep I would've liked last night. After hanging up with Javier, I'd cleared my plate and moved into the bathroom to probe for any potential stray hairs on my already sore chin. Satisfied only when my skin began to burn, I'd proceeded on to my eyebrows, over-plucking if only by a few hairs, given my blood-alcohol level. I'd then also considered shaving my legs, the wax I'd gotten before the trip already expiring, but my vision was too blurry with all the wine, so I'd called it a night then.

"Did I wake you?" Jamie had asked in a whisper when he finally came home—Abbott's home. It was well past midnight.

"No," I'd whispered back, fairly grotesquely, hugging Abbott's sheets close to my body, which was dressed in an old Talent's spring musical t-shirt (stereotypically, it just had to be Cats).

We didn't need to turn on the light to inevitably find our way to each other. This seemed to be the only thing we did anymore—late night whispers and contortions. Each time our bare skin touched, I felt a small victory over fate, a minor jolt to my system. The infatuation I'd felt not so long ago was actually something tangible now—I made it happen against significant odds. This was a turn-on. George was now mute to protest; and I was barred from George, anyway.

"Where were you?" I'd asked when his tongue swirled around my earlobe.

"The studio."

Only a week back on the American soil and this studio was beginning to sound like the other woman I'd have to keep an eye on.

"So he lives on Staten Island, who gives a flying you-know-what?" Sophie dismissed back in the practice room, skipping down the two steps from the stage to me, the cello peaceful in its sarcophagus behind her back.

"Sophie, you're emulating someone way out of your league. You're saying what Paz would say, but you can never match her artistry," I spat out when our bodies neared each other's. Her breath smelled of bubblegum. "I'm serious, Sophie—you're ruining a man's life!" I hissed when she tried to pass by me.

"Are you living with Abbott now, Ms. Levit, is that it? It's his turn now, is it? Does that mean Sola is available again?" Paz had a solid future in pedagogy. If the acting thing wouldn't pan out for some reason, she'd need to look into teaching. "And he's ruining his own life, thank you very much," she added when I found myself at a loss for words. "It was ruined before I ever stumbled upon the honeypot."

"That may be so, Sophie, but you'll be the nail in the coffin. If he really didn't do anything to you, and you're just blackmailing him for a grade.... Look, I guarantee he'll give you at least a B+, but you have to stop it right now!"

Still dizzy, my heart pounding so loud, I was sure no sound insulation would keep it from disrupting Ms. Stein's math class, I stared Sophie down, determined, her afro at my eye level. My intestines contracted from the adrenaline flushing through my veins. Sophie's feline eyes, I saw, were childish when she wasn't playing.

"You can guarantee that?"

I would have to now.

"Ms. Levit, what's in it for you? Why do you even care? He's going down one way or another. He did have an affair with a student! It wasn't me, but he did!"

"She was seventeen at the time—"

"Apologist."

I'd heard that descriptor before.

"Why do you even care?" she repeated.

This was a good question.

"Because one mistake shouldn't have to undo everything," I muttered, half-sure.

~ ~ ~

The distance between the ferry and the isle of Manhattan grew by the second, as if we were actively pushing away from it (which, I suppose, we were). The skyline glistened in the sun, putting all of its reflective surfaces to good use. Abbott and I sat in companionable silence on the outside deck, tourist-watching. This being a free ride, it was not a bad boat to take if you were a visitor. Huddled along the perimeter of the deck, their bodies hanging dangerously over the railings, the Norwegians to my right were taking pictures of Ellis Island, while the Koreans to my left smiled posing against the backdrop of the Statue of Liberty. Each speaking their own language, they rattled merrily along about something I'd never know. They smiled and giggled and pointed. I envied them. To think just over a week ago, across the ocean, this was all of us.

I leaned my head on Abbott's shoulder and closed my eyes; twenty more minutes to the island that was my new temporary home—the Island of Staten.

"I talked to Sophie today," I told him.

"I appreciate the sentiment, but I doubt it'll do much good. The paperwork is in—I'm out at the end of the term either way."

"And if Sophie goes on with her lies, all thanks to

Paz?"

"I don't know." I felt Abbott shrug under my ear. "I really don't. She's seventeen now? I don't know when she's saying I allegedly started in on her, but I guess we'll find out." His Scottish accent made him sound like a sage, and his calm was as enviable as it was infuriating. I considered contesting, but that seemed fruitless.

My phone lay limp in my grip, my hands in my lap. After working overtime in Europe, it no longer burped at alarming intervals; it was now a phone again, not a pager. Even Words with Friends was slower now, Jessica apparently choosing not to use her scarce free time to challenge me at strategy. Couldn't say I blamed her.

Perhaps because of its newfound silence, the bubbling ringer of my Skype app was now a startling phenomenon rather than the annoying distraction that it was back on our spring break. My head flew off of Abbott's shoulder and was at once up right, my pulse immediately painful in my temples due to such a sudden change in position.

"What's wrong, Javier?" I asked when his likeness appeared before me. He wasn't inside his apartment—I could see that sterile fountain of his courtyard behind him. He looked pale.

"Are you living with that Portuguese guy?"

His English precise, the volume of my phone set to the max, I was sure that everyone around me heard him.

As I scrambled to my feet and gathered my belongings, I saw Abbott's eyebrows shoot up as if seeking to conjoin with his hairline.

"She's living with me, mate, whoever you are, and I'm Scottish," he called into my phone. His eyebrows still arched, he mouthed "what the fuck?" before I could run off to a less populated part of the boat.

If Javier heard Abbott, he didn't show it. His free hand (the one not holding his phone in front of his face in a way that was anything but flattering), his fingers long but crooked, were raking through his hair, over and over, as if his five-inch-mop needed constant touching up.

"Did you read my mind last night? About these calls being expensive, I mean? Thanks for Skyping, because I can't afford any more of these this month, I swear!" I stammered with a smile bordering on maniacal, hurrying mistakenly inside only to immediately lose reception.

Rattled, I ran back out, accidentally jabbing another tourist in the shoulder en route to the back of the ferry, further away from Abbott's prying eyes. I heard some bitter muttering in my wake but knew that I couldn't spare a moment for an insincere apology.

"Stupid American pig," I heard yelled in my direction just as I reached the doors. I barely flinched this time.

"Hey, sorry. What were you talking about

before?" I asked breezily as soon as Javier and I were reconnected, hoping to be able to change the tone of his voice from a distance.

"Why didn't you tell me you moved out of your parents' house? You moved in with that guy from the trip?"

I hadn't seen that face in a long time: face-to-face in pretty darn close to a decade, and computer screen to computer screen—months. It was soft and pleasant, if slightly rounded—clean-shaven cheeks with remnants of a goatee, slightly hooked, wide nose. Unlike Jamie's, it didn't have any sharpness or precision to it, but it was an altogether comforting face. His hair was slicked back. And I'd almost forgotten that he had an earring.

"Honestly? You really want to know? This is why," I breathed, beckoning the mild spring afternoon sun to mask my flush. I wasn't sure how much of me Javier could see in this light to begin with, but I couldn't let him see me fluster. "Who told you?"

"Jessica!"

"Why?"

"Besides the fact that it's the truth?"

"Well…yes!"

"She was upset I told you we'd kissed back then." Looking at him as he said this, I could see that he was ashamed. It was as endearing as it was comical. As if it still mattered. As if it ever had or would.

"Javier, I don't care what you guys did."

"Well, I care that you lied to me."

"I didn't. I didn't!"

I heaved once, twice, and was then suddenly crying, much to apparent bewilderment of those few around, as well as myself. My hands trembling, I was afraid I'd lose my phone in the blackness of the water below. I swatted at my face, hoping, baselessly, that that'd be enough to dry it. It was as if a dam broke within my chest and, without any floodgates there, now everything was getting soaked, soon to drown altogether.

"Hey, it's okay. *¿Puedes oírme?* Can you hear me? It's okay," Javier shushed from a place too far away from me to hear. It was late evening where he was. I'd have to let this man sleep every once in a while.

Jessica: between her marriage falling apart and the infant-induced sleep deprivation, she clearly no longer had my best interests at heart. Although, if what Javier relayed of their time together in Seville was true, she maybe never had.

"I can't live with my parents, Javier, so I moved in with a friend. And yes, the man you're referring to also lives there, all right? The commute was ridiculous and I feel like I'm stuck at twelve years of age in perpetuity when

I'm over there. Why do I have to justify myself to you—you're my friend! You should be on my side!"

Apologizing, explaining, justifying. I'd once thought that, at some point in time, I wouldn't need to do these things anymore. Maybe once I'd reach the age of majority, I'd reasoned once upon a time, or maybe when I'd graduate from college.

"Are you and that man…together? *Sólo dime la verdad, por favor.*"

There was no anger left in his voice. Not anymore. It was just resignation now. He smiled, assuredly, to encourage me to speak, to be honest, but that only prompted more tears. I tried to think about it. What defined "together," anyway?

"Truth? I don't know."

"But you want to be, I understand? You took steps to get there?"

I said nothing, careful to let out a sigh through my tightly pursed lips (twisted so to prevent my jaws from trembling). Javier, meanwhile, emitted a strained bit of laughter. I watched as he stood up from his seated position by the fountain, presumably to walk back inside the house.

"So what was with all that Morocco talk, then? I thought you wanted to come with me, finally."

"I…I thought I did…. I don't know…."

"I love you, Helen," I heard him whisper a split second before his image froze on my screen and the call was officially ended. As if to do me a favor and save me the effort, the app closed on its own.

"Call me a name, Javier. Make me hate you," I typed, deleted, and re-typed into our Words with Friends chat before deleting everything all over again. Coincidently, I saw that he had played a word earlier—"truth."

Chapter Sixteen: *Too Difficult*

Though her mousy hair was as greasy as ever, Veronika was back in my class. Her face comprised of small and predictable features, she was a welcome sight to see. It was out of character for this girl to be out this many days. In a school full of kids whose parents scheduled castings at all hours of the day, be they smack in the middle of my class or during lunch, Veronika had always been a breath of fresh air—her attendance record near perfect. We smiled, knowingly, at each other as she took her seat, although the "knowing" could only be one-sided, in our case. She sure had dirt on me, but I no longer knew what was going on in my favorite pupil's life. I hadn't even realized how much I'd missed her until I saw her again.

My thighs painful, my stance hunched and awkward, I sat behind my desk, watching my seniors settle in.

"Did you go horseback riding or something?" Wisdom asked in that sing-song way that came naturally to her. Most things uttered by her sounded like a question, but this one actually was. She didn't seem to be joking, either. With her head tilted and her ponytail limp, she looked like she was legitimately curious if I had indeed gone horseback riding.

"No, Wisdom. I just rode a bike for the first time in a few weeks," I confessed, getting up from my seat whilst trying to display as little difficulty as possible.

I did—I rode Abbott's bike. I rode it earlier that morning, when I woke up with the piercing sunlight that felt like the worst of hangovers and realized that Jamie was not next to me. Still in my pajamas, I rode up and down the block of Abbott's building before packing it in mere minutes into the attempt, just in time to shower and board the ferry. Those hills were prohibitive—the descents scary, the inclines near impossible.

I raised my arm to begin filling in my "Aim" for the day, my notes in the grip of my left hand, but, feeling Veronika's eyes peeled on me, writing "What role should international precedent play in the U.S. Supreme Court decisions?" on the board in front of me proved too difficult. Despite Jamie's earlier insinuations that the girl had a crush on me, she'd never paid me that much attention before, especially non-verbal. It made me nervous.

"Don't they say that riding a bike is like…riding a bike, or something?" That was Sage. I tossed my notes on my desk and turned to face the class.

"It was like riding a bike, Sagey-girl. I'm a bit sore, but yes, I was able to indeed ride it. I'm not in pain because I fell off or anything," I snickered just as the bell let out a ring, announcing that anyone who'd cross my threshold now would be officially tardy (if that meant anything at all to a room full of kids who'd be graduating in a few weeks' time). Just then, Paz and Ofir hopped in in an almost choreographed unison. "Right, people, so we have single number of weeks left. I can't even bring myself to name the exact number for fear of breaking down in front of y'all."

"Nine," announced a voice from the back.

"Thanks, dear Liam. I feel much better now," I groaned, throwing in a snicker for levity to avoid any miscommunication. "So, anyway, for some reason—feel free to call it laziness—I don't feel like teaching today. I want to actually talk to you for once. I'm going to miss you, after all, believe it or not. And I'll let you in on a little secret—we do have a day or two built into the academic calendar just for this kind of waste of time. So let's talk—who's doing what come June? Come August?"

"So are we not talking about taking foreign precedent into consideration today?!" Paz exclaimed, her perfectly blown out hair effortless on her shoulders. "I actually did the reading for you today, Ms. Levit."

Her knees crossed tightly, her top foot wrapped around her rooted leg's calf, Paz peered at me with a twinkle of her beautifully lined eye. The precision there was uncanny; one could see this even with her heavy bangs.

"Paz Terranova is over-prepared for once? Will pigs fly?" I gasped, theatrically. I made a show of plopping dramatically down in my chair, which hurt the backs of my thighs. That bike of Abbott's sure did a number on me. I rode it the night before, too, not just that morning. Following my inexplicable meltdown on the ferry earlier that afternoon, with Jamie at the studio (again), Abbott had wordlessly taken me down to his storage unit and rolled it out for me, saying, "Take it for a spin, why don't you," as if I were a schoolchild. And that's what I'd done. In a state of lucid thoughtlessness, I took the bike out, riding up and down those agonizing, San Franciso-esqe hills, past the expired colonials, until my palms hurt from my desperate grip and my crotch felt like it would continue to hurt violently in perpetuity. I didn't yet know I'd feel the need to ride it again in the morning.

"You're home!" I'd cheered, stupidly, when I'd limped back in last night, wiping the sweat from my brow. Eight wasn't early—it was unheard of. Of course, I'd soon learn that he wouldn't be back for the night once he'd step out the door again.

Jamie had only smiled in return. Leaning over, he gave me a clinical peck on the forehead.

"Feeling better?" Abbott had asked, thus making me open the eyes I'd just closed to savor the contact with Jamie, the warmth of his lips making its way through me, confusing me. Inevitably, I had to be brought out of the momentary trance.

I could see that Jamie raised an inquisitive brow at this question.

"Everything okay?"

"Levit spoke to her friend in Spain on the ferry over, and apparently something upset her to tears,"

Abbott'd rushed to explain. I'd closed my eyes again, waiting for further inquiry from Jamie, but none came.

"Dinner?" Abbott had offered, seemingly losing interest in my crisis.

I could only shake my head.

"None for me, either. I actually have to head back out," Jamie had announced just as I'd bent down to kick off my boots.

"Oh?" I'd barely whispered on my way back up to full height, my spine still curved, my feet now bare.

"I won't be late, I promise."

I'd tried my tongue at a plea or a rebuttal but could only mutter unintelligibly in response. Before I could say anything that would sound even remotely like any human language, he was gone for the night.

"No worries, we'll be back to our scheduled programming tomorrow," I reassured Paz back in my classroom. "Think of it as no homework tonight."

"Oh, good, because, you know, I was seriously worried," the girl smirked back, popping her gum mid-sentence.

Just as I crossed my fingers across my belly and leaned back in my chair in an attempt to exude confidence and ease, I saw Jamie pass by my door. He paused at the small, rectangular window and waved, timidly. My heart, too, paused. We'd missed each other at lunch (on account of a parent of a freshman of mine requesting that I make a homework packet for her son who'd be gone for the remainder of the school year, away on some theatre project). Our eyes locked now and all I could think was that it was as if nothing had changed since before we were formally introduced—we'd regressed back to distanced glances. It seemed I would never get out of high school.

"Right, well—" I stuttered.

"Oooh, Ms. Levit is all distracted, how cute!" Paz whooped. "Hi, Mr. Sola!" she shouted. "Miss me?"

Regular classrooms not being soundproof, it looked like he heard her. "No," he mouthed, before waving at me again and moving on.

Heat rushed to my cheeks. There were no secrets that a teacher could keep in that school. Or maybe any school. Everyone was at once engulfed in giggles. Ver winked at me, flashing a smile full of less than perfect teeth. She was the comforting constant I'd grown accustomed to having around, like a pet one grows used to over its short lifetime.

"Thanks for that, Paz. Now, before we all get too busy with graduation robes and textbook collections, et cetera, maybe let's take today to just talk about who's going where for college and where we each see ourselves in five-year's time, maybe even ten. Paz, since you're the one with the loosest tongue around here, maybe you start?"

Paz unfolded and refolded her limbs and rearranged her sweater before leaning in closer, her elbows square in front of her.

"Ms. Levit, I think talking about international precedent is safer. Why discuss our futures? It'll only remind you of your own place in life: right here is where you'll always be."

Low hoots and whistles could be heard. Grateful that Jamie was likely out of earshot, I leaned in on my own elbows, closer to Ms. Terranova.

"Yes, I'm like a tree, Paz—a reliable evergreen you can always visit," I smiled sweetly, speaking over the pulsating ache inside my ribcage.

More hoots and whistles. "Owned!" someone shrieked.

This was just one of the many reasons why I wanted to teach teenagers—their blessed predictability.

"You should really think through your metaphors, Ms. Levit, because something about tress…and dogs…," Paz winked at me, her sweater revealing her full bust. I thought of Abbott. "But okay, let's play. It's Yale School of Drama for me."

"And five-years from now?"

"It's bad luck to talk about all the awards that will be bestowed upon me."

"Is it?"

"Well, it can't be good to brag preemptively."

Would I miss these standoffs? Unlikely. I was pretty sure I'd be happy to unleash this one into the world. I couldn't wait for there to be a screen between us.

"More power to ya, my dear," I nodded with a tap of my open palms on my desk for effect. "Who's next? Veronika?"

I regretted calling on her the exact moment I heard her name uttered out loud, almost surprised at the sound of my own voice. There was no good reason for me to make this child talk about her having to give up her career before having properly begun it (and all because of her parents' refusal to accept her sexuality). You couldn't be Veronika Horvat and play the guitar as a hobby whilst assisting in a merger—this was akin to clipping her wings. And now, thanks to me, everyone was going to know her shame.

As if it'd help matters, I stood up from behind my desk and walked over to hers. When I saw her hesitate, I squatted down by her seat and rubbed her arm in an act of encouragement, if not desperation, hoping she knew that my calling on her wasn't an act of cruelty so much as helplessness, simple thoughtlessness, even. I could've called on Liam, I could've called on Jordan...

My thighs burned as I waited for her to speak.

"I'm going on tour with Mr. Sola, actually. Well, not with, per se, but he'll be doing the bass for the headliner and I'll be playing with the opening act. All summer stages. We'll be on the road for a few months, with a few days in between to do the laundry, so to speak. It'll be fun. You should come out, Ms. Levit."

Chapter Seventeen: *Groupie*

When I stopped blinking maniacally, Veronika looked equal parts eager and apologetic. Paz looked triumphant.

"Well, you know I will definitely be coming out."

"Once a groupie, always a groupie," I all but muttered out loud.

Andrew spoke about his plans next, as did Ofir after him. He was predictably called a Nazi for going to support a Zionist regime that was guilty of ethnic cleaning against the rightful owners of all that desert land—the Palestinians. I remained crouched on the floor by Veronika's desk, but this did not raise any eyebrows.

"There was never even such a country! It's just what the British or someone called it or something. It's a relic of colonialism, right Ms. Levit?"

On a different day, I would've been profoundly disappointed by Ofir's knee-jerk reaction to such a simplistic accusation thrown his way (I was sure I'd taught him better), but in that moment, I couldn't focus on anything past my own blood whooshing violently in my ears, my heart bruising itself on my ribcage.

"There were people living there, despite what you'd rather call the region—"

"Are you a self-hating Jew, Ms. Levit?

"Ofir, watch it," I barked, easing myself up, leaning on Veronika's desk too obviously. There were no heels on my feet that could act as an excuse, if not exactly a justification. "I'm just pointing out a hole in your argument—you can't explain away the people who'd lived on that land before the inception of the State of Israel regardless of any name given. And I'm not a self-hating anything," I barked, not fully believing myself. "The way to a permanent and peaceful resolution doesn't lie in pointing out that there was no country named X, case closed. That's not productive."

Feeling my already sore legs grow weak, I retreated to my chair behind the desk.

Ofir and whoever sat behind him continued to go at it. There was talk of the peace efforts and the various Intifidas, religious and water rights, not to mention—Soda Stream. Eventually, Ofir made a joke and batted an eye, at which point all was calm again. A wink of his lashes, a sideways smile, and he had supporters. Maybe Israel could use more Ofirs. He'd be fine—be it on stage in tights or with a rifle at border patrol. I, on the other hand, feared I was about to suffer a stroke in front of him and his classmates.

Feeling dangerously on the verge of vomiting, I soldiered through everyone else's plans post-graduation. I was no longer happy I'd asked. That bell couldn't come soon enough. Veronika, the merciful, approached my drooped-in-the-shoulders form on her way out as I rubbed my temples, my pulse increasingly painful.

"Mr. Sola hasn't told you?" she whispered when she checked over her shoulder to make sure that Paz wasn't listening. I shook my head. "Well, he'd only just found out two days ago. At least that's when I found out. He got me the audition after he got the gig, himself. He heard the opening act needed a touring bassist—"

There were more details peppered in there, surely, but I couldn't make myself pay attention. The burn in the back of my throat was too severe.

"And your parents?" I asked, almost cruelly.

"You're right—it didn't have to be like they said. They don't want to support me—I'll make my own living. I'm not going to be an indentured servant."

I'd created a monster. And now it was going to be living my life.

~ ~ ~

My belly soft, I stumbled out of my classroom after Veronika and headed downstairs to Jamie's. I knew I was going to be late for my next batch of kids, but it didn't matter. Once the bell announced the beginning of next period, I dared a peek through Jamie's own door's rectangular window. About a dozen pimply-faced freshmen sat in a semicircle, their faces tilted up toward Jamie, as if he were a cult leader and they were willing to commit mass suicide on command. There were no guitars in sight—this was a vocal section, I reminded myself a fraction of a second before warm-ups could be heard emanating shyly out of their room. The door not closed fully, their sound insulation was violated. I must've missed the breath relaxation and the tongue trills I remembered from my own brief time in musical theatre, because what I was hearing Jamie do now were two-octave scales. His own voice already warmed up, it sounded smooth and enveloping, his sound traveling its intended and deliberate distance. Just as I closed my eyes to take it all in, I heard the door yawn open and closed, a girl I did not know rushing past me armed with a hall pass, practically jogging in the direction of the bathroom. I walked in the opposite direction before I could be spotted; it was high time I headed back up the stairs to my own class, anyway.

I didn't bother checking the guitar rooms after my last period. Instead, hightailing it for the exit along with my most eager to leave students, I ignored three calls from Abbott, my mind blank but feet determined. They were taking me somewhere without consulting me first. Veronika quoting my own musings on life was unnerving to say the least, but Jamie leaving for the summer without so much as informing me created a bubble of fury-colored haze around me. Before I knew it, I was parked inside a bus shelter by the school—the same bus shelter that had once afforded me that memorable look at Jamie all those months ago. That rainy afternoon in December, that ragged blue umbrella, that shiny with moisture leather jacket, that guitar case, those bright eyes, that stark black hair.... That sighting once seemed to have changed everything. So serendipitous, it was even reciprocated—he'd noticed me, too. I sighed as I landed my weight on a narrow metal bench.

By the time I disembarked my old cross-town bus, I was a little more than queasy. All muscle memory, my feet carried me without any direct commands from my brain. It was getting too hot for my coat, but I hadn't yet unpacked anything lighter. I didn't think I was going to need to at first, but now spring was slowly inching its way toward summer and I had no appropriate wardrobe.

No keys to my old home at the Kasun's brownstone, I wrestled out of coat and settled on the stoop. My bag full of final paper proposals from across all my grade levels, I shook it off my shoulder as if it were possessed. It was silly to come all the way up here; it'd only add to my commute back to my latest temporary shelter in St. George. With Jamie gone, it suddenly dawned on me that I probably would no longer be able to justify staying with Abbott. To prevent likely hyperventilation, I lowered my head between my knees, preemptively.

"Helen!"

My old downstairs neighbor was at my feet. George's apparent guardian angel, this aspiring actress waited tables at a restaurant down the block. It was the same restaurant that used to feed the first homeless man to whom George had gifted my old bike; maybe the same guy now owned two bicycles, for all I knew.

"Amanda?"

"No, I'm Ashley. Amanda's my roommate."

"Right! Hi!"

Lightheaded from having thrown my head up too quickly, I scrambled to my feet, my brand new Uggs skidding.

"George mentioned you were away before…you know…before all this. That was a long trip you went on! But anyway, how is he? How is George now?"

"Oh, he's better," I lied with some difficulty. "I just forgot my keys." It got easier once you got going.

"No problem, let's go," Ashley cheered as she wrestled her own set of keys out of her faux-bohemian purse (likely purchased from Zara or the like) and pushed the door open.

"Thanks for calling 911, by the way," I muttered as I followed the girl up the stairs, unsure what I was going to do once I got to her floor—it'd be impolite to reject an offer for a cup of tea from a woman who saved your (former) fiancé's life.

"No, no, that was Amanda. Well, we both heard him take a tumble, but it was Amanda—she actually called the paramedics and waited for them downstairs. What happened to him, exactly?" she asked in a whisper when we got to her apartment door. There was one more flight for me.

In her multiple barrages of me, Dr. Kasun failed to give me any instructions for situations like this. I stammered.

"Umm, he had an adverse reaction to some cold medication he was taking," I whispered back.

Ashley made a face that I could only imagine was meant to express pity and/or fear. Something told me that her theatre training wasn't much better than my own.

"Ouch!"

Indeed.

"Well, tell him we hope to see him back around here soon. He's such a great guy. You're so lucky," she squealed, giving my shoulders a squeeze. Was I the only female on the planet who never learned to do this? Well, Veronika and I.

I nodded too aggressively, struggling to keep my bag on my shoulder and my coat on my bent arm. One of us had it wrong—either Ashley (or was it Amanda? I no longer remembered) was mistaken in her estimation of George, or I'd just burned all possible bridges that led to a real life. "Do I just burst her bubble?" I wondered. "Disappoint her?" That seemed unnecessarily cruel. I nodded along, figuring it was more merciful to allow her to live vicariously through me—live the life she imagined me to be living, that is. Not many could possibly be jealous of me in my actual, real life, so it was tempting to let this one slide.

"Thanks!" I did my own version of squealing before throwing my foot up on the next stair in the hopes of losing Ashley (not Amanda!) for good. Her bouncy curls were giving me vertigo. "Okay, bye!"

I took to the stairs two at a time, hurling my things off by my old apartment door. Squatting down next to my belongings, I unwrapped my scarf and fingered my chin, finding one stray hair on the third run. No matter how regularly I plucked these out, they'd always be back, I knew. It was an uphill battle. I considered just saving myself the time and the pain from there on out. No matter the effort, I'd always be back where I started.

Chapter Eighteen: *Maintenance*

I wasn't sure if it was that fourth Manhattan in my bloodstream or the sight of Jamie's bitten bottom lip up on that stage with a guitar strapped across his chest that was making my head swim. Whatever it was, it also made my thighs vibrate and my crotch burn. I was no longer drinking Ginger Ales, that was for sure. And those Manhattans only sounded good in Sex and the City. Next to me, Abbott was sipping another beer.

"He's sexy, that beast up there! Who knew?! So scrawny and shit, and just look at him go…hair flowing, spit and sweat flying…."

Maybe this was his third, or even fifth, beer.

We could've driven in to see Jamie play, but, rightfully anticipating the temptation of alcohol after the couple of weeks that we both had had, we'd decided on the trusty ferry and the good ol' subway. Jamie, of course, made it in hours ahead of us—sound checks and all.

It was Abbott'd who picked me up by my old apartment door the day before yesterday. I'd reluctantly answered the phone on his fourth attempt, confessing where I was. By the time I'd gathered my students' loose-leaf pages and staggered downstairs, he was already there. I'd registered a distinct ping of disappointment when I didn't see Jamie at his side. "He wasn't home when I left," Abbott had explained receiving my bag without request, preempting the question I couldn't bring myself to ask.

"Those faces he's making though—ouch! Is he smelling something foul up there?" Abbott hooted at my side at the bar. Manhattans or not, I loved Abbott, I told myself with another gulp of some rye whisky and vermouth. "What's up, sweet Levit? Why so grumpy?" I heard him ask over the music, but my mind was too busy swimming with the warmth of the alcohol and the sway of Jamie's hair to answer; those strands, partly braided on the right, were at least as intoxicating as my drink, maybe more, I decided. His powerful eyes glaring into the spotlight, hovering somewhere on the brink of agony and ecstasy by the looks of it, that skinny frame hunched over his instrument, squeezing melody out of just six strings that had my heart gripped from the sizable distance between us.... It beat so fast, it drummed in my ears, leaving the rest of me tingling with numbness. I couldn't see if his ring was still on, no matter how hard I squinted. "Earth to grumpy Levit!" Abbott nudged me in the ribs. We were sitting at the bar, with our backs to the stand of it, our eyes to the stage. Stage right is where Jamie was positioned, so naturally that's where my attention was. Abbott, on the other hand, was just background noise—he blended with the hum of the hall, the chatter of the bartenders, and was just about drowned out by the music pushing its way out of the many sizable speakers. Giving up, eventually, Abbott turned his focus away from me and, instead, to the two women on his right. I glanced in their direction, taking comfort in the fact that they likely had to be carded in order to get in. Someone must've made sure they were of age.

My phone jumped on the bar—that wood panel

only about sixteen inches in width that separated us from the wall of glistening liquors. Mom. This wasn't the first time she'd called. I usually clicked the red "ignore" button, but this time, my finger warm and soft, I almost picked up. I quickly changed my mind, however; it was too loud to talk, anyway, I reasoned before deciding to send yet another call to voicemail.

Mom wouldn't appreciate the sound of this music. It was a lot heavier than I would've expected out of Jamie's gentle hands, myself. I realized that, short of hearing him play "Spanish Caravan" in our hotel room in Paris, I didn't really know what kind of music he played for a living. Maybe it was heavy metal all along.

"Oh, he plays in various genres, Ms. Levit. The man of his talent and caliber can do anything," Veronika had whistled in my office earlier that day. She'd come to apologize for putting me in an "awkward position" the day before. She was here, at the brewery, too, of course; she wouldn't miss an opportunity to watch her accessible idol play.

"Will this be the band he'll be playing with this summer?" I'd asked Veronika while eyeing my Words with Friends cheat on my phone screen. My finger occasionally hovered over the exit button, but I kept my eyes glued to it, anyway; so she'd know I cheat at Words with Friends, so what? It's the truth, after all. It was better than looking her in the eye. Adults cheat, too, Veronika.

"No, this is more like progressive rock, whereas

the festival guys are more old fashioned rock-n-roll, so to speak." She'd told me the names of both bands, but they told me nothing. Besides, I wasn't sure if it was necessary to spare any memory capacity for any of this, anyway. Not with Jamie leaving. I hadn't yet told him I knew of his plans, partly due to lack of opportunity, but mostly out of perverse curiosity as to how long it would take him to tell me himself.

She didn't travel to the venue with us—Veronika, that is. Though one could say that any right to dispense advice on boundaries that Abbott ever used to have was now long gone, if not forgotten, boundaries were still a good idea. As though thinking the same thing, back at school, Veronika had promised she wouldn't bring Paz with her. Then she'd muttered her goodbyes to my folded and half-hidden form and skedaddled right on out of my closet of an office.

She kept her word—she came alone. She beamed brightly at us when she'd first walked in, on her way past the bar to her reserved seat at a table up front. That's where we all were supposed to sit, as Jamie's guests, but I thought it'd be wise to begin acclimating now. I had a leg up on this challenge. I already had quite a bit of experience watching this man from a distance.

~ ~ ~

My head spinning, I led Jamie down the hall and toward the disabled bathroom. My hand firm on his belt, my still-not-repainted fingernails just grazing his skin-I was determined. Compliant, Jamie followed, his limbs loose after a ninety-minute set. Once the door was closed behind us, I turned the lock. Our acquaintance progressing rather quickly—from never actually speaking, to sharing a room, to doing it often and intensely—a bathroom date wasn't entirely out of left field.

"What are we doing?" he panted in my ear as he pressed his pelvis against my hip, making sure I feel him.

"You're leaving," I breathed into his damp with sweat hair, throwing all my chips on the table without a second thought. "So who cares what we do?"

"I can't stay." His kisses did not stop as he said this; instead, they made their way up my neck and around my earlobe. His scent—deodorant competing with sweat—only thickened the haze of all that whisky within me. This was how that groupie made him stay, I remembered. I'd have to be lower maintenance than that.

My fingers simultaneously rigid and restless, I struggled with his buttons and the buckle of his artful shirt (which lay across his chest, akin to a straight jacket). My thighs shaking from balancing my weight on the balls of my feet, back in my ambitious heels now that it was Friday, I ached for some skin-to-skin contact, for the warmth of his body. When my fingertips finally got their way, I gasped, the air around us thick with Febreze or the like—stale and suffocating. I felt it come into contact with the burn of my multiple drinks in the back of my throat, making me want to retch. Fighting the sensation, I reached for Jamie's pants, feeling the hardness of him against my open palm now. It was exciting, increasing both my heart rate and, predictably, the nausea. As he kissed his way down my chest, his wide hand confident on my breast, I continued to breathe through my nose. In and out, doing my best to suppress every single thing on my mind, I breathed at regular intervals, forcing air into my lungs steadily just before expelling it again.

I thrust myself into him, hoping that it would make everything better. And just when I thought it did, I felt my body propel itself forward to immediately hunch over the toilet, thankful that it was a high one, it being the disabled bathroom. Our clothes in disarray (shirts untucked and pants unzipped), Jamie snatched my hair out of my face just in time.

Chapter Nineteen: *Lover's Bridge*

As if the actual hangover didn't already feel like imminent death was upon me, the room seemed to be drowning in sunlight. My eyes were not accustomed to such luminosity and the rays stabbed too deep, seemingly keen on probing the depth of my aching skull.

My eye sockets sore, I was intermittently awake ever since the proverbial crack of dawn. Grudgingly exhausted to the point of physical pain, my hair stuck to my face, I tried to lift my head off the pillow, but that goal proved too ambitious. I took comfort in the fact that Jamie wasn't repulsed enough by me to sleep on the floor rather than next to me; I threw my heavy arm on top of his warm body in appreciation. My tongue unresponsive and glued to the roof of my mouth (and my mouth feeling as if it were stuffed chock-full of cotton balls), screwing my eyes shut in hopes of more sleep did little to further the goal.

I let my fingers roam underneath the couch in search of my phone, but all I stumbled upon were a few dust bunnies. I gave up only to try again minutes later. Eventually, I found it and squinted just precisely enough at its screen to see that it was seven in the morning. It was time to wrestle my way out from between the sheets before I would inevitably wake up Jamie with my attempts to unglue my tongue from the roof of my mouth.

Eternally clumsy, clearly never to become that elegant and effortless adult of my dreams, I landed on the floor with a thud, glad to find myself still in my street clothes. On all fours I crawled into the bathroom. There was no way less dignified to say goodbye to Jamie; I was grateful that his eyes were closed believably enough. Until I'd gulped a mouthful of tap water in the shower, I hadn't even realized that the sensation that wasn't letting me fall back asleep all along was indeed thirst. I hadn't drank that much alcohol since Spain.

Abbott and Jamie still sound asleep (as any working adult should've been at seven thirty in the morning on a Saturday), I didn't want to risk turning on the blow drier. Instead, I parted my hair down the middle and gave myself two messy braids; a child smiled back at me in the mirror when I was done. No matter how fast I ran, how hard I kicked, it seemed, nothing ever changed. Not for long, anyway. Every time it seemed that enough distance was put between me and that insecure, suburban teenager, there she was—inside that murky glass in need of a good Windex treatment. All my running was done in place.

I undid my braids in a huff and made my way into Abbott's wasteful kitchen. A pair of fuzzy socks on my feet (and a mismatched set of clothes I'd pulled out of my bag on my fast escape out of the room earlier on my body), I opened the refrigerator to find a few unopened packs of cold cuts and a gallon of orange juice. Juice it was. Satiating, it cooled my burning throat on contact. I gulped it down like a convicted glutton.

Trying to keep my grunting low as I pushed open

the kitchen window, I crawled onto the fire escape. Years of sleeping next to one but this was my first attempt at the cliché. The morning air too chilled to be comfortable, I folded a few kitchen towels under my ass before folding my legs into a George-worthy lotus and sipping more juice straight out of the container. I could see the water down at the foot of the hill, but without my lenses, I couldn't see any ferryboats shuttling people between the two shores. They must've been there, of course, whether I could see them or not. They didn't need me to bear witness.

I fingered through my social media on my phone and glanced at my Words with Friends. There hadn't been a word from Jessica in days; I'd tried calling but not that persistently. She was busy, she was broken—I got it. What did I know of these things, anyway? And whatever bones I had to pick with her right now would not be picked for reasons aforementioned. We were better off in our respective corners for now.

Javier, however, played a word—"stubborn."

"You're no longer mad at me?" I asked when he picked up. Skype would've saved me a penny, but my slightly puffy with alcohol face wasn't ready for his hazel eyes beautifully set on that plush, round, friendly face.

"Remember when I used to wait for you to say everything in Spanish, even if it took you forever? Even if you were wrong?"

"¿Sigues estás enojado conmigo?"

"Better," Javier commended. "And no, I'm not mad. I have no right to be mad. At anything. Well, not at you, anyway. You can live with whomever you want. You owe me nothing." There was a barely audible sigh on the other end, but he was trying.

My exposed arms cold in the morning breeze, I wrestled one kitchen towel from underneath my own weight and wrapped it around my shoulders.

"Nah, you do. I lied…by omission, at any rate. And you're literally the only friend I have left." This was more of a moan than a statement, my mouth still dry and tongue still uncooperative.

"Ah, that's quite an exclusive status."

"You know what I mean—" Not having thought through the rest of the plea, I gave up.

"I do, I do," he assured, anyway, forever more merciful, kinder than I deserved. "Anyway, I don't know about you, but I'm going to Morocco this summer. Although, I'd also never been to Paris. You and your Portuguese friend have—"

"Javier, we're not together," I protested, barely able to contain my disappointment at the fact. "And he's leaving on tour soon…," I added, definitely failing to hide it now.

"Are you going to do the whole long distance thing?" Javier asked after a tasteful pause.

I closed my eyes against the sun that seemed to grow brighter by the minute. It still did little for the temperature, but the sight of it sure intensified my headache.

"I doubt it. He hasn't even technically told me yet."

Were we on Skype, I'd be able to watch Javier struggle to pick his words, maybe even see his facial muscles twitch as he tried to suppress a smile.

"If he cares about you, he'll call it quits now, because he wouldn't want you to sit and wait for him—"

"That's convenient advice, Javier!" Above me, someone was smoking out on his own fire escape. I wrinkled my nose at the odor wafting down.

"No, hear me out! He's a musician, right? That's what Jessica said. He knows what life on the road is like, and you guys can't already be that serious, you know? So if he'd rather put an end to whatever this is now, it'd be the right thing to do. It's not that different from what you did to me…with me, back when you were leaving."

The symmetry was nauseating. I couldn't break out of these circles, doomed to continue suffering from this self-imposed vertigo. I needed to make amends or else I'd continue to repeat myself, man in and man out, I suddenly became convinced.

"Is there a lover's bridge in Paris?"

"What?"

"A bridge where people leave locks with the names of their lovers and throw the keys into the water? I heard it's like endangering the structure of the bridge over there. Isn't that something—that a bridge can crumble under the weight of love?"

"Well, locks, technically," I couldn't help but correct. "It's the weight of the locks that's crumbling it, not love or whatever." I had a vague inkling as to what was coming.

"Did you see it in Paris?" Javier asked without missing a beat, as if what I'd just said wasn't actually said out loud.

I shook my head, which wasn't a welcome sensation. I forgot he couldn't see me.

"No, but I think the automated tour guide voice thingy on the evening cruise we took over there mentioned something like that."

"Hmm. Well, I was thinking maybe I'll go put one up there before they dismantle the whole thing, you know? I heard they will be removing all the locks soon."

Reluctant, I opened my eyes and shook off the kitchen towel. In the distance, if I squinted, I could just make out the outlines of an orange ferry on its way to the city. Of course, without my lenses, it could've just as well been a mirage. Still, it seemed to be gliding peacefully enough for me to want to be aboard any vessel of similar destiny. Anything to move from my place.

"Don't they just put those locks anywhere now? It's like a world-wide hipster movement. There's probably one somewhere in Morocco, too. Hell, I think there's one in Brooklyn."

"Do you want me to come to New York, then?"

~ ~ ~

I told him that I didn't. It was the right thing to say, or at least so I told myself when my heavy tongue had almost blurted out a tempting yes.

I'd stayed out on the fire escape longer than felt comfortable, but eventually, Jamie woke up (and then Abbott), and I felt compelled to climb back in.

"Don't forget to wash your hands, spring chicken! Who knows where that fire escape has been! You got us washing hands round the clock, so don't be a hypocrite," Abbott teased helping me in, lending a hand as I jumped off the counter. Jamie stood in the doorframe, arms across his chest. Throwing up all over the bathroom stall last night was not something that was going to help me keep this man around, I suspected.

As I lathered and rinsed my hands under the kitchen tap, I watched the girl Abbott had apparently brought home the night before stumble on her way out of the apartment, her heels in hand. You'd think he was the rock star.

"Feeling better, sweet Levit?" Abbott asked, pouring me a tall mug of coffee without asking if I wanted one, ignoring the click of the lock after his one-night stand. "You were pretty legless last night!"

"Legless?"

"Drunk! I bring you slang from across the pond—you're welcome! You'd think you'd treat me with some modicum of respect for the cultural attaché that I am! Jesus Christ!"

Jamie smiled, I could see that much in my peripheral vision without turning to face him face on. I couldn't bring myself to do that. An artist of suspect talent, I could now trace Jamie's face in my sleep if I had to. I knew the curve of his jaw, the line of his nose—the strong chin, the large lips, the almond eyes. I didn't need to look at him to know each tiny wrinkle, every lash as it was. It would be best to keep my eyes on the eggs that Abbott had put in front of me on the dining room table just so as not to involuntarily memorize any more finite details. On the other hand, those soft yolks made my stomach twist in on itself. I could've sworn to myself that I would never drink again, but that'd be another promise to myself that I knew I would inevitably break.

"She wasn't so bad," I heard Jamie say before reluctantly picking my head up. With his hair gathered in the back, only a few pin-straight strands down around his face, Jamie looked like a child grinning. Open and unabashed, that smile could look caricature, clownish even, if you did not know that face, the way its features fit so precisely together; if you didn't spend hours fantasizing about it like I did. So impossibly cruel it all was.

I squeezed his knee under the table and shoved a forkful of eggs in my mouth, putting mind over matter to try to keep the gag reflex down.

"So what's the plan for today, kiddos?"

"I'm in rehearsal," Jamie answered through a hearty swallow of whatever of Abbott's orange juice that I didn't get the chance to down out on the fire escape. "Of course," I shook my head to myself. "Do you have any more fire escape phone conversations planned for today, Helen?" he asked as he set his drained tumbler back on the table, glass clicking against glass. Flushed on command, I felt the eggs hesitate at my esophagus, contemplating a way out; I all but swallowed my lips whole, swirling my fork around my plate, to try to dissuade them.

"It wasn't George," I defended with my voice small.

"Ooh, was it that dude from Spain? The guy you stayed with over there?" Abbott always was too eager to help.

Jamie nodded in assent, as if he knew whom Abbott meant, but neither he nor I said anything out loud. I puffed once or twice, but nothing I had swirling around in my brain as a viable alternative at a comeback seemed wise enough to be uttered at any reasonable volume. "You're leaving, anyway," seemed too petty; "why do you care?"—too immature. It was better to focus my energy on keeping those eggs down.

"Well, alrighty then, children. Stephanie is popping in today, so I suppose it bodes well for all y'all not to be here for a while," Abbott whistled, waving Jamie jokingly away with his fork before he could say anything. "So, sweet Levit—can I buy you out for the day? Maybe go to the library to work on that Teacher-of-the-Year speech of yours?"

"My brother!" I suddenly called out. The stress of having to fill an empty Saturday on demand appeared to sharpen my senses. I had only a few homework assignments to page through; I could hand out those checkmarks on my way up the stairs to my office on Monday, if I wanted to. I wasn't going to spend the day alone inside the Staten Island Public Library, just down hill from Abbott's apartment. "My brother's wife is away like every weekend now, I think, which tends to improve his mood, dramatically, so it seems like a good time to bond." With the room swimming, it was my best attempt at a joke. "The speech can wait. Not like anyone is going to be on the edge of their seat waiting to hear it."

My men nodded.

"Where does he live?" Abbott asked, collecting the dishes from us.

"Jersey City."

"I'd offer you a ride, but I should probably clean up for Stephanie," he said, tossing the remains of our breakfast in the trash bin. "Which way are you headed, Sola?"

"Williamsburg."

Of course!

~ ~ ~

The view from my brother's condo was always breathtaking on a sunny afternoon. Granted, I didn't visit often, but, if anything, that meant that every time I was there, I could appreciate it more. Even with my sunglasses on, the river shimmered, as did the city on the other side of it.

Out of the two of us, it was Vlad; if this were a competition, he would be the winner, and by a long shot. Education, real estate, family, paid-out student loans—he's the poster child for what a son of two Soviet almost-Refuseniks had to be. "We could've ended up in Israel! You could've ended up in the army! You could've been dead from a terrorist attack already!" my mother would occasionally threaten when either one of us brought home a grade that slipped below our routine As. Ofir would love to hear this story. "Your father was a Zionist for all of five minutes, worry not. But he wouldn't last a day in that heat. Believe it or not, I think my heart attack actually helped us get to America. You know, you had to use whatever you could to your advantage—even if it was pity," she'd sum up. "Vlad's asthma helped a bit, too." Obviously, Vlad listened, took all this in, whereas I was to become the reminder of all those sacrifices made in vain. They may as well have gone to Israel, sent me to the army.

"George still not dead?" my brother asked as I plopped down on the grotesquely uncomfortable couch contouring his twentieth-floor bay window. When he first put a down payment on the apartment, my parents had gasped at the sight of it. "You'll have children one day! Do you want them to fall out of these floor-to-ceiling monstrosities?!" Of course, they said all this in Russian, so the "you" unambiguously meant Vlad alone, as if he alone had all the requisite body parts to do the deed that would provide him with the aforementioned suicidal children. And by "they," I mean mother. Dad did what he did best around mom, which is nod vehemently and agree in no uncertain terms. He was more pliable one-on-one, his opinions occasionally his own then, and quite different from those of his life partner.

"Well, I've been banned from all contact by the good Doctor, and I haven't been invited to a funeral, so I can only presume he's alive and well.... Well, if not well, then at least alive."

The couch was white—a dangerous choice with twin toddler boys, of course, but my sister-in-law didn't compromise anything for her idea of style (which managed to somehow blend ultra-modern utility with old-fashioned tackiness). The back of it low, when folding yourself down onto it, you really did experience a moment's fear that you were going to tumble backwards and down to your death. Once you were safely seated, however, the rush of it was quickly gone.

"The new boyfriend?"

"Gone as of this summer."

"Are you hiding bruises over there? What's with the sunglasses?"

I hadn't even realized that I still had my aviators on. Squinting preemptively, I pulled them off my face and dragged them up on top of my head. My hair had dried spottily along the way—a bit aboard a ferry into Manhattan, and then some more along the way to Jersey City. Uneven waves fell sloppily on my face and shoulders. These frames were just the headband I needed.

"Rough night?" My brother scrunched up his face at the sight of mine.

"I haven't drank that much since downing pitchers of sangria in Spain," I confessed, sucking water thirstily out of the bottle I held on to with bloodless fingers.

"And why do you think that is?"

"What, are you Alla now? You want to psychoanalyze me? Psych 101 at Rutgers is the only psychology class you've even taken!" I snorted, uncertainly.

Vlad rubbed his eyes and reclined in the armchair positioned directly across from my sofa. It was equally ugly.

"Fine. Have it your way. We can do what we usually do—shoot the breeze with some dopey bull and call it a day. I'm going to have a good day, sister dearest, no matter what you insist on doing. Alla is—"

"Why are your kids away when she is?" I interrupted before gulping down some more water.

"What do you mean?"

"They are four! You can take care of them for two days on your own."

"So can Alla's mother. And she's better at it than I am."

"But they are your kids!"

"And her grandkids! Jesus, you're making me sound like I'm a neglectful prick! I'm providing them with care…good care!" my brother shrieked, shooting up from his seat without having thought through where to go from there. The stomping in place that I was witnessing took a bit of drama and flare out of the gesture. "I work fourteen hour days! I deserve a day or two of mindless solitude! Especially with everything coming…," he drifted off and I didn't feel like following up.

"A break even from your children?"

"Especially!"

I successfully ruined his day, I knew. The satisfaction of that knowledge quickly gave way to guilt.

"Fourteen? Really?"

"What?"

"You really work fourteen hour days?" I asked, quieter, decidedly less bratty.

"On average," he answered with a shrug, matching my tone and sitting back down. "Look, I know I give you a hard time for being difficult and insisting on your way—"

"My God, that makes me sound like a bohemian artist or a mime or something! I just wanted to be a damn high school teacher!" I couldn't help but groan. I leaned back, half-expecting the top of my head to meet with the glass behind me, but of course, it was too far.

"Did you have to go away to school to do that? Go abroad? Go to an expensive grad school?" Vlad peered at me, leaning in closer, with his elbows on his knees.

"Well, not everyone can make a career with a community college degree, like your wife," I scoffed, my grip too tight on the now empty water bottle. It caused the plastic to crinkle. I shoved it in my purse.

"Helen, stop it! I don't want to do this. My point is this- I bag on you all the time—I know I do, and I'm sorry. It can't be easy listening to mom's nagging, and dad's sighs, and my passive-aggressive nonsense, and Alla's quasi-educated conclusions about your choices and sanity."

"Sanity?!"

"Again, I get it. We can all be assholes to you. I'm sorry. But if you think it's easy to be me, you're sorely mistaken." My brother paused for dramatic effect before fixing his t-shirt, which stuck unflatteringly to his slack body. He probably could benefit from some weight loss, given the family history of untimely heart attacks, but were I to bring it up now, I'd likely hear about his long work hours again (and, more than likely, this time around also hear about my short ones, too).

My coat folded in my lap, I scrunched it up further and pushed it toward the arm of the couch before lowering my head onto it. Without removing my shoes, letting my feet dangle for fear of leaving a smudge on the white linen surface, I lay back.

"Okay, fine, let's roll back and do it your way," I said, closing my eyes against the hideous pretend art-deco chandelier on his ceiling. That TV on the opposite wall was probably the only thing my brother picked out in this house.

"What was I talking about?" he asked with a sigh that sounded cleansing. I heard him settle back in his chair.

"I think you were asking about my hangover."

"Ah, you were saying how it's been a while since you drank that much—since that summer in Spain. Now, why do you think that is? And, by the way, a beer should help with the headache."

"Why is it that I hadn't been getting hammered with more regularity, you ask?" I laughed with my eyes still blissfully closed. Hearing my brother join in the laughter made me laugh harder. I kicked my legs up, involuntarily. My sneakers were now on the white couch.

Chapter Twenty: *Single-Room*

The sun was once again brutal on my face as it hung there high in the sky, peering in through the poorly shaded bay window of my brother's high-rise living room. I needed a bed—a real bed. Since I'd gotten back from Europe, I'd spent all my nights on unfolded couches, I realized as I rubbed my burning eyes awake. My single-room in London, the one where Jamie and I began, now seemed far away and a long time ago. I missed it.

We'd been drinking beer and playing video games until some ungodly hour the night before. Only when the lights of the city across the river began to gleam bright in our window did my brother retreat to his marital bed, leaving me where I was. He'd offered me the boys' room (and then their office), but I was too warm and heavy to move. Abbott had called to inquire as to when I'd be home (now decidedly paternal), and I'd volunteered my whereabouts to Jamie before falling blissfully asleep, trying not to focus on the fact that he hadn't asked. I was out before he had the chance to reply (which was hours later and with a simple "Ok," at that; the buzz of it woke me up enough to allow me to part my lids to read the two letters, but not enough to send me reeling and cost me the rest of the night. Small blessings).

I tried to ignore my vibrating phone now as I clumsily rubbed my eyes with the heels of my palms. It was tucked dangerously away underneath the weight of my makeshift pillow—my coat. The buzzing was insistent, but I was too desperate to latch on to as many fragments of the previous night as possible. We had never been that brother and that sister, not even as children. And he was right-—drinking beer did seem to help my hangover. He said our father shared this bit of Russian wisdom with him when he was in college. It took all I had not to ask how many intimate conversations they've shared over the years that didn't involve me.

"Hello?" I eventually croaked into my phone without checking who it was first, my lids too heavy to lift.

"Hi, Helen."

George.

My heart leapt into my throat, choking me at once. Trying to contain my immediate hacking for fear of waking up my brother (whom I imagined to be sleeping splayed across his king-sized bed, what, between his long work days and his wife being away), I put my hand over my mouth.

"You there, Helen?"

It was unmistakably George. I hadn't hallucinated. I opened my mouth to speak, but with my heart still swelling in my windpipe, I struggled to breathe.

"Helen, if you're not going to talk, I need you to at least listen."

It sounded like George, but there was no snarkiness, no cruelty. At least not yet.

"I was banned from talking to you, you know?" I guess I felt the need to maintain some kind of equilibrium. If he wasn't going to be unkind, I was.

"Ditto, but I need to talk to you. My therapist thinks so, anyway. It's practically one of the terms of my release—to get off the suicide watch and all."

He sounded the same—his vowels short, his timbre low. But he was hoarse, which made him sound simultaneously intimidating and powerless—a disorienting combination.

"Wow, you didn't get your mother's permission to do something, for once?" I cringed at myself.

"Yeah, I didn't get it when I swallowed a couple of bottles of Tylenol, either. So I hear you're back?"

"Where?"

"The country!"

"Yes, soon after—"

"Soon after I tried to off myself, yes, that's what I was told."

Folded in two, my head between my knees, I tried to picture him the way I saw him last. Was he still inside that glass cubicle uptown? Was he still wearing a backless gown or was he allowed to put on pants? Was oxygen still force-fed up his nostrils? Was his hair spiky, or still collapsed to the side? His lips—were they as dry and cracked as ever?

"A couple of bottles? That many? Maybe they were small bottles," I thought, involuntarily screwing my eyes shut.

"I heard you've been stopping by?"

I nodded, forgetting that he couldn't see me. The motion seemed to almost dislodge something in my throat. I made it a point not to move anymore.

"I'm going to assume you nodded in agreement," I heard George say. Feeling my lips stretch into a smile, I pulled them back into their thin and straight formation.

"Does that mean you're back? Like, back-back?"

Against my own interest, I shook my head.

"Is that a 'no?'" His voice was now more familiar; I felt a row of goose bumps inch its way up my spine in response.

"Correct, that is a 'no,'" I confirmed, my eyes shut so tightly, I was starting to see red dots swim before them.

"Of course not. Not when things are hard, Princess Helen. Anyway, I was just calling because I was told to tell you that you are not responsible." Though he pronounced the words with bona fide due diligence and attention to each syllable, they sounded simultaneously forced and also flat, somehow. He was trying.

"Not by your mother, I gather," I muttered into the lackluster redwood parquet of my brother's floor underneath my naked toes, my eyes now open. I must've taken my socks off when we were playing Wii tennis. Or maybe it was Guitar Hero? No, that was unlikely, because Guitar Hero had quickly dissolved me into a puddle of warm tears and snot, thinking of Jamie, so we'd moved on from it pretty quickly. I squinted across the room to locate my shoes, but without my contacts, I could see neither my shoes nor my socks. I didn't have backup contacts with me either. I'd have to go blind the rest of the day.

"Well…," he hesitated. He didn't mean any of this, that much was obvious, but it was important to let him finish; that much was obvious, too. "I need a new liver."

"Good times," I breathed as my forehead hit my denim-covered knee. Even Abbott approved of jeans on a weekend.

"Sorry to bum you out so, precious Helen," George mocked, his voice nearing a tremble. "I'm not asking you to donate or anything. What a waste of time talking to you is each and every time! You know what? Since I got you on the phone against my better judgment, I may as well tell you something else. And this isn't from my mandated shrink—straight from the heart. I never loved you!"

He was back in control. In fact, his voice was now so even, the words so precise and therefore convincing, that I almost mistook them for my own. At least he wasn't asking for a liver.

Uncurling my spine slowly, I threw my head back. These should've been liberating words to hear. In my wildest dreams, I wasn't expecting the release of my leash to be this easy. This couldn't be it. But, then again, this really could be it….

"So why try to kill yourself?"

"Brought you right back, didn't it?"

"And your parents said you weren't ambitious…."

The back of my sister-in-law's couch was too low to rest my head comfortably. My neck bent backward with no support, I opened my eyes, registering just the tops of the structures making up the Manhattan skyline. I quickly grew dizzy and shut my lids.

"Oh, don't pretend to be heartbroken now. You never loved me, either," he sneered. "I was convenient for you, just admit it. It's okay—you were for me, too, but you were so obvious…so transparent! You kept harping on and on about not having a place to live by the time you'd need to start at Columbia—it was too easy dangling those apartment keys in front of you."

"So, what is it that you got from me, then? I used you for an apartment, or so you say, and what did you get out of it?" I breathed, my face ablaze. Was it outrage, disbelief, or shame? I couldn't quite decipher.

"You!" George laughed. When that booming laughter erupted out of him, I could finally focus on his old image in my mind's eye. Yes, there was his wide forehead, there were the acne scars on his chin.

"What do you mean, 'me?'"

The inversion my contortion was imposing on my head was giving me a head rush. I had to change my position.

"Okay, once again, for the slower people. I got what you got, silly—the apartment!" he snorted. "Having you meant having that apartment. My parents would've never let me live in that stinky walkup hole alone! Too irresponsible or whatever. You made me look more…more together, I guess."

So we had more in common than I thought.

My de facto standoff with Jessica was as good as over now—I simply had to deliver this news to her. And in person, too. She'd get a kick out of it, I was sure. Maybe it'd even restore her faith in some universal justice.

Slowly, carefully, I unfolded myself and pushed through into an upright position. My legs were soft, but I stumbled over to Vlad's kitchen and turned on the tap. Letting the water run, I bent over the sink leaning on my elbows. The position brought me right back to my pathetic attempt at sex with Jamie inside that disabled bathroom not two days ago. I clicked my tongue in disgust at myself.

"Don't go all high and mighty on me now," George clicked his tongue. "You, of all people, get it. And it's not like we didn't have a good time along the way, because we did. I liked you…you know, for a while, anyway. And I admire your perseverance. No matter what I did, you wouldn't leave! You must've really liked living there, 'cause I know you couldn't possibly be that in love with me! How someone who isn't a cat can be so attached to a physical place is beyond me," he roared with amusement. "Father did always say it was hard to evict tenants."

Splashing some water on my face, I stood back up, cool droplets streaking down my face. I was glad I hadn't bothered with makeup the morning prior.

"So why in the world did you summon me back every time with your goddamn threats to kill yourself?" I shrieked. "And, again, why did you take this extra step? I don't get it!"

There was no way this wasn't going to wake up Vlad. I listened for the shuffle of his feet.

"I'm just that messed up, Helen!" He was laughing hard now. Tears were likely the only natural next step of this hysterical outburst. If I stayed on the line long enough, I would likely hear this progression. "I'm just that fu—" I heard him scream again before I managed to end the call.

Chapter Twenty-One: *Silly*

Before he was due to pick up his kids at their grandparents' house and dutifully wait for his wife at home, my brother was expected at our parents' house for our regular Sunday brunch. This was a weekly pilgrimage for Vlad, but even when she was in town, Alla, his wife, rarely made these, opting to spend her day off at the hair salon, instead. Considering the volume of her hair, I could hardly blame her, but one way or the other, those children always spent their weekends in Riverhead, Long Island (this made Alla's coaxing me into having a child of my own a little less convincing).

I often tried to stay away from many of these myself, so I couldn't judge Alla with any air of moral superiority. There wasn't much for me to do there, anyway. The itinerary was always the same: food, lectures on financial irresponsibility of Vlad's clients, discussions on the subject of the various delays that Alla came across in her early intervention/occupational therapy practice (as well as related debates as to whether or not such delays could've been caused by the MMR vaccine), more food, followed by a dessert of summations of my accomplishments (which, in all honesty, did plateau sometime after high school). These shindigs usually ended the same way--with hoarse throats and indigestion. If I could avoid shrieking at the top of my lungs about how my life did not only not harm anyone, but was actually the future (you know, by way of children being our future, as the song goes), I usually did. Besides, my childhood friend did give birth fairly recently; it was simply imperative that I visit her. I didn't even need to come up with an excuse this time.

Another ferry and a subway ride later (having hugged my brother tentatively on my way out, still not sure if our fragments of intimacy could really be taken as a sign of things to come) and I was in Brooklyn. Showing up at Jessica's unannounced (and likely becoming her punching bag for the day) sounded like an act of charity to my ears still buzzing with George's confession.

The wind off the bay on Emmonds Avenue blew harshly. Occasionally, I tripped on my feet, the beer still warm inside me, and had to grab ahold of the railing for balance, the chipping paint of it harsh against my fingernails. The smell of fish attracted seagulls but curled my lip. Neither helped the vertigo. The birds beat their wings so vigorously, so harshly against their bodies, I couldn't believe they weren't hurting themselves. I had to cross the street to stop watching.

"You should've called first," Jessica grumbled as she shuffled away from the door she'd opened for me, disappearing further into her dim apartment. I'd spent a night on that living room floor years ago—on an inflated mattress, to be precise. It now seemed ages ago, but once, when I'd allegedly embarrassed George in front of his guru, he thought it was wise to ask me to leave. Armed with three suitcases, I'd changed three subways to come to this apartment that night. Jessica and Max had been living here since the day they got married. She was in college back then, and he was bussing tables at the nearby

Applebee's—it had "young romance" written all over it (I was the reluctant maid of honor, having to sport a dress the nauseating shade of olive-green).

Her home was quiet. Not the relative quiet one would expect in a house with three children, but the literal, dead quiet. No low static of Internet radio, no TV on for background noise.

"Sorry. I just didn't want to go home," I mumbled, kicking off my shoes as I knew she'd insist I do, anyway. Not doing so in a Russian-speaking household is akin to an act of domestic terrorism, after all, so I was surprised when Jess waved her hands animatedly at me, clearly instructing me not to bother.

"Where is home for you, nowadays? Still with the Turk?"

I reluctantly stomped back into my shoes, not asking why I was allowed to do so, and uncurled my spine to meet her face. She always was significantly taller.

My coat slid off my arms and coiled at my feet, its buttons sounding out a clear clink upon contact with the floor.

"Staten Island. A friend's couch."

"That Turk's?"

"No, it's not his place. But he's there, too." I didn't bother correcting her identifier of choice for Jamie.

She laughed at that. Hard. So hard, tears spilled from the rims of her eyes. Her ordinarily pin-straight and stiff hair now in a frizzy ponytail, with the light seeping in from between the blinds pulled shut being minimal, she looked mad.

"Life is just so hard for you, eh, Helen? So many men, so many available couches!" Her face contorted, her voice thin, she didn't just look mad, she sounded possessed. "So why did you not want to go home then? And where are you coming from, anyway?"

I stumbled backwards, as if pushed by an invisible hand.

"I don't know if there's anyone there, and I didn't want to be alone. And Vlad…Alla's away, so you know—"

"Jesus, what's your issue with that woman?"

Jessica's eyes narrowed as she asked this, her hands at her hips, like a professor expectant of a sub-par answer, fully prepared to fail the student. Never one to disappoint, I gave her what she wanted.

"I don't know," I muttered.

"Ah, so perfectly reasonable, as always. Glad I asked." When I refrained from adding fuel to the fire, Jessica nodded in pretend-thoughtfulness. "I see," she concluded. "So why haven't we moved back in with our parents for good, then? They hardly ever leave the house, from what I remember, so you'd never be alone."

She crossed her hands across her chest and popped out her hip. Squinting in the poor lighting, I tried to size her up. This wasn't her usual state of upkeep—not with those ripped leggings, not with that tank-top that was paired with them (the one barely containing her obviously even fuller than usual breasts).

"I don't want to."

"You don't want to?!" she demanded.

"It's a long commute to work!" This was a stupid thing to say; a stupid reason not to move in with my parents under the circumstances, too. I knew as much when the words first escaped from my lips and I heard them, myself. Speaking of lips, I suddenly missed Jessica's coral lipstick. She was less intimidating with it on, as it turns out. This fullness didn't work in nude.

"Oh boo-hoo, you, Helen-dearest."

Though she screamed this, there was no real bite in that last statement. It was flat—it hurled itself from her throat, leapt from her mouth, but then just collapsed. In the quiet of Jessica's living room, I almost thought I would be able to hear it fall to the floor with a flop.

"Jess, are you okay? Where are the kids?" I asked, quietly, as if afraid to wake her any further. I wouldn't be able take her on were she to get any more animated.

"My parents'. I'm leaving Max, Helen. And I don't have the luxury of nomading my way around Europe and then the five boroughs. I don't have single men with couches available on demand. And even if I did, who in the world would take me in with three children, including one infant who can't sleep for more than two hours at a time without screaming her giant head off?!"

"Well—"

"Well, what?!" she cried as I took another step back, stumbling over something that I immediately realized was a toy fire truck. The sirens of it blared, sounding so full-bodied, it was hard to believe they weren't blasting out of a real fire engine in a rush to put out a raging fire somewhere.

I had no convincing follow-up ready.

"Don't you make enough—" That was probably not good, either.

"Yes, I do, but I will need a bit of help, won't I? I'm entitled to that, at least, aren't I? For the time being? No? I haven't earned that much? I need to run this by you?"

"No, of course not…. I mean, of course you deserve—" I faced dozens of teens a day—I even faced off with Paz—so why did Jessica make me so nervous?

"I don't have the luxury of turning up my nose at free lodging at my parents' house, like you do, so excuse me. I have to pack up my children and move back into my childhood room. You can afford to do otherwise, I can't!"

I breathed hard, all the while trying not to make a sound.

"Do you need any help?"

"Help? From you? You can barely help yourself! What, there's room for four more over there at the friend's?"

Jessica pulled the blinds open in one harsh pull, as if erecting sails against unforgiving winds. Her face was at once illuminated, making me miss the dark. She was swollen and puffy, her features colorless without the customary makeup.

"I can help you pack. I did tell you that Max can't be trusted after—"

"Yes, I forgot what a great expert at men you are, Helen—what a brilliant judge of character," Jessica mocked. Turning on her naked heel, she abandoned me by the window in favor of squatting down on the floor to shove too many toys into a box that'd seen better days. "You screwed a man you thought was married not a week after leaving George!"

"Jessica…"

The smart thing would have been to just let her talk. But I was not smart.

"He's not married."

"But you thought he was when you wanted to!" she exclaimed so loud that, were I looking at her in that particular moment, I'm sure I'd see spit fly out. "Does he have kids?"

"He thought he did. Well, he thought he knocked up a groupie. It's someone else's, though, so he left." Surely, this over-simplification wasn't making anyone look good.

"Classy, Helen. So, any interest in the kid now?"

"He was helping out, but I think he's going on tour this summer." Unexpectedly, my heart set off on a journey into my throat, settling painfully mid-trachea, breaking up my attempts at breathing again.

"You think?"

"Yeah, he hasn't told me himself yet. I heard it from a student." I coughed to prevent myself from saying anymore.

"Wow, that is something, Helen. So he's just going to leave this kid?" Jessica was back on her feet now, standing tall over me.

"Well, it's not his kid—"

"Wonderful!" Jessica exclaimed, clapping her hands intimidatingly loud and close to my face. "You sure know how to pick 'em. I think I'll be better off without your help, if you don't mind."

With that, she turned her back to me, returning to a pile of toy trucks at her feet. Her shirt rode up her back, revealing a thin layer of fine, pale hair.

"Wait, this friend with the couch—is that your friend or the Turk's?" she asked from her crouched position on the floor, turning over her shoulder briefly to reveal a tentative smile.

"Mine." I knew I'd have to either immediately busy myself with some unsolicited folding or get the hell out of dodge before Jessica's tongue took to harsher things. That's the fear with old friends-they know too much to not be able to hurt you when necessary.

"So, did you get him a place on this couch?" she asked, shooting back up, clearly unable to contain her glee.

I squatted down to pick some random plush toys to pass to Jessica, but she ordered them back on the floor. My fingers released them on command.

"No, we were going to room together, so I thought while we look, he could stay at my parents' house with me. They said 'no—'"

"Right. Right! So you got him that couch, basically. Finally, somebody using you, for once." She laughed so hard, her balance threatened to give out. "And, now that he got a free cot out of you, he's leaving. Now, that's karma!"

Perhaps someone of Veronika's breed would be

happy for her friend being able to find laughter during such a difficult time in her life. Not me. Feeling myself color, my heart awkward on its slow descent back down to its proper place from my throat, I left Jessica's apartment.

All relationships have expiration dates. That's what Paz had once said in class. She was, of course, referring to the fall of the Soviet bloc, but she wasn't wrong, in general. I'd commended her on such profound insight at the time, but forgot all about this piece of wisdom until I found myself in Jessica's slow, airless elevator. By the time I reached the lobby, I was convinced that that is what this was. We were merely past our expiration date. A sensational girl, that one was, really—Abbott's crush. Despite the crippling age difference and the less than savory circumstances, I was beginning to see what he saw in her. Her words resonating in my mind, I pushed the lobby door open to stumble back out into the street. The afternoon sun was high and bright, but the breeze off the Bay took away some of that young spring warmth. Instantly shivering, despite the profound flush, I stopped in my tracks when I realized that I forgot my wool coat upstairs. Hesitating, I turned back twice but decided to leave it be. I didn't know the woman living upstairs anymore.

Chapter Twenty-Two: *Invincible*

It seemed that I now got all my information from Veronika. The girl sat biting her nails at my desk as she waited for me to say something in response to all she'd just left at my disposal. Her nails were now generally in better shape than before, as was the rest of her current level of upkeep, but her nail varnish was hardly newer than my own; mine was nude, hers—black.

"When, again?"

"Well, I have another two weeks, but Mr. Sola is supposed to leave by the end of this week, I think."

I sat as still as a statue for fear of splitting neatly in two were I to so much as blink. My throat seized when I tried to speak.

"To— Bu— But the tour is this summer," I eventually stammered. I still hadn't heard anything about the tour from Jamie, himself (if you don't count the few words exchanged during our drunken fumbles in the bathroom).

"Well, there's rehearsal and then the European leg…."

I scratched my head, painfully.

"And school?"

"You're the last teacher I'm supposed to speak to.

Everyone else is on board. I can complete things via mail. I still qualify for an actual diploma."

"Well, you earned it! Are you not the valedictorian?"

"Nope, second in command," she smiled. I saw that row of crooked teeth and felt my eyes fill. "Salutatorian, it's called, I think? Good thing I'd be skipping graduation, because no way can my parents pronounce that!"

As I sat there trying to contain the tears that were filling my actively swelling throat, I already knew I'd miss everything about this child: the squeak of her Doc Martens, the sway of her flannel shirts, the roominess of her Disney sweatshirts, the shapelessness of her overalls. Of course, the liberation she was currently experiencing by way of standing up to her parents and pursuing her calling instead of being shamed back into the closet also caused her to suddenly tap into an apparently deeply hidden sense of style, so the girl in front of me was no longer wearing the aforementioned staples. I'd been missing a lot of things happening right under my nose, lately.

"I see."

Veronika bit her lip and wrinkled her nose. The dry skin on its bridge folded in a way that looked like it hurt.

"I'm so sorry, Ms. Levit. I was looking forward to your Teacher of the Year speech."

Maybe it was the light in my windowless office, but it looked like Veronika's eyes were also glistening.

"Oh my God, what a waste of time that thing is going to be!" I groaned by way of transparent deflection. "How do you even know about it? I thought it was supposed to be a surprise."

"It's seriously the worst kept secret, Ms. Levit! Every year!" I'd miss the way she repeated my name after every other sentence. "Last year I knew about Mr. Abbott even earlier."

"Paz?"

"Paz."

She squirmed in her seat.

"I'm sorry I jumped the gun back in London, Ms. Levit. I had no way of knowing about Sophie. She's just so precious, who knew she was a bigger bitch than Paz!" This new, confident Veronika was refreshing. She'd kill it on tour.

"Hey, I thought you guys were friends!" I blew my nose into a wad of Kleenex.

"We are! I love Paz! I know she's a bitch, but we can still be friends. Those two are not mutually exclusive things."

News to me.

"Has she gone to talk to the principal, do you know? About the timeline? About Sophie?"

"I don't know," Veronika confessed with a shrug so innocent, it was endearing. I would have to give this girl the hug I'd been meaning to give her since ninth grade before she rolled on out of my life aboard some tour bus. "Okay, I also have to tell you something kind of related. This is between us, though, Ms. Levit, okay?" she whispered, leaning in closer to me. Instinctively, I met her half way. "I think she actually does have some feelings for Abbott. Paz, I mean, not Sophie, obviously. Why? Beyond me, but I think she does. She works his name into every other conversation now. You know, like when you're all giddy and crushing on somebody. I kind of used to do that with you," she blurted out.

Here I shrugged a shrug of a different character—a skeptical one, ignoring her rosy flush.

"Paz could be putting you on, Veronika. Wouldn't be the first time—"

"Ugh, I'll miss you so much, Ms. Levit!" This was probably the first time Veronika had ever successfully squealed without Paz there to coax her. "Come out with us this summer, please! I guess you can't leave now, but maybe after graduation?"

I looked down in my lap and brushed my tears away as bravely as I could.

"Maybe," I lied. "But I'm learning about all of this

from you. I'm not so sure Mr. Sola and I are as meant to be together as you and I once thought."

Veronika nodded, solemnly, as if expressing her condolences.

"So what do you think you'll do this summer, Ms. Levit?"

In the effort of demonstrating thought, I bit my own lip.

"I was thinking to go visit Morocco. I've been meaning to do that since college. With a friend of mine."

I winked for levity, but I didn't mean it.

Chapter Twenty-Three: *As Warranted*

"So much for one day at a time, huh?"

Picking a fight—one way to go.

"What are you talking about?"

With Abbott in the kitchen making dinner that nobody remembered requesting, I tried to control the volume of my voice. I struggled out of the chunky cardigan that now functionally replaced my missing coat and stepped out of my boots. My hands shaking, I tried to steady them by lacing my fingers at my hip. Jamie stood watching, visibly readying himself for what I had in store for him. He looked preemptively tired.

"You're leaving within a week?"

"Veronika?" he asked as his shoulders collapsed with a sigh. I couldn't summon more than a nod of myself in response. "I didn't want to upset you…you seem like you have a lot going on…like you have a lot on your mind…."

"Were you just going to up and leave? And not tell me? Would I not notice? Would that not upset me, you think?" I clenched my jaws so hard, I could almost feel my teeth sway under pressure.

"Of course not, b—"

"Do you know how embarrassing it is to find out

that your boyfriend is leaving from your student?"

"Boyfr—"

He cut himself off and threw his hands up. Then, in a move more graceful than one would anticipate, he threw his whole body down on our couch, falling flat on his back. His long fingers rubbed the almonds of his eyes, the veins on his hands so prominent, I could've sworn I could see them throb with his blood.

"I never signed up for this."

He sat abruptly, with his knees spread wide apart, his slim elbows squarely on top of them. I wanted to focus on anything but his smooth as velvet voice, but Abbott's guest room was clinically uninteresting (albeit overfurnished). Jamie's sleeves down for once, I couldn't even study his roses any further; who knows what else I'd been missing in there besides the skull. Even the ring was no longer there.

"What?" I finally huffed. It took all the self-control I still had not to stomp my foot.

"You knew I'd be leaving," he smiled, his mouth so wide and tempting, I felt my knees begin to soften. "Eventually, anyway."

"But you never told me!"

"I'm a musician, Helen—it's what I do. It's what I have to do. I won't be on the road forever, but I only took this teaching job in some lame attempt at doing the 'right thing.' It wasn't ever going to be permanent. I'm sorry."

"Even if Zoe was yours?"

"Maybe…or maybe not. I can't just make that up now—I'm not an oracle."

Hiding my eyes behind the palms of my hands, I rolled them.

"Even if I'm yours?" This had to be my rock bottom. At least so I hoped.

"Helen—"

"I thought we were going to look for a home together…."

Still averting my eyes, I imagined Jamie struggling for words—squirming on Abbott's sheets.

"Helen…do you even want to?" I eventually heard him scoff.

I sat myself down on the couch next to him. Jamie's fingers reached out and brushed my cheeks, my neck, my collarbone. His touch was silk. I scooted over closer, in spite of my pride. I considered begging, but bit my tongue. Physically.

"And the kids?"

"It's literally weeks until summer. I'm not going to make or break anybody in this time, anyway. The department is divvying up my sections."

"So I'm literally the last one to know about this tour thing?"

"Helen, I can't stay in this room with you forever."

I'm not a short girl. I'm not tall, but I'm certainly not short. But when Jamie took my hands into his and gave my fingers a squeeze, using his spotless eyes as warranted by peering directly into mine, as if trying to reach me beyond the surface, I felt like a tiny, insignificant speck that would fly away with a snap of his fingers.

"Yes, yes, I know, because you're a musician," I whined, stifling a heave in my chest.

Across the hall, we heard Abbott banging pots. I wondered if he could hear us. How is it that I could do everything right as an adult and still be so behind the expected emotional development?

"And also because I'm not in college anymore. I can't bunk with you here indefinitely." Even with his hair taking up half his face, he still looked heart-meltingly stunning. I looked down to his Adam's apple as he swallowed. It was so prominent, it looked painfully wedged in his throat. I wanted to kiss it. "You can come with me," he whispered when I said nothing, my fingers still in his.

"Why can't we still look for a place here?" I asked, pointlessly.

"Helen, you spent half the time we've been back here inquiring after your ex, and the other on the phone with some guy from Spain," he laughed. Not cruelly—compassionately. He tucked his pin-straight hair behind his ears.

"But—"

"Helen, I like you, but you're not here with me. I appreciate you setting me up with this room—"

"Oh God, I did not!" I protested, Jessica's voice loud in my head, sending my face ablaze. "You didn't get this damn couch because of me!"

"Helen, please, he'd never offer if he didn't know about us," he chuckled with a wink. I focused through the thin film forming before my eyes, aching to hold on to the chocolate of Jamie's eyes beyond it. He shook his head. "But this is clearly not the right time for you…or us."

"I didn't use you, Jamie!" I shrieked, surprising both of us.

"I didn't say that." There it was again—that lopsided smile of full, luscious lips. Come next week, I would no longer be able to study them, kiss them, or trace my thumb over them in his sleep. "Come with me!" he called, tugging at my hands, as if to wake me.

"I told you I can't. And I can't leave the kids—finals are around the corner," I answered, quickly, bitterly, and with a loud sniff.

"See?"

I tried to picture my summer and beyond.

"I can't," I finally confessed, shaking my head for my own conviction.

Chapter Twenty-Four: *As you Wish*

"You'll have to take mom's call one of these days, you know." Vlad bit into his burger before continuing with his mouth full. "She's worried. Says you haven't called since you left that day in that Englishman's car. And, allegedly, you don't pick up when she calls, either."

I swirled my spoon around my soup bowl made of bread. I wasn't sure why I'd ordered soup on a sunny, warm day, but it seemed daintier than a sandwich, and I knew that, once the summer came, I probably wouldn't be able to eat anything with this much cream in it. I certainly was all about trying to preemptively fill my cravings that month.

"Yes, yes, I know," I eventually groaned in response, my spoon heavy in the thick dairy. "I just don't know what I can possibly say. I'm still me and nothing has changed in my life. At least not in any regard that would make her any happier…well, Jamie's leaving, so maybe that's something. Oh, and tell her Abbott's Scottish. He'd take real offense to that English nonsense. I had to talk the man off a ledge when that whole 'we will secede' business didn't take."

"You mean that guy who was with you at the airport is leaving? The younger one, with the guitar? You mentioned this back at my place, right?"

I nodded while Vlad continued to work on his burger. I couldn't remember the last time the two of us had lunch, or any meal together, for that matter; the luncheons at my parents' house didn't count.

"So what's the plan now? Jersey?"

"Well, I know that's what you want. And Alla. And our parents." I stuffed my mouth full of soup before I could undo the magic that brought us there—to a chain eatery in downtown Manhattan for a spontaneous late lunch—in the first place.

My brother picked up a paper napkin and wiped his lips, thoroughly, left to right, pondering me.

"We're not the enemy…well, at least I'm not the enemy. And the parentals aren't, either. Now, Alla…well, that's a separate conversation altogether, but I wouldn't say she's the enemy, per se. She just likes to hear herself talk. In order to get her off your back, you just have indulge her every once in a while—let her talk as you nod, repeat her name at the end of sentences—"

"That's how you do it?" I picked at my bread bowl. Was this the root of Veronika's habit? I suddenly wondered. Or did she really confess a crush?

This was refreshing. I missed this Vlad. Actually, I'd never even met this Vlad.

"I understand, Vlad," I nodded when he didn't say anything.

"See?! Works like a charm."

Vlad was due back in court by four, as I'd been informed upon my hurried arrival. We only had half an hour for whatever this was. I'd already had my salad back at school (half hoping that Jamie would come knocking, half hoping that he would begin to continue to disappoint), but these invitations weren't common, so right after my last period, I'd jumped on the 6 and rushed down to the very tip of the island, the subway cars sparsely populated going in this direction that time of day. Were it a different day, when we'd be done, I'd be right by the Ferry Terminal—closer to Abbott's hostel. But, today the school was hosting a Year Book party, so I'd need to turn right back around after—to chaperone. Jamie and Abbott were on the official roster, too; their professional obligations were coming to an end, mine were continuing.

"Are you going to stay where you are, then? At your apparently-not-English co-worker's?"

I wasn't going to finish that soup. I put my spoon away and cleared my throat. Outside the floor-to-ceiling window to my right, I saw suits running to and fro. Between the Stock Exchange and the courts, at this hour there were more New Yorkers than tourists down here, which was a rare enough scene. I tried to picture myself among them.

"Probably not."

"You're not going to follow the guitar man, are you?" Vlad asked through a burp of his coke before he took his fist to his chest. "Excuse me."

"I can't afford to do that even if I wanted to," I snorted, landing my chin in the palm of my hand, my eyes still on the busy people outside. Workday wasn't nearly over for most of these people, so why were they out here? Then again, why were we?

"That's your explanation for many thi— Sorry! Sorry, reflex! Old habits and all," Vlad laughed when I shot my eyes back to him. He threw his hands up, conceding defeat.

"Well, it's the truth. Y'all win—I'm a big fat loser," I shrugged, my arms instinctively crossing across my chest.

"And you really don't want to move in with mom or dad?"

"And be subjected to daily rehashings of my failures? No. I can just call Alla on a more or less than regular basis for that. And living there adds like a crap-load of time to my commute."

I could see the old Customs House just across the small, cobblestoned plaza. That's where Vlad was headed after this—the Bankruptcy Court. It occupied a wing of that old historic building, along with the Museum of American Indian. I took my juniors there once, but they'd spent most of our time posing for selfies in the rotunda. Something about the muted lights of the place, I guess.

"You don't work summers, though."

"That's even worse—being stuck there without a car."

My brother sighed. I was afraid that another sigh would mean the evaporation of our newly developing bond.

"I see," he sighed, again—carefully, this time, probably fearing the same thing. He looked handsome in his blue shirt, trimmed with that white collar. If he had a tie, it wasn't around his neck; perhaps it was in the pocket of his blazer, which lay folded on the windowsill next to him.

"You know, Javier has been asking me to join him for vacation this summer." I'm not sure why I said this. The words formed and ejected themselves from my mouth before I could weigh their propriety, or even give Javier proper consideration, myself. "I think he might be in love with me or something." This I couldn't say without blushing. Javier was too good a man for my boasting.

"Is that the guy from your summer abroad thing?" Vlad squinted, remembering. He waved his hand to get the attention of our waiter, signaling for a bill—the universal mime for a checkmark. I nodded, which was likely visible only in his peripheral field of vision. "You told me about him, right? How you guys have kept in touch, et cetera?" I did; on that white couch of his in Jersey City, sometime during our boozy night—between my weepy attempt at Guitar Hero and my fourth beer. "You guys hooked up over there, in Seville, right?" I continued to nod, my neck beginning to hurt. I didn't need a mirror to know that my cheeks were blazing red. "I think love is like this chemical thing we have rushing through our bloodstream in the beginning. You know, when you meet someone and all you want to do is talk to and about them, incessantly touch them, or whatever? The rest—you know, after that—is just the idea of someone—the knowledge and satisfaction that they are there, that they are yours, and that they'll always be. Most of us move right on up to that territory, and the rest of us skip that altogether and go straight to resentment, but anyway…sounds like this Hector—"

"Javier."

"Right—Javier. It sounds like Javier is stuck in that early stage. It's stagnation of sorts, I suppose."

I wrinkled my brow.

"Ugh, I don't know if I'm explaining myself at all here, and I have to go now," Vlad hardly clarified as he hurried to sign the check. He waved me off when I half-heartedly offered to at least cover the tip. "Anyway, there's so much freedom in that! You cannot disappoint and he cannot be disappointed, so you can't screw up! It's marvelous!"

"Great, thanks for the pep talk, bro. So it's resentment for you? Really?"

"Yeah…I don't know. Oh my God, screw it. I'm full of it, okay? Go on vacation, I say, Helen. A real one this time! Go hang with that guy—Hector, Javier, I don't care what his name is, really. I'll cover your plane ticket, just smile once in a while, okay? You've had the same sour expression on your face for nearly a decade. It's aging you. You were always the better looking sibling, so you have a reputation to protect." Vlad grinned at me as he put his arms through his suit jacket sleeves. He bent down over me and planted a kiss on my forehead—the most physical contact we've had probably since the day I was born and he was told to pose for that obligatory photo where the older sibling is instructed to hold the younger one with the expression that reads fear for self-preservation more than anything else. Sometimes I hate him for not dropping me then. "I'm the smarter one, but of course, so I have to go get some idiot out of debt and get paid for it."

"Why are you so happy all of a sudden?" I called when he was half way to the door. "Why did you call me here today?"

"Oh," he snorted, taking a step back toward me. "Alla's been cheating. There are no weekend conferences—it's a splendid, scandalous affair!" He was beaming. He looked glorious when he smiled, his face practically radiating light; my face has never been that capable. I realized that I hadn't seen my brother happy in quite some time, either. He was vaguely inspired when his twins were born, but this was different.

"This is good news?" I scrunched up my face in puzzlement.

"Oh yes! It's oh so liberating. She says it's some

kind of a new chapter for her, a new leaf or whatever."

"And the kids?" I whispered, thinking about little Zoe. There was relief in the knowledge that she was not Jamie's back in London, but his leaving her still resembled betrayal, somehow, even in the vaguest of terms. Although that, too, should've been good news for me.

"What about the kids? I'm not leaving them—only her. They are my kids—they are my responsibility."

Chapter Twenty-Five: *Yearbook*

It was too early to be having a yearbook party. When I was in high school, we didn't have ours until it was legitimately hot out; a week until graduation, and only then were we all packed inside our non-air-conditioned cafeteria decorated a la "Hawaiian luau on a budget," our necks sweating through those neon plastic leis. We sipped quintessential punch, swearing that we'd stay in touch forever, writing similar insincerities in Sharpie markers in each other's books. Of course, I'd only stayed in touch with Jessica. There was this one girl who'd gone to George Washington, but, as if conspiring so from the get-go, we avoided each other at the Amtrak station whenever we were headed home from DC on the same day. Nobody ever stayed in touch. In the effort to reinvent yourself, you make the mistake of attempting to shed your past, foolish enough to think you can actually succeed. The same was bound to happen to these kids, too. It was inevitable. Now ladling a familiar-looking punch into my red plastic cup inside Talents' gymnasium, I knew that eventually I'd have to admit to myself that the only difference between then and now was that I now had a full-time job and a 401k.

Everything about this party was ill-conceived. To start with, it was on a Tuesday, slated to last from 6:00 P.M. to 9:00 P.M., while classes were still scheduled to continue as usual tomorrow morning. And there was no theme I could discern, which was out of character for Talents. The more I looked around, the more I became convinced that this had to be just an excuse to distribute yearbooks the students had dished out $150 each to receive (that's not counting the twenty they would have to pay in order to enter) as early as possible. This was technically the kids' last school party until graduation. Of course, normal high schools had proms around this time of year, but Talents believed it was best to hold off its prom until after graduation. There was some logic to that approach—graduate, then dance. Logistically, this was admirable, as well. The hedged bet was that, with various summer plans, fewer kids would be able to attend, or even want to, then, and therefore—crowd control. This yearbook party must've been the planning committee's compromise.

"Ms. Levit!"

I jerked when I heard my name, full ladle in hand and all. The purple punch was now all over my white, boxy blouse trimmed with lace.

"Sorry, Ms. Levit!" It was Sage. That whiny voice delivering every statement with a question mark attached at the end of it would not be missed when it'd graduate. I dabbed the stain with a paper napkin that disintegrated in my fingers in a matter of seconds. "Really, I'm so sorry," the girl added, quieter. "Maybe some baking soda would help? Or vinegar? I heard about one of those working magic on stains. Or maybe it was both?"

I looked down at the circular stain spreading across my chest, slowly seeping into the fibers.

"Do you happen to have these ingredients on

you?"

"No, Ms., why? Oh my God, is that Sophie?"

On second thought, maybe I would miss Sage.

I straightened my back to watch Sophie stroll into Talents' souped up gymnasium. It made little sense that such money was ever spent on renovating this place when, in a school full of performing arts demi-gods, not many could dribble a basketball. This was excess. But we couldn't justify another dance studio, and the surplus budget simply had to be spent.

Petite by nature, Sophie looked somehow taller that day, her curly hair natural and soft on her shoulders. Her walk was regal, almost Paz-like. The little wallflower who only seemed to ever come alive behind her cello was no more. A few weeks ago, I would have taken two Sophies over one Paz, but now I'd do anything to have Sophie graduate early and keep Paz behind a year. Or better yet, ship them both out and keep Veronika around for another two.

"It sure seems to be Sophie, yes, Sage," I nodded before turning to face the girl again. "And, this is not your fault, don't worry about it," I smiled, pointing to the stain of now rather sizable circumference between my breasts. "It's from like Express or something—nothing I can't replace."

Sage wasn't listening; she was watching Sophie.

"She's a junior—what's she doing here, anyway?" she asked with audible contempt.

"I don't know. Maybe she worked the junior yearbook committee. Look who's territorial, all of a sudden!" I continued swatting at my blouse, knowing full well that doing so was akin to simply wishing it away—neither was likely to yield results.

"Well, yeah! Have you heard what she's been saying about Mr. Abbott? Don't you care about him?"

I looked up at Sage, wondering how much she really knew before I spilled too many beans. The concept of keeping anything a secret was a foreign one in a high school environment, I knew that much, but I had no way of knowing their details, my spy no longer my own. The only thing Veronika seemed to share with me anymore was Jamie's itinerary.

"We all know about Paz, Ms. Levit," Wisdom placated, materializing as if out of thin air and immediately reading my mind. "That's not a secret anymore. Never really been, either, but Sophie made sure it would never be."

"What has Paz been saying?" I dared just as the DJ took to his laptop up in the bleachers. Half of these kids were musicians, so it was hard to understand why on earth they'd jump up and down for a guy just playing with his levels. The speakers, of course, were state of the art. Having been fortunate enough to student-teach here before being offered this permanent position, I never got the chance to visit many other high schools around New York, but I suspected their gym classes weren't held in rooms equipped with Bose speakers mounted along the perimeter. George did always speak of my luck.

"Nowadays, I don't think Paz is saying much of anything, really. She mostly winks and pops her gum when she hears this," Wisdom reported, throwing a few honey mustard pretzels into her delicate mouth.

"Yeah, it's Sophie who volunteers all this stuff to anyone who'll listen. I'm in Abbott's French class, you know? I don't know how he manages with all the murmurs."

I did my best to keep my face from contorting in a way it ached to do. Abbott has been his usual self around school—an amusing combination of indifferent and witty. Besides bringing me up to speed a week or so ago, there had been no more forthcoming updates. At home, he cooked, he ate, he slept. On weekends, he apparently picked up girls in bars whenever his middle-aged girlfriend wasn't around. Nothing seemed different, as far as my less than observant eyes could see, anyway. But this was the most coherent I'd ever heard Sage and Wisdom be; I had to take advantage.

"So, what has Sophie been volunteering?"

"Oh, you know, how he makes her do different things to bring up her grade…like in his office…and, like, it all started with Paz and she can back her up et cetera…."

Wisdom went on, but all her intel was predictably vague. My mind wandered as Jamie caught my eye from across the room. It looked like it was his turn to man the sign-in table. Beams of light traveled up and down the length of the gym, pools of white and blue illuminating his frame as it hunched over the folding tabletop. Like an inmate due out on parole, you could tell that Jamie was counting down hours to his release. It was in his tensed shoulders, his bit bottom lip. His sharp chin cupped in the palm of his hand, his bored eyes roamed the room absent-mindedly. Veronika, forever a faithful volunteer for any extracurricular activity, was at his side. It was like the girl ached to fill every free moment of her life with bona fide responsibility. When another student strode up to sign in, Jamie took her ID to lazily examine it before signing the girl in, his free hand raking through his loose hair.

"Oh, there's Paz!" Sage exclaimed over the music.

"What?"

"Over there!"

I choked on the punch I still dared to continue to drink when I realized that the student Jamie was checking in was indeed Paz. Some more purple goo seeped onto my shirt.

"Would you sign my yearbook, Ms. Levit," Wisdom whined in my ear as I tried to peer through the thickening crowd of students to make out more of Jamie and Paz. The light was scarce and there was too much black hair between them to make out much of anything.

"Sure," I mumbled, taking the fuschia-colored Sharpie from her hand while trying not to let Jamie and Paz out of my field of vision. I scribbled a note on the inside cover of her yearbook: It's been a pleasure getting to know you, Wisdom!

"Thanks, Ms. Levit! I'll miss you," the girl cried.

"Yeah, me, too," I smiled, exaggerating just a little.

"Ooh, do me, do me!" Sage shoved her yearbook in my hands before I could think of an excuse and hurry to the sign-in table, myself, now that I saw Abbott entering the gym. He shook hands with Jamie and then buried his in the pockets of his slim jeans. Before I could scratch a message paraphrasing the one I'd just left in Wisdom's book and make the few strides I was expecting it to take me to make it over there, Abbott and Paz could be seen departing the gymnasium altogether, leaving Jamie to shoot up from his assigned position at the table with his glorious mouth agape. The lights still manic, I could see him squinting, his eyes scanning the room. He waved at me when our eyes locked. He gestured at the double-doors and summed it up with a shrug.

It's been a pleasure getting to know you, Sage! I eventually scribbled in Sage's book. There was no sense in paraphrasing.

Chapter Twenty-Six: *I have a Dream*

"Hey."

I must've repeated "hey" about five times since Jessica's "hi." Other words just wouldn't form, my brain too full with both anger and apathy.

Water cold on my skin, I scrubbed my hands until they were red and raw. The ferry, especially in the afternoon, never seemed sanitary to me, no matter the predominant smell of anti-septic. Between the occasional tourist and a few homeless men, I often felt the need to take a shower, not just wash my hands, as soon as I disembarked, especially on days like today, when neither Abbott nor Jamie accompanied me back to Staten Island. With the weather getting warmer, aromas only intensified. Forget soap, I needed a steam room to exorcise all that. But now I had no time for anything of the sort, given that Jessica caught me just as I was about to put my shoulder into Abbott's sticky door, the key alone never enough.

"Hey," I repeated, again, as I wiped my hands on a hand towel that was still damp from this morning. While Abbott gave each of us our own bath towels, the three of us continued to share the one hand towel by the sink. Soon, it'd be just the two of us.

"I'm three doors down from your folks," Jessica said. I heard the whoosh of a sliding door leading out to her parents' deck. About five more steps and she'd probably be at the foot of that pseudo-lake over there. It always did look more like a swamp to me, but ducks had been known to grace the residents with their presence, so who knows what the proper term for that body of water was.

"Wave hello three doors down, then."

I took off my cardigan and threw my bag down on my current bed. It bounced off, thudding to the floor with my laptop inside. My arms, now bare in my camisole, grew instantly cold; I'd left the window open just a crack this morning, whilst contemplating Abbott's whereabouts. As if an inch of an open window would help him return safely and without Paz.

"I have your coat."

"Keep it."

"Kind of you."

"Have to spread the good fortune, given that I'm just so lucky in life," I scoffed as I kneeled at the foot of the couch to inspect the damage to my computer. It seemed intact. Already on the floor, I crept to the window to close it. I stayed there, huddling up to Jamie's guitar for warmth that was unlikely to come from a cold and hard as a turtle shell case.

"Look—" I heard her sigh.

"Why did you tell Javier I was living with Jamie?"

"It's the truth!" Her giggles came frustratingly easily. I felt a flush rush to my face.

"That's what you said when I asked you why you told him I was rooming with Jamie in Paris."

"Consistency is key."

"Who are you, then? The Associated Press?" I sneered back, adjusting my position on the floor, leaning forward, knowing full well that it would not bring me any closer to Jessica (not that that's where I wanted to be).

"Why are you so mad he knows? Who cares? So what if he knows? You and Javier aren't together—you keep forgetting that. You just keep that poor guy on a leash, so I thought I'd help him along."

My chest was beginning to burn. "Is this what my mother felt that evening in Ladispoli as she was suffering that untimely heart attack?" I wondered. No, I was just hungry. Having run around all four floors of the Talents building looking for Abbott at lunch and after school, I'd forgotten to eat. Jamie hadn't seen him either, and neither had my office mates. I'd asked Jordan. I'd asked Andrew. No one had seen him all day. And Paz wasn't in.

"Is that why you made out with him, too?" I challenged, pressing my knees into the floor with my elbows.

"What?" The cough that came with the question betrayed the put-on surprise in her voice.

"It's the truth, isn't it? Javier felt guilty and spilled the beans. Guess you didn't."

Her screen door swooshed open and closed again.

"Oh, please! That was, like, a hundred years ago!" she protested in a voice too paper-thin for her usual husky, voluminous delivery.

It was quiet where she was. Could the kids already be settled into day care centers and schools?

"You didn't know that we wouldn't wind up together at the time, though, did you? And you knew we were hooking up," I snapped back, practically growling. I could hear the immaturity in my voice, imagined how she must look listening. If she were back inside the house, she was likely in the living room, just by the fireplace, still looking out at the lake/pond. A cemetery lay just across it.

"Oh, I knew better than that," she puffed, eventually.

"Than what?"

"Than to expect you to carry that thing through beyond the day of your last final exam over there, give me a break!" I imagined her plopping down on her parents' couch, their corner unit similar to the one my own parents had installed in the same corner of their own living room, their townhouses identical.

I exhaled, my brain too scattered to string words

together.

The floor underneath me still cold from the nine hours of spring airs it got through the open window, I scrambled to my feet, my socks slipping. I tried to hold on to Jamie's guitar case to remain upright, but it failed me. We both fell. Adrenaline pushing its way out of my skin, I stumbled out of Abbott's home office less than gracefully and hurried into his wastefully oversized kitchen, leaving Jamie's precious guitar lying where it fell. Once in the kitchen, I spun around three times before realizing that I'd picked up a carafe of water when I wasn't even thirsty.

"What do you mean?" I took bait when the silence continued, filling me with more dread that felt to be the density of cement.

"What do you mean, what do I mean? Like I would've ever believed, even for a second, that you'd stay in Spain with Javier—a chubby tour guide living with his mother—"

"He was in school then—that was his part-time job—"

"Not after you had just spent the entire evening before showing me George's Facebook profile: the muscles, the allegedly rich parents—"

"And he's not chubby!"

Jessica was laughing; I could finally hear her real laughter when I stopped breathing for a second. Stumped for what to do next, I stomped into the bathroom and threw on the overhead light. The mirror here was not lit nearly as well as it should've been. Undeterred, I dug out my tweezers from my Clinique cosmetics bag (the one I got as a gift when shopping in London just so recently) and went to town searching for any hairs I may have missed that morning, jamming my phone in the crook of my neck.

"Okay, so he's not that chubby, and maybe he's got an actual job now. What does he do, anyway?"

"He's an engineer!" I cried, tweezers hard at work at a stubborn stump of a hair just on my jawbone.

"Fascinating! Still lives with his mother?"

"Yes, but—" I attempted to defend.

"Right. Well, anyway, you weren't going to stay there, and it was obvious to me that he'd never leave his mother to come back here with you, either. Has he ever even visited?"

"He wants to go to Morocco this summer. I may go, too."

"Ooh, score! I beg of you, Helen, give me a break with all this. I know too much to buy into any of this. You couldn't stop talking about George and all the witty little notes he'd been writing you that summer! Javier was just there so you wouldn't be alone." I could hear clatter on the other end; she was probably making coffee now. "I was trying to do you a favor—distracting him, to make it easier on you to leave."

"You were doing me a favor by kissing a guy I was dating?"

"Okay, you weren't dating—you were screwing! Don't be so dramatic. Jesus, everything just has to be your way, doesn't it?" The mug she was likely holding could be heard landing on the counter with a thud. If there was coffee in it, it was probably spilled now. "Why are you wasting my time with this ancient bull? He was just your crutch over there. You're just that independent, aren't you, Helen? I'm going through a divorce, I just had a baby and, unlike you, I don't have the luxury of turning up my nose at free housing like an ingrate— Look, I called to apologize for this Sunday and you're bringing this up? Like I'm a home-wrecker or something?! Talk about the pot calling the tea kettle black! Have you completely lost yourself in your own imaginary world?"

She was screaming. I was grateful that it was only a voice I was hearing; I didn't want to see her, even though I did wonder if, now that she was at her parents' house, she was wearing tights that weren't ripped (and if they were paired with a shirt that fit). Still, feeling at once small at the sound of her full voice, which boomed big and confident again, I knew I'd be much better off not knowing. From my general knowledge of my old friend, I could imagine her skin growing pink now.

"How is this going to end?" I finally spat out,

throwing my tweezers down into the sink, listening for the clank.

Puffs and scoffs could be heard in response. I turned off the light in the bathroom and shuffled back toward the bedrooms. I peeked into our room before succumbing to curiosity and looking into Abbott's. Like the room he so kindly gave us, his own room was generously lit by natural light. His bed was sleek and low, his bedding white, making the room appear larger than it was. It was neat. The nightstands were impeccable. When I saw a large mirror mounted across from the bed, I knew it was time to shut the door before I was laden with too many unwanted images of what my mentor potentially liked to watch happen in that mirror. There being no living room, I eventually situated myself atop of one of the dining room chairs and brought my knees to my chest.

"How's this one going to end, Jess?" I asked again.

"What do you mean?" she muttered, her damn screen door yawning open and closed one last time.

"So, let us gather what we have thus far, shall we? Let's list everything you've told me you think about me in the past few weeks. Honestly, a decade and a half of friendship and only now do I find all this out?" I snorted, unnaturally. "So, let's see: I'm an ingrate, I'm lucky, entitled, I use people, I'm shallow…am I missing anything?"

Silence. I think I heard those stupid ducks.

"Oh, and you were doing me a favor by kissing Javier back when, as far as you were concerned, we were together. Quite selfless!" There was no response. "Right, so, given that I'm a pretty pathetic human being who uses people, I think it's best if we don't talk for a while," I concluded, shrugging to myself in summation.

Just as I was removing my phone from my ear, ready to end the call, my heart, large and uncomfortable inside me, I heard her voice again.

"I'm glad he's using you now—that Turk. Got free lodging out of you and off he goes—that is brilliant! Downright poetic. I always dreamed something like this would happen to you, but this is better than anything I could've imagined. See why George was so mad now? See how it feels from Javier's perspective? He deserves so much better than you, by the way. They all do. Everybody does! So what's next for you? The teacher housing y'all freeloaders over there? Going to do him later?"

Chapter Twenty-Seven: *From the Horse's Mouth*

I only realized that I'd been sitting in that same position at the dining room table, humming the funeral march to myself in honor of ending my friendship with Jessica, when Abbott walked in, Jamie on his heels.

"Found him!" Jamie proclaimed as he turned the light on in the dim room and locked the door behind them.

"Where?" I croaked. My throat dry from not speaking for a necessary period of time, I wondered what would happen if I'd continue being mute any longer.

I threw my heels off the chair. My neck was sore from the contortion I'd imposed on it for hours, sitting with my head atop my knees, while my knees themselves felt leaden now. I wasn't ready to stand up.

"What were you doing sitting in the dark, spring chicken?" Abbott asked, wrestling out of his chunky wool cardigan—the same outerwear, I noted, he was wearing the night before, inside the school gym. He looked well put together for someone who clearly did not spend the night at home. Even the stubble on his face managed to look artful. The man refused to age.

"Oh, literally just downstairs. We walked into the building at the same time," Jamie answered my question over Abbott's. Though I said nothing, I was grateful he bought me time.

With his pin-straight hair put up in a haphazard ponytail, Jamie looked even younger than usual, which was a feat. The slim, black blazer on top of his similarly black t-shirt failed to tab on any years, either.

"And you were…?" I watched as they each kicked off their shoes in the hallway. Heavy-limbed, I continued to sit on the edge of the chair, my head empty.

"Wrapping it up at the studio." Jamie's eyes were on his laces. "Have to finish up before I—" he added under his breath before cutting himself off.

Right.

"And you, Abbott?" I eventually dared when I saw both men walk on in and continue past me, into the bathroom. In my short time here, I'd managed to get them to wash their hands as often as I did. Small victories.

"Paz."

"Paz?" Jamie and I shrieked in unison.

"God, seriously, just the name of the girl makes me dry-heave," I could hear Jamie groan from the bathroom. Abbott, a bottle of water in hand, meanwhile, walked back out and settled across the table from me, his chair painfully screechy against the floorboards. I could lean back in my own chair now, which was a relief to my achy bones.

"What? She's pretty," Abbott shrugged

defensively.

"Paz?" I asked in half-whisper. My muscles were sore, my head heavy with fog. This time, it was most probably just allergies. I sniffled.

"Si," he smiled in response, winking an eye. That wink was always just a bat of an eyelash away, so I didn't assign it any more significance than usual. His breath was bitter with coffee and peppermint gum. I caught myself thinking that I should check on him in the middle of the night to see if he chews it in his sleep, too.

"Paz?" Jamie scrunched up his face to ask, now standing at the head of the table with that musty hand towel in hand. "But she's a child."

"Yes, people, Paz! Enough already! And she's hardly a child, come on! Don't make me sound like a pedophile. Eighteen is not a child. And seventeen is not a child," Abbott waved us off before taking a swig of his water. "Levit, you look like hell. Drink some," he tsk-ed, sliding his bottle over to me. "Are you okay? Sick again?"

"Probably allergies, but never mind that! You were with Paz? Where, and most importantly why?"

"Jeez, Levit, what are you? My mother?"

Jamie placed his large palm on my forehead, checking my temperature, before coming around to sit down at my side.

"You know, in Portuguese, her last name literally means 'new earth' or something," Jamie reported, absentmindedly.

"You speak Portuguese?" I slurred.

"A bit. A little bit of Turkish, too."

"We needed you like a week ago, when Levit and I tried to figure out what her last name means in Spanish. So apparently it's Portuguese, not Spanish, eh? Maybe you guys would have more in common than she and I ever did, what do you think?" Abbott chuckled rhetorically, his sarcasm fairly well disguised, all things considered. "Anyway, it's over, so y'all don't have to worry now."

My eyes still adjusting to the light, I said nothing. Instead, I shuffled in my seat, contemplating whether or not I should cozy up to Jamie to my right. It was tempting, but I stayed rigid.

"Meaning?" Jamie voiced my own question.

"She's sorry and all that," Abbott shrugged, lowering his eyes to his lap. "I give her an A-, she calls Sophie off. Allegedly, she can. In fact, she swears she can. And for an A, she said she can tell the school nothing ever happened between us, period. Meaning, she'd say that she'd made the whole thing up, but that's not true…and I've already fessed up to everything, myself, so that ship has sailed, anyway," he shrugged, fidgeting with his nails. "So it is what it is. But, the good news is that she was seventeen when we started, and the administration is on my side, technically speaking. A scandal at a school for all the oh-so-gifted and oh-so-talented? Especially with a teacher like me? No way do they need that going public. I mean, if it were someone like Jamie over here, they could probably use it as a selling point—put it in the brochure, even! Get horny girls from all over the country to come apply for the privilege. But an old geezer like me? Nah," he tried to laugh but wound up whistling, instead—the air emitting out of his lips stifled and unnatural. He removed his glasses and squeezed the bridge of his nose. Out of the corner of my eye, I saw Jamie cringe. "So it's over. I'm given the honor to drum out the year, and then I'm outta there…and everywhere, really. Guess I can use the time to finally write that great American novel…or would that be a 'great Scottish novel,' in my case?" When he looked up, his eyes were full with moisture threatening to overflow.

"And if you don't?" Jamie asked, my own eyes on Abbott, who was now trying to appear busy wiping his glasses.

"If I don't retire voluntarily?" Abbott cried, planting the glasses back on his nose, pushing them all the way up. "Are you kidding me?"

"Well—"

"Well, what, Jamie? I'm not a touring bassist, or whatever the hell you are in real life. I can't have any of this be out there." Flustered, Abbott snatched his water bottle from my hands and took a violent guzzle from it. The plastic crackled in his grip.

"But since she was of age or whatever—" I attempted, knowing full well it was futile. I was with Abbott on this one, and there was no point in my solidarity with Jamie now, anyway.

"Are you for real? There's enough whispering going on. I fight this and they'll stop whispering—they'll speak full volume! Unlike you, Mr. Sola, I've been a teacher for more than five minutes. This thing can't ruin everything I've worked for! Believe it or not, I had a reputation before this—a good one!" Abbott exclaimed, landing his open palms on the table with a thud. He was standing over us now, shoulders hunched, eyebrows arched.

He breathed in and out, forcibly, a few times. Then, he muttered something under his breath and turned on his heel to stomp toward his room. His chair fell behind him, but he didn't stop to pick it up.

"So, where exactly were you last night?" I called when Abbott was one foot in his bedroom.

"Just walking," he called back without turning around.

When he all but shut the door, Jamie asked, "With Paz?"

"Yes, with Paz. Can I go now?"

The door banged closed with Abbott inside just as I leaned over the table to have a place to land my elbows.

It was getting hard to keep my spine upright. Before I could catch my head in the palms of my hands, Jamie checked my temperature again. "I really can't get sick this close to going back out on the road, but I don't think you have a fever," he concluded.

"It's probably only allergies this time around, not to worry," I muttered under my breath, gathering myself to try to stand up. "I'm going to bed," I said, my feet downright asleep as I forced them to support my weight and move forward.

"It's still light out, Helen," Jamie called. "How can you sleep, especially with Abbott's latest revelations?"

"Sleep is the only natural thing to do—if you wait long enough, it'll come," I sighed mere feet from our door. Then, in spite of myself, I took two steps back and turned to face Jamie, again. My spine curving all too willingly, I bent over him. His wide, full lips were ready. "Come with me?" I whispered into his mouth.

Chapter Twenty-Eight: *Secret*

Most of my clothes still in boxes, my options limited, I had to repeat my outfits more often than I would've liked. Surely, these artsy teenagers noticed. I really needed a closet big enough for all that luggage that I kept dragging around. Following Paz, I felt altogether too self-conscious for an adult my age.

"Ms. Levit, I'm buying. I just need five minutes of your time."

Paz was a polite girl, but there was always a bit too much saccharine to her delivery, which inevitably lent itself to sarcasm. This was the first time such was not the case. This amused (if not perplexed) me. I watched as she jogged down the steps of the school, ahead of me, leading the way. I followed her, dumbly, past the bus stop where just half a year ago Jamie stood in the rain, armed with a guitar, a backpack, and that tattered blue umbrella. Just looking at it made me feel cold and wet again; I even reached for the phantom engagement ring that's been off my finger for weeks now, aching to turn it over to feel the sting of its three stones digging into the skin of my palm.

"Where are we going, Paz?" I called after the girl, allowing myself a chance to appreciate her effortlessly put together outfit of straight-leg jeans and a cropped sweater. On me, straight jeans never did look entirely straight, always clinging to my thighs in a way that made them seem more like jeggings than straight jeans, per se. On Paz, however, they looked custom-made. Perhaps it was my denim situation that inspired Abbott's no jeans rule in the first place ('cause we all know it sure wasn't those infamous boundaries).

"Anywhere, really—Starbucks, for all I care," she answered over her shoulder, her luxurious hair flowing elegantly in the wind. You'd think the girl traveled with her own wind machine.

"And we couldn't talk in my office?"

"No, because it's not school business," she rebutted when we reached a coffee shop that appeared to contain the least number of our Talents compatriots. She held the door for me.

"You don't have to pay, Paz. It'll be my pleasure to order you an espresso and get you even more…I don't know—are you wired, would you say?" I tried to joke as I settled atop a white wicker chair. It was the best I could do given the pressure that being in the presence of this girl seemed to put me under.

"I don't know, would you say I'm wired, Ms. Levit?" Paz squinted her black eyes at me, inquisitively.

I blushed.

"No, I guess not." My sinuses heavy and painful again, I squeezed hand sanitizer into the palm of my hand with my eyes lowered.

"Is Sola waiting for you back there?"

"Where?"

"Back at school?"

"No, he isn't," I confessed for a reason unknown to me. She needed no ammunition as it was.

"Sorry he's leaving, Ms. Levit," Paz said, blowing on her caffè Americano with her smooth, glossy lips just slightly pursed. They were painted the color of deep plum.

"Didn't you say you were going to go visit Veronika on the road? You'll see him again, won't you, then," I snapped, taking a gulp of my own scalding chamomile tea. My eyes watered upon contact, the roof of my mouth immediately peeling skin.

Paz's laughter caught me by surprise. Unlike her usual sarcastic little yelps akin to Hollywood's representation of evil laughter, this was a laugh that sounded genuine, even kind of sweet—light and melodic. She pulled on the sleeves of her beige sweater, hiding her palms within.

"I say a lot of things, Ms. Levit. Believe it or not, I don't mean all of them."

"Like all the stuff you told Sophie to say about Abbott?" I smirked as I ran my tongue over the now raw top of my mouth.

"Look—"

"Paz, why am I here?"

"I want to talk to you about Abbott. You're living over there, right? I'm not sure if he's hearing me clearly now, after everything that's happened, and I was hoping you'd talk to him for me."

I felt my right eyebrow lift of its own volition.

"Say what?"

"Just listen to you, Ms. Levit, using the cool-kids slang!" Paz laughed, again. This was a hybrid of that laughter of hers that I was well familiar with and the new kind. She was exhausting. She must've seen as much on my face. "Okay, fine, I won't take much of your time. I just—"

"Do you know that his career is over?"

"I know," I heard Paz from behind her palms, her fingers now concealing her face. Her nails, manicured to perfection (and painted nude), grabbed a hold of her own hair. "I'm sorry, really," she sniffled.

I could've said it was okay, but it wasn't.

"If you're so sorry, why did you blackmail him? Why did you sic Sophie on him?" I stopped to take a sip of my tea before continuing. As mad as I was at Paz for simply being, as it would seem, I had to be careful not to excuse Abbott's own behavior—a delicate balance, as a female and a teacher.

"I started it, but he was in control—he was always the adult…and he's a man!" Paz protested, leaning back in her chair. It could've just been my eyes playing tricks, but this was the smallest I'd ever seen this girl appear.

I nodded. She was right.

"You're right! And he's paying for it. As he should! But Sophie could've made everything that much worse…."

My allegiances murky, I could feel my head begin to swim, suddenly afraid that my neck would roll were I to stop paying attention.

"God," she groaned, folding her sleeves up and over her elbows only to hide her face behind her fingers again. "I was just mad. I wanted to bring up my average, he didn't want to…. I was mad, I was just mad! I was mad…," she kept repeating maniacally, over and over. "And Sola was there—so much younger, and just stunning, Ms. Levit! You did well. Keep it up and all that!" she tried to explain, revealing her face for a moment to give me a thumps-up.

I watched the girl's shoulders shudder. She was crying. I was the bully now.

"Look, it doesn't matter now. Just make sure you go to the principal and tell her everything. The real, actual truth," I whispered before reaching hesitantly across the table to Paz, to try to stroke her surely-moisturized-to-perfection elbow, but none of her was within reach.

“I will,” she sniffled, her face still veiled.

Uncomfortable with the uncharacteristic display of emotion in front of me, I checked my watch (and then my phone) for distraction. The café was still on the empty side, likely to be filling more closer to the evening. It was not even four o’clock in the afternoon, so besides a couple of students from Talents, there weren’t that many people around to drink coffee at this hour (and those who were, likely preferred Starbucks). It was still light outside, but it was growing cooler the closer the sun came to setting. My trip back to Abbott’s was bound to be chilly and sad. We needed to wrap this up.

“Well, then you would’ve done everything you could. Again, not like this is all your fault—Abbott really should’ve known better. You were a minor—”

“Well, I was seventeen,” she objected, revealing a tear-stained eye. “It’s not that creepy. He’s not as big a pervert as Ver makes him out to be.”

“—And a student,” I continued, pretending not to hear her. “He was your teacher…it was all kinds of inappropriate,” I summed up, professionally.

“It wasn’t all cold and calculating, Ms. Levit. Not all of it,” Paz eventually challenged in response. “I’m not the bitch I like to often appear to be.”

My stomach suddenly filled with ice, I was afraid to ask for clarification.

"I care about him…. I love Abb—"

"Oh, Paz, give me a break, would ya?!" I moaned over the blood now thudding in my ears. "He said you two negotiated a grade the other night, so, as far as I can tell, you're done."

"No, it wasn't like that! Please, he offered me that stupid grade bump as some kind of reparation! I don't care anymore. None of it matters. God, I'm so stupid! I was jealous of that old hag he brought on the trip—"

"Stephanie?"

"God, yes! That bow-legged dinosaur! So between that and…I started mouthing off…oh God, and I got Sola involved…I'm really so sorry about that, by the way, Ms. Levit. Please tell him that."

Shocked mute, I sat with my face in a contortion and my lip curled. Paz resembling me more than my once-upon-a-time protégé Veronika blurred my vision, throwing everything upside down. Surely, the planet itself would be thrown off its axis any moment now.

"I'm happy for you…well, that you two hooked up, not that he's leaving. And if I'll go visit Veronika, it wouldn't be to pursue Sola, believe me," Paz continued, trying to appease me, visibly worried by the sight of my stupor. "I—I care about Abbott. And I don't think he'll believe me now—"

"Can you blame him?"

"No, of course not…. I know, this is all such a mess. It did start with just a grade, but, ugh, then I started feeling things—"

My mind going blank, my vision blurry with the influx of images, I suddenly caught myself thinking that this furniture we were sitting on was probably never meant to be inside. In a few weeks' time, it'd probably be lining the sidewalk. It's nice that it has a plan, I thought. It's nice to have something to look forward to, to be able to not only anticipate the future, but to be certain of it.

And then I continued listening.

Chapter Twenty-Nine: *Goodbye*

"Sweet Levit!" Abbott called from the kitchen, spatula in hand, when I walked in with his bike at my side. "Dinner?"

"No," I shrieked. I had to get out of Abbott's for the sake of being able to continue wearing my old jeans, if nothing else. Summer was coming and I'd finally be allowed to wear those whenever I wanted. I couldn't afford a whole new wardrobe on top of everything else.

"Coffee, then?"

I shook my head, my eyes down as I pulled the zipper of my right boot toward the floor, having parked the bike by the coat closet. I'd have to tell him about Paz—about her quasi-confession. The entire ride back to Staten Island, I racked my brain for an angle. And I continued to search for one pedaling around St. George, too. The only thing I could come up with was that maybe this was Paz appealing to Abbott's vanity. Of course, these kids were no strangers to ego themselves and this could also be a game. Those crocodile tears were so out of character, they were hard to accept at face value. Was there even a face value to Paz?

My socked feet slippery on the floor, I approached Abbott with small, penguin steps. Wrapping my arms around him from the back, I laid my cheek to rest on his shoulder blade.

"Whoa, spring chicken!" he exclaimed, whipping around until my face was on his chest. His arms immediately tight around my ribcage, he whispered into the top of my head, "I love you, spring chicken, you know that, right? Are you okay there?"

Nodding, I screwed my eyes shut. Was this the time to tell him that I just had tea with the one girl who managed to grab ahold of him so strongly that he managed to undo his entire career all by himself?

"Yes, just expressing my support, is all," I chirped into his sweater. He'd soon be fifty, but he felt younger.

"Well, you may want to redirect that supportive energy right now. I'll be just fine, but peek into your room." Whenever he was tired, Abbott's Scottish accent seemed harsher, rougher around the edges. And despite the fresh pot of coffee to his right, no matter his strutting his feathers like a peacock, he did look tired. Even that cloud of peppermint emanating out of his mouth couldn't veil that.

"Jamie?" I hiccupped, raising my head off of his chest. "I didn't see his shoes—"

"Veronika."

"Veronika?" Maybe I could use a cup of that coffee. These kids were crossing all boundaries. "What is she doing here?" I whispered, blushing at my own language in regard to my quasi-baby.

"No clue," Abbott mouthed, returning to his sauté pan. I didn't see what he was making, but it smelled good. "Showed up here in tears, asked if she could wait for you. Didn't even ask about Sola, believe it or not. I thought she was smitten with—"

"You know she's gay, right?" Maybe I wasn't the last to know this, after all.

"Really?!" he gasped, facing me again, his spatula in the air. "Go figure. And here all this time I thought she was in love with Sola. That shows you, I guess—you never know with these girls. Hey, didn't you used to think I was gay?"

Indeed.

He was back to his dinner before I could catch my breath and stammer out any of what Paz had left me burdened with. Given that neither Jamie nor I ate with Abbott with any regularity, it struck me as impressive that he bothered to cook at all. I stood and watched in silence before backing my way out of his massive kitchen. If I ever so much as dared to live alone, I knew I'd wind up living on takeout, thus wasting my already limited resources and likely expanding my soft waist.

The dining room dark, no light peeking out from underneath the door to Abbott's office, I stood still a few long beats before wrapping my fingers around the knob. I looked back to the bright kitchen as I put my shoulder to the door to open it.

Our couch still unfolded (and made only by way of having Abbott's old blanket thrown on top of our sweated sheets), Veronika sat curled up at its foot. I tiptoed past her skinny frame to pull the shades open, lighting the room in pale orange glow. This made the hunched form twinge alive.

"Ms. Levit, I'm sorry," it croaked, audibly struggling to make its tongue comply.

I knelt in front of Veronika and picked her hair out of her tear-streaked face. She was trying makeup now and it was all over her cheeks.

"What's wrong?" I whispered, hoping it sounded soothing. The girl scrambled to sit up straight, her long limbs uncooperative.

"What am I doing, Ms. Levit?" she asked with a sigh so deep, it sounded painful.

"Here in Abbott's apartment? In my temporary room?" I tried to distract Veronika from her apparent distress, relieved when I saw her face stretch into a reluctant smile. When it looked like it was going to crack and give way to more tears, I told her to breathe. Tapping into my deepest George reserves, I timed her inhalations and exhalations until she looked calm again.

"Well, yeah, I'm not exactly sure why I'm here, either. I just didn't know where else to go. I called Sola and he said to come here—that you'll know just what to say."

"And where is this Sola?" I tried, half-heartedly.

"I think his ex and their little girl are leaving tomorrow and he wanted to say goodbye. Well, it's not his little girl, per se, but you know what I mean."

I registered my heart flinch but blinked the sensation away—if only one of us was privy to this information, it made sense that it was she.

"So, why are you here?" I asked, unenthusiastically landing on the floor, next to the girl.

She sighed (twice), before breaking into more tears. I rubbed her chest until the heaves subsided.

"I was okay with what I had to do—"

"Meaning?"

"The deal I had with my parents, which was that I was to stay and do something normal under their nose…ugh, look, coming out to Balkan immigrants isn't the easiest thing to do. That was an unfair expectation to have. They can't be expected to just accept me on command."

"You're their daughter—"

"Not the kind they wanted, apparently."

"Well, it's too late to go back to the store to pick out another!"

Veronika sniffled, a strip of moisture accumulating on her top lip.

"Okay," I continued when she said nothing, "so then how did playing the guitar enter that?"

"They can keep a better eye on me if I study business, not so much if I'm going from gig to gig, or so the reasoning went. But you…you inspired me," Veronika implored, looking up at me with her eyes open so wide, it unnerved me. She hurried to stand on her knees, kneeling before me. "Look at you—doing what you want, at all costs, no matter what anyone says! Your fiancé almost killed himself, but you stayed strong! I want that for myself!"

It took the composure I was never aware I possessed not to laugh out loud. The muscles of my abdomen flexed in preparation, but I kept my lips sealed. Highlighting our conflicting points of view on the matter would be no different than taking a sledgehammer to my reputation.

"Well, not my fiancé attempting suicide, of course, but you know what I mean," Veronika hiccupped. "I just mean doing what I want. So now I signed up for the damn tour and…and they threw me out. My parents, that is. I only just now told them about it, as you may have gathered." She gestured toward the door and I noticed her duffel bag—the same one I saw fall out of the closet in the room she shared with Paz back in Paris. "Don't worry, I'm going to Paz's after this. I'll stay there for now. Tight quarters in here already, I can see," she giggled, quickly wiping the snot pooling under her nose.

I rearranged my limbs, shifted my weight side to side, looking for a position that would not feel as if my legs were about to snap off.

"So you just told your folks about the tour, huh?"

"Yeah," she snorted before blowing her nose with a wad of Kleenex that looked like it had already served its purpose and more. "And they followed through on their promise." The note in her voice was a familiar blend of tears and hysterical laughter—a relatable register for me as of late.

I hung my head low to let my hair envelop me. I twisted right and left to hear my spine crack—pop, pop. Still no words of wisdom came.

"It gets better," I tried.

"No, it doesn't!" She was skeptical.

"You're right, it doesn't."

"What?!" she snorted, that hysterical laughter winning over now. "You're not supposed to say that! You're supposed to make me feel better! Is this what you're going to say in your Teacher of the Year speech at graduation?" When I lifted my head, my neck sufficiently strained, Veronika's eyes were pleading. Green and desperate, they were looking for something. Maybe she didn't need me, per se, but she did need my words. I gritted my teeth.

"All right, look—it does and it doesn't get better. You'll always be you, your family will always be your family. Your circumstances will change, your place of residence will change, but it's hard to escape yourself, your…I don't know, baggage!" Veronika pointed to my fort of boxes, beating me to the punch. "Believe me, this much I know and I'm not even done running. And no, I won't be saying this in my acceptance speech…I'll paraphrase."

"Wow, inspirational," Veronika smirked, her green eyes a shade lighter. "Never work at a suicide hotline, okay?"

"Ah, well, there is an upside to all this…the trick is to stop caring. Or at least learn how to try to not care. Or care less, in any case," I attempted to recover, the setting sun behind me warm on my back. I tugged at my sweater. "Can't change your circumstances—change your attitude toward them. There—I'm an inspirational poster. All we need now is a high resolution photo of a kitten hanging from a tree branch with the graphic, 'Hang in There.'"

Veronika listened attentively, the way she'd always done in class. She cocked her head to the right, as if to rest it on her shoulder. Another minute and I expected her arm to shoot up with a question.

"Is that how you do it?"

There was no arm raised, but there was a question.

"Do what?" I finger-brushed my hair, combing it over to the side. It was not as smooth as Paz's looked it would be to the touch. I suppose I could ask Abbott to compare.

"How do you appear so effortless, so comfortable in your skin?" She whisked her tears away and stared at me wide-eyed and expectant. Her brows were beginning to heal, I could see. Perhaps Paz was finally taking the girl under her wing. It'd be a crime to send her out on that tour as her old self. She had a part to look, a part to dress now, something to look forward to. She clearly had too much riding on this. "How do you do it—stick to your guns no matter what others think or say?"

I shifted in place, again, before giving up and standing up altogether. Avoiding the girl's inquisitive eyes, I marched over to the light switch. At once lit brightly, the room appeared somehow smaller than it did in the pale orange glow of the sun.

"I'm not entirely sure what you mean, Veronika," I finally said, sitting myself down on the couch, Veronika now at my feet.

"Ms. Levit, I know we're not supposed to know certain things about our teachers, but we do. One way or the other—rumors spread. And some of them, strictly statistically speaking, have to be true. So I know your family is not always behind your choices—personal and professional—"

"Let me guess—Abbott?" I rolled my eyes, mainly to avoid Veronika's.

"No…well, not always, anyway," she laughed. She finally really laughed—a feat! Behind the streaking makeup, I could see her—a child with dry/combination skin. "So how do you do it?"

I stroked the sheets that wrinkled underneath my weight, feigning deep thought. Her words weren't making sense. I wasn't effortless. I was anything but. An anxious, nervous wreck with no idea how to make her ends meet, a lonely woman with no prospects—that's who I was.

"I don't." My fingers gripped Abbott's sheets.

"Okay, what do you mean by that? We all know you, Ms. Levit. We watch you. The way you dress, the way you carry yourself. The way you speak, et cetera. We know what we see—we all talk about it. Even Paz agrees! We all kind of want to be you when we grow up."

I laughed then, channeling Jessica—my head thrown back, trachea exposed.

"Well, I don't know what to tell you. It's gotta be like a transference thing."

"Like when you develop feelings for your therapist or something? But that's not really the same thing. That has to do with early childhood experiences or some such." Of course she took A.P. Psychology!

"I guess, because I ain't got a clue what you're talking about, sista!"

"Okay, Ms. Levit, this ghetto thing is not cute on you," Veronika snickered, hunched at the couch. Her chin-length hair traditionally oily, she rested her elbows on Jamie's pillow, folding her hands as if in prayer. "And I don't have feelings for you. Not anymore. Not like Paz does for Abbott, anyway—"

I stopped her short. "So that whole deal is for real?"

"Beats me. She claims so, anyway."

I rubbed my eyes, thinking of what I could say to send this child out into the world with a modicum of confidence, with some peace of mind. But Jamie was going to be out there, too, I remembered, and he was better for her, anyway—he was a clearer picture.

I leaned into her, cradled her face in the palms of my hands, and kissed her on the forehead.

"I'm none of the things you paint me to be. I'm just me. If I project anything different, it's because different is what I want to be, and different is what you want to see," I said with a smile as confident and professional as I could muster without rehearsing in the mirror beforehand. The dean who signed off on my change of major in college would be scandalized—I was a slightly better actress than he agreed I was. "And for acting tips—how to act like you don't care…well, Paz is a better resource."

Chapter Thirty: *Moot Point*

"Why do you have to go?"

This was a moot question. In one of its definitions, anyway. More than that—it was embarrassing, shameful that I should even voice it out loud. When he said nothing, I tried something else: "Where were you after school?" This wasn't a test; I was just comparing notes with Veronika.

"My neither underage nor Argentinian groupie ex-wife is reconnecting with her Korean drummer baby-daddy, who now resides in San Francisco. So I went to say goodbye," Jamie admitted as he turned on his side to face me.

"With Zoe? Your daughter?"

I wasn't expecting an answer.

I'd stayed at George's door for a length of time I refused to measure. I wasn't even sure how I'd gotten there. All I know is that Veronika left and I'd followed her out. The rest was a blur. I'd say it was an out of body experience, but I didn't exactly observe myself making the trip, either. One moment I'm hugging Veronika goodbye, and the next I'm at the walkup steps. I occupied myself mostly with my Words with Friends and its complementary cheat. "Forgot my keys again," I'd mouth at each former neighbor returning home from work.

"Where's your bike?" those who didn't already know would ask.

"George donated it," I'd joke in response.

"Again?"

Apparently, most of them knew more about my life than I'd given them credit for. Did Ashley, too, know more than she'd let on last week? In that case, my nodding at her estimation of my lucky love life back then was just plain sad.

Before I could contemplate this to exhaustion, and just as I'd lost another game to Javier, Jamie came to collect me, appearing as if out of thin air.

"How did you know where I was?"

"Abbott ventured a guess."

Traveling in companionable silence, we'd transferred trains, boarded a ferry, and hiked up the poorly lit hill. And then we went to bed. All roads lead to Abbott; I should've learned this much already.

"She's not my daughter. It's that Korean drummer they are going to see—he's the one, remember? I hardly have a claim to her." On the couch next to me, Jamie nonchalantly shrugged, at least as it looked to my burning eyes. I'd spent too much time in that dim hallway uptown and it was taking me forever to adjust.

"And yet you felt the need to say goodbye," I challenged, my pulse reactionary.

"Well, I did live with her for months. I'd watched her grow before she was even born." I could recognize a tone that was defensive in my sleep; I'd perfected it in my own short lifetime.

"So, fight for her, then! I'm sure you have some kind of claim, given that you took care of them all that time. You could probably stop them from moving, if you tried." Only I could be caught pushing a man of sexual interest to me to hold on to a former lover. (I guess I reluctantly inherited that word from my mother, after all—lover.)

Jamie only shrugged and pushed his hair behind his ears. There were remnants of a couple of piercings on his earlobe. I'd never registered this before.

"So that's it? Your groupie leaves, and you suddenly have no reason to stay? You're going to just hit up some festivals?"

The bridge of my nose felt tight. If I weren't careful, I feared tears would spring from my eyes—a grotesque fountain. Pinching my nose whilst screwing my eyes shut, I waited for the inevitable.

"Helen, I found you at your ex-boyfriend's house today! Why would you go there if you were serious about moving on at all? Forget moving in with me, per se? And I know you've been going to the hospital a lot since we came back—"

"Abbott?"

"Abbott," he nodded. "Helen, I like you, but I won't put my career on hold any further for another woman who uses me as a place holder for something else, whatever it actually is. I just can't."

"He tried to kill himself because of me—"

"So this is guilt? That's what you're trying to sell this as? Too easy…next!" he demanded.

I'd miss those eyes; they were so precise, they seemed feral. Those lips—long and full and with such a delicate cupid's bow, too. Less than six months ago, in the rain, we'd secretly studied each other from the distance of a two-lane avenue, and now—here we were, wrapping up what barely had a chance to properly commence. Did George do this or did I?

"I just want a home. Of my own. And that place was the closest I had to it," I eventually said, hoping the explanation sounded plausible.

Jamie's dark eyes were so stout on mine, they had a hypnotizing effect. I didn't dare move.

"Home isn't a place. You're thinking of a mailing address," he scoffed. "And, it isn't some cliché, like, 'home is where the heart is,' either. I just don't think there is anything special about that one place you happen to be living at the moment, so there is no use getting attached. At least that's the case for me. And no, I'm not high!" That infectious smile stretched across his face. "It just is what it is," he shrugged, kindly, his fingers firm around mine. "We are human beings—we move around…we pack our bags and we move on. I'm my own home—and you're your own."

"So you're not coming back in September?"

"I'm not."

"And where will you be?"

"I don't know yet. The tour is wrapping in August. San Diego is our last stop. I'm sorry you had to find out from Veronika. I wanted to tell you, but I wanted to finalize everything first."

"So I can't talk you out of it?"

We've already had this conversation.

"I don't know if you should."

This sounded familiar. How often did I let George talk me out of leaving? The symmetry of it all took some of the sting out of his words, but my blood still continued to drain from the rest of my body and pool in the pit of my stomach, leaving the rest of me cold.

"You should be happy, though!" Jamie tried to cheer.

"Happy?" I snorted. "I should?"

"Veronika took your advice! You got through to her. She's not going to Baruch, or whatever—she's pursuing her own dreams, not her parents'. Like you!"

Like me? This was almost too cruel. Veronika couldn't be like me—not if she was actually getting to live the life I wanted, alongside Jamie (even if it would be aboard a set of bunk beds on wheels). Meanwhile, I was no better off than I was a few weeks ago. No, she wasn't like me—she was better (and better off).

I squinted at the elaborate tattoo on Jamie's left arm and searched for the skull. When the film before my eyes made sure that I wouldn't be able to make out its outline, I lowered my head onto Jamie's chest and closed my lids altogether. I gripped his ribcage to me, tighter by the second, my fingertips going numb. It was slim, his frame, which, of course, made his vocal abilities even more impressive to witness. I wouldn't hear any more of those now, either, of course. This made the tears sting harder.

"Look, I'm sorry, but I have no reason to stay," Jamie stated as plainly as if he were reading off a menu in a diner. He sat up to face me and cradled my face in his large hands, the way I'd done to Veronika not that many hours ago. He used his thumbs to wipe my cheeks.

I let my head lean into his left palm, taking comfort in the support it provided. I was expecting to feel the chill of his ring there, but it was no longer there.

"What about me?"

His hair a heart-warming mess, he smiled. I wished he wouldn't have had. I had to stop repeating myself.

"I was only here because I was trying to do the right thing…and as it turns out, I was pretty embarrassingly duped. I have to get back out there. Teaching was a convenient thing to do for a while, given the circumstance, but certainly not a calling—"

"But the kids love you!"

"And I love them, but I can't be cooped up in a classroom. Not yet, anyway."

"And me?"

"Which part?" he grinned, tentatively.

"Not the love part, I'm not that pathetic."

"Helen, if I felt even for a second that this was more than what it is, believe me, I'd do my best to stay…."

He waited for me to contradict him, and I considered doing so: I opened my mouth to speak but nothing materialized, my tongue only gauging its capacity to say anything to entrap this man for the second time in his young life. But I bit my tongue; I physically bit it.

"I think it was your hair that had me, you know,"

I finally spoke, surprising myself. "How is it that it's always so straight?"

His lips stretched into that glorious smile of his, his teeth large and white.

"Keratin."

"So it's not real?"

"Not naturally, no."

"Hmm," I heard escape from my throat.

"True story. Sorry to disappoint."

"You can't."

Jamie didn't let on that he heard me.

"Keep an eye on my guitar for me, won't you?"

"Does that mean you'll be back, then?" I chirped, audible hope on the tip of my tongue.

"I try to make it a point not to etch anything in stone."

"So I've gathered. What exactly is the deal with that guitar, anyway?" I stuck out my chin at the black case in the corner. "Veronika said it was all special and that you'd never part with it or something to that effect. She was so thrilled when you let her play it in Paris."

Jamie laughed and readjusted the sheet around his chest, hugging himself with his arms. I'd miss the roses, even the thorns. I watched him as he stood up and strode over to the instrument in question, Abbott's bedding trailing on the floor—a train. I didn't even realize how warm he'd been making me until we separated and a chill ran through me.

"It's not that special," he smiled as he cradled it out of its shell, picked it up, and handed it to me. "It wasn't passed on to me by a grandfather on his deathbed or anything. It was just the guitar I was playing when I realized that this is what I wanted to do professionally, for a living. It's not that expensive or unique in any other way, really. It's simply a reminder of who I am. It's my home, if you like."

"You don't want to take your home with you?" I rolled my eyes.

"I think you could use it for a while."

Chapter Thirty-One: *Condensed Milk*

Fingers—I'd miss them the most. I caught myself thinking this more than once as they traveled up and down my thighs, gripping my flesh every few inches, stroking as if to soothe where nails had just grazed with passion that bordered on painful.

And the mouth—I'd miss that, too. I'd never experienced lips of such lush, airy plushness, and I knew I was unlikely to ever again. It was best to be realistic.

When I'd catch myself wandering, floating above us, just watching, peering, I'd open my eyes and cup Jamie's face in my palms. "Stay here," I'd tell myself mutely. "Remember."

With the floor lamp for our light, I traced the lines of his face—his nose, his eyebrows. My stomach felt soft under his gaze—his eyes lost somewhere between mental exhaust and physical ecstasy.

I tensed my legs to push him further into me, tucking my face into the crook of his neck. He moaned. Even the timbre of his moans was melodious and breathy in the most dizzying of ways. He never grunted like an animal in heat the way George did; and he didn't whisper compliments that hardly seemed sincere under the circumstances the way Javier did. "Why had I waited so long to take note of these things?" I asked myself over and over. And then I remembered that I had to stay put, soak it all in. Maybe Jamie's weight wasn't enough to ground me, after all. Or maybe I was simply destined to float.

My fingernails drew circles on Jamie's side as my lids drew closed. I felt him twitch (flutter, really), and opened my eyes. How else was I supposed to remember the exact hue of his skin—the condensed milk of it? I inhaled a lungful of his collarbone, hoping the sweet scent of it would help the memory seep in deep.

His arms outstretched at either side of my head, his palms driven into my pillow, I let myself turn my attention from the black of his eyes to the burgundy of his left arm. The rose vines seemed almost black in the dim light of the room-—black magic roses. I wanted to touch them, but removing my hands off his body was the last thing I wanted to do. The Calavera looked me right in the eye, but I didn't flinch. I had to remember everything. Everything.

I hadn't noticed when the thrusts grew more rapid. It was almost over. Though I wanted it to last—needed it to go on for hours, days, even. I let my hips grind in a semicircle and up to him in encouragement, anyway. My fingers wrapped around his (apparently less than effortless) hair of their own volition, making their way closer and closer to his own skull. I was probably hurting him, but that line was always fine.

I kissed him when I saw he was close, tasting that last gasp with him.

Chapter Thirty-Two: *Calavera*

I'd never not gotten out of bed in the morning. I did not understand the concept. More precisely, I was not allowed to understand it. If I ever so much as considered the possibility of such, my mother would always point out the invalidity of the like sentiments by reminding me that, so long as I was healthy and fed, I barely had a right to words that carried such gravitas as "depression." One's problems only being relative to one's own existence philosophy only extended so far, at least when it came to Mrs. Levit's own children.

Sure, I'd contemplated not getting out of bed before (the day after my last set of finals in college, my first morning in Seville), but never had I ever followed through. When a particular dawn felt too heavy, when it felt as if it physically pressed my body into this mattress or that, all I had to do was remember my mother's voice.

"What do you have to be sad about?"

In Russian, of course.

I'd usually say nothing.

"There has to be a reason."

"Tired" or "sad" wouldn't cut it.

"Busy yourself with something. A person needs activity."

This was routine advice.

Turning over on my stomach on Abbott's unfolded couch, I gathered Jamie's pillow under myself like an extremely possessive toddler. I inhaled deeply, trying to hold on to the sweetness of his sweat in combination with Abbott—issue shampoo. I screwed my eyes shut against the sun peeking through the blinds. If I wanted to open them again (and keep them open), I knew I would have to call my mother.

"He left," I told her as I folded my knees underneath myself, now in fetal position, my voice muffled by the sheets under my cheek.

"The musician?" my mother asked. The pity she exhibited by speaking English was enough to finally spring those loaded tears from my eyes.

"Yes," I sniffled.

"What are you doing? I can barely hear you," she barked, inevitably back to Russian. She was likely puttering around the kitchen—I heard the clank of a ladle against a pot.

Throwing myself out of my contortion, I landed on my back.

"Are you in bed?" my mother shrieked.

I muttered in acquiescence. Jamie had left early that morning. His alarm went off as set—at 5:30 A.M. It vibrated against the floor, the sound of it shrill, but I pretended not to hear—I pretended to be asleep. As tempted as they were, I kept my eyes shut, resisting the urge to steal one last peek at his face, afraid that, were they to flutter open, my arms would fling from my body to latch on to his. By the time I dared to finally lift my head, I only caught a glimpse of his left hand pulling the door closed. There was no ring. The Calavera glared at me for a split second before the lock clicked. The guitar stayed behind, snug in its case, as promised.

"Helen, it's 1:00 in the afternoon, get out of bed," my mother instructed, matter-of-factly. "Busy yourself with something. Don't just lie there, idly. A person needs to be occupied with something. You need an activity." I was expecting these words, of course (these words, verbatim, in fact), but their effect was less than desired. My palm thrown across my eyelids, I turned toward the wall, my legs prickly under our sheets…well, Abbott's sheets. I had no sheets. And, once my legs had been waxed clean, any amount of hair on them felt foreign and unnecessary. I regretted ever doing it in the first place. I was ruined.

"Why?"

"Helen, seriously, you mean to tell me you have no papers to grade, no lesson plans to write?" I heard the clink of cutlery—maybe she was loading the dishwasher now.

"No," I lied, effortlessly.

My mother sighed again, her breathing as laborious as ever.

"Helen, there will be others," she said, returning to English.

I felt my mouth begin to twitch, the corners pulling downward.

"Don't cry, Helen! No whining! I always did hate it when you whined as a child. As if you ever had reason to—as if you knew or now know what hard life is. Anyway, I promise you, there will be others," she repeated. "He was clearly temporary—look at his timing, look at your time together."

I loved it when she spoke English. There wasn't much of an accent there, and her grammar was perfect, but something about her delivery was otherworldly. She savored words, so that when they were finally released from the confines of her mouth, they sounded whole, complete, if not necessarily warm. In Russian, she was hastier, sloppier.

"How so?"

"How so? He was too convenient in timing and proximity, darling. He served his purpose. Let him go—"

"But you never even met him!"

I threw the sheets off and opened my eyes. They burned from the abundance of light.

"Get out of bed, Helen. Busy yourself with something," she ordered in Russian. "It won't always hurt. If he were the one, he wouldn't leave a child—"

"It's not his child, though," I defended, instinctively. "And how do you know about that to begin with?"

"Jessica. And that's not all that much better, by the way."

"Jessica is a b—"

"A bitch, I know," my mother finished my thought by blending English and Russian, the way so many immigrants do. "I never liked that girl, not since you two were in middle school. Her coming over here and tattling on you like that—what is she, still thirteen? Helen, I told you to go to medical school-—you could've been her boss. You're so much smarter than she is!"

My eyes adjusting to the light, I smiled into the ceiling.

"I love you, Helen, but you have to get out of bed. You are healthy and you have a roof over your head…or so I hear. You have nothing to be sad about."

And we were back.

Chapter Thirty-Three: *Chaser*

Abbott tasted much like he smelled: coffee and peppermint gum. I had no recollection of making it into his immaculate room, and I certainly had no recollection of straddling him atop his oversized bed. I was warm. And soft. And drunk.

We'd been drinking wine in his dark dining room, that's all I remembered. Abbott had actual dinner with his, but I (forever afraid of imposing having to digest a calorie past lunch on my digestive tract) just drank. Sure, alcohol has calories, but they are liquid, and I didn't care. I was out of bed, and I was dressed—I wasn't sure how much else could be realistically expected of me.

I tried to lose my fingers in Abbott's hair, but there was nowhere to go, really. One twirl of my fingertips and I was at his skull. It wasn't the same.

"Whoa, spring chicken!" Abbott exclaimed after a few reciprocated thrusts of his caffeinated tongue. I sat back in his lap, my behind on his kneecaps, my legs at his sides. My thighs tingly with the abundance of alcohol, my head heavy, I took his long face in my hands. He was smiling his open, toothy smile. For a man soon to be fifty, he looked like a bona fide child, his hair floppy after being roughed up by my fingers. "I like you and all, sweet Levit, but I thought we came in here only because you were uncomfortable sitting in that chair in the dining-room, and nothing else. I'm such an irresistible piece of man candy, though, that it must be really hard for you to resist. I understand. Half the time, I wish I could screw me."

I smacked my forehead. Ah, so that's why we were in here. "Right." I reached over to his side table for my glass—there was still a good gulp of wine left in it.

"Don't get me wrong, Levit, I'm more than happy to oblige, but it'd probably be less than appreciated in the morning. Too much drinky-drinky is all," he smiled. "I love ya too much to mess that up, Levs." He sighed, demonstratively, before kissing me on the cheek. "Besides, I'd just forever ruin you for other men, trust me."

His comedic timing seemed only sharpened by all the wine. I laughed until I was sure snot was going to rush out of my nose, and plopped off of Abbott to sit at his side.

"Please don't feel bad! I get it—I'm a sexy beast," he shrugged into the mirror at the foot of the bed.

"Has Paz been in here?" I asked his reflection.

"No. You know me and boundaries," he mocked.

"Ha, yeah, you're a real stickler for those! See, Jamie somehow knew you were full of crap and wore jeans in spite of your sage advice," I remarked, hurling whatever was left of the wine directly against my throat.

"Sola…a smart cookie that one! Though, I guess if he were smarter, he wouldn't fuck a groupie unprotected and wind up in that stupid situation he was in."

"You're one to talk!"

"I always use a condom!" he proclaimed, a drunk finger in the air. "Did you guys?"

"Eww, yes!"

"So was I meant to be your chaser, then?" he whispered, leaning into me, a soft elbow in my warm ribs. Two bottles were downed between us. I was surprised I'd been able to taste coffee on him at all after all that. I suppose that's a testament to how much of it he routinely drank.

"Gross! Is everyone familiar with that 'chaser' term?"

"That's how some of us rack up quite a number of partners, my dear."

It was full-on déjà vu now.

Crying was the next natural stage of intoxication.

"Oh man," I heard Abbott mutter. He probably regretted ever letting me into his bedroom.

"I didn't even shave my legs for Jamie before he left," I squeezed out of my heaving lungs and seizing throat.

Though it was difficult to hear over my own crying, I was pretty sure Abbott was laughing.

"Ah, sweet Levit, you're too precious!" he blurted as he doubled over and slapped his knee. "You really think we care about any of that? Women care way more about that than we do, and then y'all blame us for misogyny or whatever. Y'all get all insecure and psych each other out, that's all."

I hiccupped and wiped my nose with my wrist, surely putting the nail in the coffin to all that was our potential romantic connection.

"You don't?"

"Well, I can't speak for Jamie, but odds are, we're all similar. Relatively speaking, at least. Short of you sporting some kind of caveman…or, I suppose, cavewoman layer of hair, we're good. Seriously, so long as we're granted…you know…access, we're fine."

"Eww," I grumbled, alcohol now bitter in the back of my throat.

"What? It's a good thing!" he giggled. I watched him in the mirror. A laughing Abbott was an endearing Abbott. Even before he removed his glasses and threw them on his side table, I could see that he looked younger when laughing. And given the carelessness of that action, I decided that I could finally stop wondering if those were prescription—they clearly were not.

"At least I know where you stand on the issue. Maybe it'd do me some good to hook up with you, after all."

"You could do worse, certainly."

"Well, getting men interested in me has never been difficult. Sustaining that interest—genuine interest—that's the tricky part for me. Especially of late. It's like I've pissed off some love god out there or something. Messed up my chi or karma or some such."

"What about that fella in Spain? Wipe those tears, Levit. There will be others."

"You mean tears?"

"Those, too."

Chapter Thirty-Four: *Spanish*

"We both need a coping mechanism—a distraction that isn't alcohol," Abbott noted before passing me a mug of coffee through the window and climbing to join me out on the fire escape, himself. "God knows you like to distract yourself, so it's only a matter of finding something more appropriate than straddling me after a bottle wine. Not that I didn't enjoy that—"

"Shut up," I growled before pressing my sunglasses up onto the bridge of my nose. They kept sliding down, forcing me to squint, painfully, into the sunshine.

I heard the metal reluctantly squeak as Abbott stepped out and folded himself down next to me, knees to chest.

"How do you cross your legs like that?" I heard him ask. My head hurt too much for me to actually turn toward the voice, but I could see in my peripheral field of vision that he was pointing to my lotus.

"George," I replied, my eyes now closed behind my glasses, red spots before my lids where the sun was meant to be. I had to open them again.

"What about him?"

"He taught me. He was—still is, I suppose, into yoga. Big time. He teaches it. He used to teach me, too."

"Probably in that early 'let's impress each other' stage, am I right?" Out of the corner of my eye, I saw him unfold a blanket and throw it around his shoulders before sharing a part of it with me.

"Yeah, just about," I shrugged, tugging at the throw to make sure it stayed put. This, of course, made Abbott pull at his half, preemptively.

"I'm just not that flexible," he remarked.

"Neither am I, apparently."

His coffee was bitter. No wonder his tongue was permanently stained.

"But seriously, sweet Levit, you and I are in a similar boat right now. We need to take our minds off of things, if not just start anew. Hey, how was my bike in that department?"

"What do you mean?"

"You seemed like you couldn't wait to take that thing out of here some days. Does it help you air out your head?"

"I don't know. Maybe."

"So, why do you disappear on that bike for hours if you're not sure?" Abbott smacked his tongue in disbelief.

"Okay, well, fine, while I'm pedaling away, there isn't much else I can think about. So fine, maybe while my crotch is on fire—you know, it being painfully pressed into that triangular seat and all—it makes for a nice distraction. But then I'm off the bike and life is still here, unchanged…. What's the point?" Cringing, I downed the rest of the coffee. "That's the reason George could never get me to meditate: as soon as I'd open my eyes again, there it was again—life. It's too temporary to be effective for me. It's more like a tease," I groaned, rubbing my throbbing forehead. "Same with alcohol."

"And yet you do it all…."

"Meaning?" I croaked, flushing.

"What do you mean, meaning? We just talked about this, remember? How bad is your hangover? You shoved your tongue down my throat last night just so as not to think about Jamie!" He laughed an infectious belly laugh, while I rolled my eyes behind my shades. There seemed to be a consensus about this. Perhaps this was my modus operandi, after all. But somehow, coming from Abbott, this did not sound as hurtful as it did coming from Jessica. Maybe it was the accent.

"Well, you see? Now it's the morning after and life is just as shitty as it was yesterday. Only I'm hungover and you'll never let me forget that kiss, so, I ask you—what's the point?"

My temples throbbing, I wished I were back in

bed. But the bed still smelled of Jamie. I'd spent the night before in Abbott's just to avoid it.

"And Jamie?"

"What about Jamie?" I shrieked, my heart in my throat at the sound of his name, already knowing full well where Abbott was going with this. The heartburn I felt just at the memory of his fine braid, his childlike grin…. "Jamie was not a distraction."

"He wasn't?" Abbott gasped in faux disbelief. "Whatever you say, sweet Levit."

"Abbott, please, weren't you trying to mate us the entire time we were abroad?" I spat back, my lips involuntarily spilling into a smile at the memory. It all seemed so silly now—the small flirtations, the half-truths.

"I did—you guys look cute together! And you clearly needed each other. After everything he's been through, I'm sure you were good for his self-esteem…if I can trust the poor sound insulation between our rooms, anyway. It's just that, now, if I know you at all, I'm afraid that you'll want to go meet that Spanish beau of yours to forget this one. Or reconsider George, God forbid. So we should probably get you a distraction that doesn't involve other people. Like candle-making or basket weaving, or whatever."

"The fuck do I need with a candle without Jamie?"

"Wow, you're a downer," Abbott lamented. "And to think I was going to ask you if you'd like to take up jogging with me!"

"Let's go!" I announced, springing to my feet. I was half-inside the kitchen before Abbott could gather himself up and follow me.

~ ~ ~

We ran out of breath fairly quickly. By the time we quasi-jogged further up the hill, we knew we were going to be turning right back around. It took us longer to change into our designated jogging clothes than it took us to actually attempt this run. We were back on the stoop of his building in less than ten minutes.

"Cigarette?" Abbott offered.

My head pounding harder now that I'd engaged in some actual physical activity, I nodded.

"I haven't smoked since college," I remarked, stifling a cough as I inhaled.

"I haven't smoked since yesterday."

"I didn't even know you smoked. I saw you in Paris, during that river cruise thing, and thought I was hallucinating." I inhaled again, feeling the burn in the back of my throat. I did my best not to cringe as I tapped the ashes off with the index finger of my right hand, wishing immediately that this cigarette were shorter.

"I don't do it often. I wouldn't get to age so gracefully were I a more committed smoker. It's everything with Paz—"

"And Sophie. And Stephanie!"

"No, just Paz. The whole Sophie thing is bullshit. Always was. It was always meant to work out on a karmic level, no? And Stephanie—give me a break! Paz, though…I…stupidly enough, I thought we had something…. Ugh, don't even dare say anything," he waved me off when he saw me contemplating a response. "I know! I know, this is all wrong, and inappropriate, and stupid, and naïve, but I felt something for her, and I thought she was feeling something for me too…. Anyway, this is stupid. You know, we should probably try this running thing again. I mean, this is pathetic! And you're but a spring chicken, so at least you should do better! Maybe after the school year is over we can try again? With actual regularity and discipline, I mean. What do you think, Levs?"

He was rambling now.

I took a long and un-enjoyable drag of my cigarette to keep myself from groaning out loud again. Was I to spend two months on the tip of this island? Could I even justify staying here? Would I have to start paying rent?

"I don't know, Abbott. I don't know if I'm cut out for all this running," I eventually said, watching smoke curl out of my mouth. "And I don't know where I'll be this summer," I wanted to add but didn't. "Look, Abbott, about Paz—" I began, mostly for the distraction of it, but lost the nerve.

"Oh, Levs, please don't, all right? I know, I'm a silly old pervert."

"No, Abbott, look…Paz really…oh my God, this is so weird, but Paz gave me a tearful confession of her undying love for you."

His eyes lit up like a little boy's at a sight of an ice-cream parlor. He was about to ask for all kinds of sprinkles.

"Do you believe her?" he asked in half whisper.

What was the harm?

"Honestly? I don't know anything when it comes to Paz. We've spent three, if not four, years sparring, so anything else just feels unnatural now."

Uncomfortable with Abbott's puppy-eyed stare, I leaned forward, stretching my back, reaching for my toes. More things I'd learned from George. I was never going to shake him. Mother was right—you can never truly rinse out a glass.

"But she was crying, you said?"

"Harder than on stage."

Out of the corner of my eye, I could see Abbott's face struggle against a tempting smile. The grin was winning over. I chose to keep my eyes on my dirty laces.

"This is good," he mumbled, his accent thicker with excitement. "This is good."

I rolled my eyes, counting on him not seeing the gesture. I still needed a place to stay until the end of the school year.

"Is it though?" I couldn't help myself.

"Yes! She won't be a student much longer, and…I won't be anyone's teacher…." The sigh that followed this thought was partly stifled, but I caught it.

"But—"

"Don't even mention our significant age difference!"

"Yes, yes, you're younger than all of us combined. I don't care about the age, but it all started so…wrong…."

"It doesn't matter…."

"She got Sophie to—"

"Can't something good come out of it?"

Chapter Thirty-Five: *Effort*

It was a few days before graduation when it finally became official—Abbott's winning streak of "Teacher of the Year" had come to an end, to be taken over by none other than yours truly! I thought they'd wait until the actual graduation ceremony to announce these things, but, at Talents, logistics outweighed the element of surprise. All other categories had been announced back at the yearbook party, apparently (though I was clearly too distracted to notice), but only today were they finally printed on pretty paper and pasted all over the beige tiled walls of the school. Mr. Jamie Sola, though he was long gone, won "Best Hair." Veronika, though she was long gone, too, won "Most Likely To Cure Cancer." Ofir won "Best Looking Male," Sage—"The Loudest," Wisdom—"The Funniest." Paz won "Most Likely To Win An Oscar," Liam and Jordan won "Best Couple." Raily won "Worst Driver." I didn't get that one.

It was also no longer a feigned secret that, come graduation, Mr. Abbott was not going to be a teacher at Talents NYC. There was no longer a point in whispering; kids just flat out asked and Abbott just flat out answered.

"Congratulations!" Javier cheered from across the ocean when I told him about my little award. I was startled at the sound of English-—he usually started his conversations in Spanish. Considering what I was about to say, it unnerved me. This certainly would be some ironic timing. He couldn't give up now.

"*¿Todavía quieres ir a Marruecos?*" I asked, breathless.

I'd locked myself in my office for this phone call, afraid to lose the nerve were I to wait any longer. Days were trickling down, summer break was literally days away. I needed a place to go. The longer I thought about it, the more I knew that I could not continue living rent-free at Abbott's without there being that pesky work commute to justify it. That wouldn't be standing on my own two feet, it wouldn't be making it on my own. I could've taken on a summer course to smooth all that out, but not all classrooms were air-conditioned. Of course, I could've offered to pay rent, but that never occurred to me, either.

"Yes!" Javier exclaimed, audibly afraid to spook me. "Yes," he repeated, softer, "let's go to Morocco!"

"Let's do it! Let's finally do it," I muttered, making sure to keep a smile on my face in the effort to sound as excited about this as I should've been all along. "I'm sorry I left you hanging back then…and for so long. Let's go, now." I nodded, feverishly, to myself, for once commending myself on making this phone call the old fashioned way and not using Skype—it would've been free, sure, but then we'd have to see each other, and who knows what micro-expressions would betray what. "I can be there the day after graduation," I said before anything could be taken back. Sure, the money I was about to spend on a plane ticket would be wiser spent on the first and last rent on a studio apartment somewhere in the five boroughs, but I had to make things right first. I needed to retrace my steps. According to my calculations, I would be able to afford a good month abroad, depending on what my boarding costs would be throughout.

"We can start over, then," Javier whispered. "Helen, is there a chance? For us? After all this time?"

I swallowed hard, my throat tight. It was most definitely allergies this time, I told myself. It was the right season.

"I think so," I lied in a whisper, pacing the length of the cluttered office, barely avoiding the sharp edges of the three desks packed inside this narrow space. Someone knocked on my door just in time to save me from making any more declarations. It was easy enough to excuse myself given what I'd just promised.

"Sophie?" I couldn't help but shriek when I peeked out of my door, my phone still in my grasp, my heart still racing with my finalized decision. I was going to spend my summer with Javier (or Hector, as George surely still called him)—now that it was out there, I had no choice.

"Got a minute?" the girl asked through gritted teeth, visibly agitated. When the very petite Sophie was nervous, her precious narrow shoulders tensed all the way up to her earlobes. I wasn't about to let her into my office, so I stepped out to the hallway to meet her.

"Let me just set my timer." I fiddled with my phone for visual aid.

Our little cello prodigy was not amused.

"Hope you're happy," she hissed.

I doubted I actually looked happy; anxious, excited, flustered, maybe, but not happy, per se.

"What are you talking about?"

"I'm suspended!" she shouted loud enough for the English class across the hall from my office to hear. Mrs. Tillman peeked through her door's little window, arching a brow. I had no choice but to usher Sophie inside.

"What do you mean?" I asked again.

"What are you—slow? I'm suspended until the end of the school year!" she hollered. I considered slamming my door shut, but decided against it.

"But there are literally three days left," I said, dumbly, consulting the calendar behind my desk.

"That's not the point! It'll be on my record!"

I looked at my phone, wishing I'd never hung up with Javier. Hearing him so happy almost made me genuinely want to go to Morocco.

"All because of that pervert!"

"Abbott?"

"Yes!"

"Well, you did spread lies about your teacher. Lies with pretty hefty repercussions," I tried to reason as I lowered myself into my office chair in the effort to exude some kind of calm authority.

"I see. So he can have a full blown affair with Paz, and I'm the only one punished?" Sophie cried. Her hazel eyes glistened.

"You know Abbott has been forced to retire, right?"

"And that's it?! No investigation, no nothing?"

Chewing my lips, I tried to buy myself some time to phrase the following just right. My loyalties could be described as murky.

"Sophie, tell me the truth—has Mr. Abbott ever laid a hand on you? Has he ever made an inappropriate remark?"

Sophie puffed, Sophie huffed, Sophie put her hands on her hips, but Sophie said nothing. Her hair was in a sleek ponytail. I missed her natural volume.

"Well, there you have it. I don't think that, given your entire history, you have any right to be scandalized by any of this." Landing my phone on the desk in front of me, I crossed my legs and leaned back. "The rest is between the school and Mr. Abbott. This is of no concern to you."

"How can you call yourself a woman? What about Paz-—any justice for her? Sure, she was arguably old enough, and sure, according to her, it was all part of some evil plan of hers, but she was still a student, and Abbott was still a teacher. It's not right and you know it, Ms. Levit!" Sophie screamed as she landed the palms of her hands on my desk, her face inching closer to mine.

Paz as a victim was not a notion I'd previously entertained. Given all the revelations as of late, I wasn't sure if now was the right time to start. It was too late to start over.

~ ~ ~

Abbott poured me a glass of wine before pouring himself one and settling in opposite me.

"Sweet Levit, you're there to inspire! You can't tell them any of this nonsense."

"But you can't start over! I'd be feeding them lies as my last piece of wisdom," I scoffed after rereading my speech for Abbott. "I know for a fact that you're the same person no matter the day or circumstance!" I couldn't bring myself to tell him how I knew this. "This is your life, it's not like it's really only about to begin after a certain point, or event…Ugh, I don't know what I'm saying."

I could feel my face begin to flush. I was talking in circles and took a swig of my wine to stop. My conversation with Javier looped on repeat in my head. It rang all the way across the Upper Bay as I sailed alongside Abbott into Staten Island. I'd have to tell Abbott I was leaving.

I jotted down another asinine bullet point in my legal pad before I brought myself to look back up at him, trying not to think about Sophie.

"I'm leaving right after graduation."

"Jersey?"

"Morocco…well, Spain, first, but then—Morocco."

"Oh God, your Spanish beau from that semester abroad?"

I nodded as Abbott pursed his lips, considering.

"You don't have to…. Helen, I know you miss Jamie, but going to another guy is not a way to quell that!"

"I owe him this much. I have to make things right, somehow—"

"But you didn't do anything wrong! Choosing whom to be with is not a wrong you have to serve penance for, spring chicken. Even if that choice sucked."

I nodded pensively, feigning understanding.

"Anyway, I leave pretty much after the ceremony. Just wanted to let you know."

Abbott raised his eyebrows but said nothing. He inhaled deeply and abandoned his wineglass; he then took to draining the bottle straight up.

"Wow, sweet Levit, and I used to think you were a smart girl!"

"I used to think you were, too," I hissed, using my pencil to point to the room next door, where Paz was asleep in Abbott's bed.

We laughed then. Hard. To tears, we laughed.

TARIFA

Javier and I spent over two hours in his car, but we were finally in Tarifa—the very tip of Spain. Any further and you'd find yourself in the waters of the Straits of Gibraltar. As I stood with my head thrown back, face turned up to the merciless sun, I couldn't help but think of the circular nature of it all. See, Abbott, I've traveled for days and I'm still standing in a harbor, boarding a ferry. I'm still me, despite the difference in time and climate. I should've gone with my gut and not let you talk me out of my speech.

Last time I saw Abbott and Paz, they were back at his apartment, her graduation robe thrown nonchalantly over her shoulder. We'd come back separately—they took the scenic, ferry route, while my brother drove me in order to be able to escort me further, to New Jersey, where I was to spend the few hours I had before beginning my journey back to Spain. One look at the two of them—Abbott and Paz—eyes bright, hands eager, and I knew for a fact that I could not stay in St. George. Not without having to hear them through the wall, not without having to think back to her fingers inside Jamie's pants, and therefore not without thinking about Jamie…and where there was Jamie, there was George. No, we had to untie this tangle. Maybe I wouldn't have to go further than Javier. Maybe we could fix it right here—just at the Straits of Gibraltar.

Javier turned over his shoulder to check on me. He winked, his sunglasses on his head, a smile now seemingly permanently etched on his broad, friendly face. We hadn't seen each other in almost a decade, but I don't think either of us looked that different. It barely felt different, too—a familiar desperation on our breaths.

I nodded and smiled in return. There was a queue to see the ticket agent; Javier was fifth in line. I planted myself on a bench and took out my phone while I waited. Habits, addictions, they are hard to break, isn't that what Paz once said?

Jessica, I saw, started another game with me in Words with Friends. I did not accept. This has been a routine exercise for weeks now. Javier, though feet away from me, was still playing and winning by a few dozen points. I pretended to put up a fight with the word "pun" in this game. The number of my opponents having dwindled over time, the game no longer occupied much of my time, cheating included. I was ready to exit the app altogether when I saw a new game request. Despite instinctual reservations, I checked to see who it was. George. "Touch" was his first word. My hand hovered over the screen as my heart tried to find its rhythm, and my brain, against its own better judgment, considered my letter options. Swallowing hard and breathing fully, I had no choice but turn to Facebook, neither accepting nor rejecting George's request. At least he wasn't asking for a liver.

My kids seemed to have only been half-listening at graduation (as expected, of course) and were now accepting my Facebook friend requests, after all. And I did request them, I wasn't kidding. Ofir, Jordan, Liam, Andrew, Sage, Wisdom…. Everyone was posting pictures from the ceremony: white gowns, square hats, gold tassels, everyone's teeth visibly whitened, their hair blown out, their eyes bright. They embraced as if they indeed would miss each other, be they in Berkley School of Music, Yale School of Drama, Tisch, Julliard, or the IDF come August. My thumb and forefinger zooming in and out, I squinted behind my sunglasses, studying the faces I would no longer see day in and day out. My beautiful Ofir, my silly Wisdom.

Quickly done reminiscing, eager to do anything else, I searched for a "Jamie Sola" only to find three James Solos. There was no Jamie Sola on Facebook, only an apparently long ago abandoned professional page, the profile photo of which managed to make a man of stunning, seemingly hand-picked features look menacing; after an unnecessarily long consideration, I decided not to "Like" it. Instead, I headed over to Veronika's profile, where her crooked grin and Jamie's lopsided one met me as soon as the pixels of the page cascaded down. They must've taken that selfie at that ill-fated yearbook party, her skinny arm draped in a tasteless see-through polyester sleeve around his neck, making a mess of his hair. There was also a video of the two of them pretending to try to outdo each other at some sound-check, their mastery way over my head, their slender frames hunched and swaying, their hair flowing. My insides pinched. I shut off my phone.

I looked up, and there he was—Javier. His aviators reflective, I saw myself, really. Distracted, I took to taming my hair, which was frizzy with the sea breeze, and readjusting my own sunglasses and my bra straps.

"*Helen, por favor, para.* You're perfect!"

Before I knew it, we were sailing south. It was supposed to be a short trip, from what the brochure told me, anyway. Still lightheaded with the jet lag, my allergies slowly drying up, I rested my head on Javier's shoulder, my phone in a tight clench of my fist in my lap, Jamie's guitar at my feet. Javier's skin was darker than George's, surely, but it was a toss up when it came to comparing it to Jamie's. I stroked his arm, the fine hairs on it, as his face, his soft cheek, slowly landed on top of my head. Before long, the sun scorching on my lids, I eased my neck up, along with Javier's, and wrestled my old red umbrella out of my purse. We needed a shield from those blinding rays.

With your eyes closed, if you managed to forget that you were indeed nearing Africa with every splash of a wave, you could almost forget that you were moving at all.

ABOUT THE AUTHOR

Marina Raydun's published works of fiction include a compilation of novellas "One Year in Berlin/Foreign Bride," a suspense novel entitled "Joe After Maya," and Book One in this two-part series—"Effortless." Born in the former Soviet Union, Marina grew up in Brooklyn, NY. She holds a J.D. from New York Law School and a B.A. in history from Pace University.

Made in the USA
Middletown, DE
15 November 2023